Joyce Reiser Kornblatt   *Photo by Barbara Nehman*

Joyce Reiser Kornblatt was born in Boston, but grew up in Pittsburgh, Pennsylvania. She attended Carnegie-Mellon University, then received a Master of Arts degree in English from Western Reserve University. After working for some years as a community organiser, programme planner and political speech writer in Ohio, she decided at the age of thirty to return to full-time writing. One of her first short stories was published in *Transatlantic Review,* and in January 1979 'Yellow Springs' appeared in *Atlantic Monthly* as an 'Atlantic First'. *Nothing to do with Love* is her first book.

Joyce Kornblatt is at present Assistant Professor of English and co-director of the Creative Writing Programme at the University of Maryland. She lives with her daughter, Sara, in Bethesda, Maryland, and is working on a novel.

Joyce Reiser Kornblatt
Nothing to do with Love

The Women's Press

For my daughter Sara

First published in Great Britain by
The Women's Press Limited 1982
A member of the Namara Group
124 Shoreditch High Street, London E1 6JE

Copyright © 1975, 1978, 1979, 1981 Joyce Reiser Kornblatt
First published by The Viking Press, New York, 1981

'Nothing to do with Love' appeared originally in *The Atlantic Monthly*
under the title 'Yellow Springs'; 'Memoirs of a Cold Child' and
'Ordinary Mysteries' in *The Ohio Journal;* 'Thanksgiving' in *Plum;* 'Relics' in *Sybil-Child;*
'Richard' in *Sun and Moon;* and 'Balancing Act' in *Transatlantic Review*.

British Library Cataloguing in Publication Data

Kornblatt, Joyce Reiser
  Nothing to do with love.
  I. Title
  813'.54(F)   PS3561.0/

  ISBN 0-7043-3891-2

Printed in Great Britain

CONTENTS

NOTHING
TO DO
WITH LOVE

PART ONE

JANET

My daughter's name is Robin and her lineage is conventional. A mother and a father. The usual birthright of forty-six chromosomes, two genetic histories fused in a moment of passion or tenderness or a physical urge no less, no greater, than a sneeze.

I have studied conception, but not in the ordinary sense. That is: I am a geneticist—Dr. Janet Sorokin—and my focus has been on the hatching of unfertilized eggs. Parthenogenesis. The absence of the father, the spermless embryo. I have monitored the phenomenon in bees and aphids.

You are familiar with other claims. Mary of Nazareth. The teenager down the block who insists they were only kissing. The patient in the abortion clinic whose husband had a vasectomy three years ago. I am not defending the claims, but merely attesting to precedents in nature, in other forms of life.

At the Bureau of Missing Persons, the officer in charge says, "Describe your daughter, Mrs. Sorokin."

He is a hulk of a man, elephantine. A cigarette lodges like a tusk in the corner of his mouth. Ashes scatter over the papers on his worn blotter. I am certain he has been here, in this

3

room, with these forms, for centuries. His blue regulation shirt is wet under the arms, stains dark as ink. He points at me with his ball-point pen. He repeats: "Mrs. Sorokin. Your daughter. Tell me what she looks like."

I give him the customary details. Height, weight, the color of hair and eyes, the mole on the left shoulder, the clothing worn when last seen. (Yesterday morning. I have not seen her since yesterday morning. She wore her raincoat to school, a clue I should have noticed. It was not raining at all. Rain was not predicted. The sky was crayon-blue, the flawless kind of sky she colored as a child. What would she have said to me if I had thought to ask her, "Robin, why are you wearing a raincoat this morning?" Her feathery voice would have ruffled with anger. "I am fifteen years old, Mother. Don't you think I'm capable of dressing myself?")

The officer writes down what I tell him.

I have told him nothing.

Which is not to say that descriptions are without value. I believe in description and little else. Observe and record. At some point, a synthesis, an insight, a realization of what we have been watching without having been aware of it.

But he does not have enough data.

He never will.

I have access to evidence he can never acquire. It has come to me slowly, day by day for forty years. The knowledge of her cells in mine. A long evolution of sorrow and love. An undocumented genealogy, stored in the archives of my brain. Down my nerves, inside my bones, the buried code taps itself clear to me: *When I find Robin, I will have found us all.*

I am speaking of a family in which disappearance is a dominant trait. People losing one another even as they face each other across a room, even as they sleep beside each other in their common beds. Example: my former husband, Brian, remembers, better than he would care to, the way his father vanished each night into alcoholic oblivion on his expensive leather couch. Example: my mother always sat at the supper table with one arm hooked over the back of her chair, her body angled sideways, so that her knees pointed in the direction of the door—a woman always on the verge of leaving. On our coat of arms, etch a suitcase and inscribe the

4

family motto: "Good-bye." (From the Old English: God be with you.)

The officer clears his throat. He rises, huge and official, behind his scarred desk. He tells me he will be in touch as soon as he has a lead. Sometimes these things are slow, he says. Thousands of runaways out there. Thousands and thousands. The ash lengthens, as if his very words were flickering out and dying in his mouth. I shake his hand, mutter thanks, knowing I have no intention of waiting for him to call me with his first paltry facts.

Eli says, "The first thing you have to do, Janet, is get in touch with Brian. He has to know about this. The second thing you have to do is put on your lab coat and get back to work, because there is no way in hell you are going to do a better job than the police. I think you already know that. If you don't, I'm telling it to you now."

I am sitting beside Eli Bell on the nubby tweed sofa in his office in Building 46. Eli is the director of the laboratory in the medical complex where I work as a research associate. It is one o'clock, and he has drawn the linen drapes to mute the insistent September sun. Light filters through the beige fabric. His desk lamp is on, and the room has taken on the quality of dusk. As he speaks, Eli fills his pipe with Borkum-Riff from the leather pouch he carries in his jacket pocket. He tamps down the tobacco, lights the pipe, contemplates the flavor, I suppose, or perhaps the sting on the upper palate. Hard to know from his expression: Eli's face always maintains a fierce neutrality. I have learned to read him by more obscure signals: whether his left foot is jumpy or still; the angle at which he holds his head. I have even grown sensitive to the calibrations of his breathing.

I have just asked him for a leave of absence. I spoke calmly, each word forming itself like a crystal I could put in a specimen jar: "Robin's run away, Eli. I have to find her. It will take time and I need you to give me the time."

As I spoke, I felt in my throat that catch, that tug at the base of the tongue, and I feared I might cry. Neither of us would be comfortable with tears. For me, crying has always been a relinquishment. As if I am losing something I need for

5

strength. As if I will jeopardize my relationship to gravity. My mother cried herself empty and collapsed like a deflated life preserver. I have learned to patch my own leaks. I do not trust catharsis, and I am wary of hearts that melt, pour out, or undergo other suspicious transformations.

And Eli would be embarrassed if I cried. He is not at ease with pain. He is a physician without patients. He trained to work in the wards; in medical school, his mentor predicted that Eli would be a great surgeon. Once I asked him why he switched to research, and Eli answered tersely, "Let's just say I was batting a thousand in the wrong league." Now he ministers to microbes, grant proposals, articles in prestigious scientific journals. He has never married. He pretends I am not divorced. I gave up trying to seduce him a long time ago.

A long time ago I did not think of it as seduction.

Seven years ago, after Brian and I had separated, I thought of it as love.

By "it," I am referring to a benign mass of feeling that had grown in me for the five years I had worked under Eli. At the end of my third month in his laboratory, I knew I *could* love him if I were not married to Brian, but I refused to allow it—love—to trouble me. Loving Eli was not pragmatic, and still, the unreasonable love I had not found feasible for all those years had spread inside me silently, exerting minimal pressure on bodily organs, remaining essentially undetected (surely there were symptoms I ignored), surprising me finally with its substantial presence.

Eli recognized my affliction. I asked him to dinner. He accepted, a doctor reluctantly paying a house call. Robin was with Brian for the night; I was picking up the last of her toys when the bell rang. I opened the door and Eli said, "Janet," not smiling, stiff, awkward about taking off his trench coat. Undoing each button became an operation demanding his full attention. I wore a long velvet skirt, a lacy blouse, polish on my nails, my hair full and shining from three shampoos and a special balsam rinse.

Eli said, "You've been looking very tired lately."

In the dim candlelight, I served him beef stroganoff, green beans amandine, Caesar salad, and a good California wine. His hands shook as he extracted the cork. I asked him about his childhood. He talked about the latest HEW allocations for basic research. I joked about sex. He quoted from a paper he had just read on the moral problems of genetic counseling.

I remember sitting there, hearing little of what he said, thinking repeatedly *I love this man*, each word predictable as a pulse throb.

Did I simply want to get him into bed?

How simple is desire?

Eli's diagnosis, after cheesecake and espresso: "Don't try to make our friendship into something more than it is."

"What is it?"

"Friendship." I could see him struggle for exactitude. "More than colleagues, less than—"

"Than?" I wanted him to say *love*, to commit himself to the word if not the reality, as if simply giving voice to it would open it up as a possibility between us.

He folded and unfolded his napkin. "Just . . . less," he said.

"I'm not married anymore."

"Legally, you are still married, Janet." He was relieved to have the conversation returned to externals, to truths that could be categorized.

I pushed for a different sort of information. "Is that the reason—"

"No." He was definitive. "That would not change anything."

I said, "I don't believe you," but I did. His *no* carried within it the weight of solid research, of conclusions reached after painstaking study. I understood then that he had been analyzing his feelings for me for a long time, maybe years, perhaps for all the years I had denied my feelings for him. Both of us, then, engaged in the same work: rationalizing the irrational.

He allowed my statement of disbelief to stand, for which I was grateful. He knew, of course, that I *did* believe him. Eli's words earn their authority: they rest on the strength of his thought. He is a factory of cerebration, an intellectual steel mill, furnaces blazing, ideas forged like ingots, theories zooming like freight cars along the tracks of fibrous tissue.

He said, "Maybe you and Brian will—"

"Absolutely no chance," I told him, and myself. "None."

"You think that now," he said, "but you may see things

7

differently . . . once things have sorted themselves out."

Things sorted themselves out, and I did not see things differently.

Now I tell him, "I can't get in touch with Brian. He's on a boat with Fletcher somewhere off the Florida Keys."

Eli gets up. Paces. Turns back to me like Darrow in court: "Don't tell me Fletcher McPherson is incommunicado. Politicians have phones implanted into their bodies like pacemakers."

Eli makes nothing easy for me ever. I come to him with simple propositions and he transforms them into complicated hypotheses that require a withering scrutiny.

I tell him: "Fletcher isn't the president *yet*. Senators don't have hot lines. He and Brian left right after the recess on Friday; they won't be back until the end of the week. You know they take off like this sometimes. They may have jumped off the end of the earth, that's how incommunicado they are."

Eli is unperturbed by my testimony. "Janet, you seem to forget that the man is Robin's *father*. What about your *own* father, have you called him up, talked to him about this? Of course not. This is a *family* emergency, and you're playing it like Joan of Arc."

He is trying to goad me into anger. To crack my determination. This is part of Eli's technique. Eli uses technique in lieu of love, and I am not speaking now of the sexual dimension.

I tell him quietly, "I'm sorry you feel I'm handling this improperly. I am asking you again: Will you give me the time."

He sees my resolve. He turns up his hands in resignation. "How much time are we talking about."

"Start with a week."

"Do you have the slightest idea where she is?"

Again, the constricted throat. "No. But I'm not thinking in those terms now. You *taught* me that, Eli."

"Taught you what?"

"The solution to any problem depends on knowing which questions to ask, and in what order. Quote, unquote."

He nods slightly, in reluctant assent. I gather myself up from the sofa. I feel like an odd assortment of mismatched parts, but I have learned, in Eli's presence, to adopt a balanced stance, a posture of grace. I am at the door when he says, "Janet." I steel myself, turn around, and Eli Bell, eyes glistening, instructs me: *"Just be damn careful."*

In my own office, I write up instructions to my assistant, putting him in charge of the cell-fusion experiment that I have been supervising.

I abdicate to him such a wealth of procedure.

I leave behind me all my old measurements, my familiar materials, the valuable equipment I proved to Eli, item by item, I needed for my work. I feel as insubstantial as my shadow that falls across the warm asphalt of the parking lot. I drive the usual eight miles home, and landmarks loom strange. I am traveling through territory I once knew, before, but now I am unable to name those places, I have no map, and I am, for all practical purposes and for purposes impractical and quite mysterious, a missing person.

Even to the lost, there is weather. It defines itself, demands of the senses an attention the mind resists. Today the sky is the color of blue parchment, and the sun glows behind a scrim of clouds. It is hot, but there is a good breeze, and the leaves move in its current. The air is clear and dry.

Sometimes in Washington, the summer air is so thick with moisture—an old swamp of a city, after all; quicksand and slime under the marble monuments and the wide concrete roads—so thick that it loses its transparency, ceases to be an element with which you deal involuntarily. Breathing becomes a decision, each breath an act of will, more like a swallow than a breath.

It is like that, mostly, in July and August, sometimes into September.

But not today. This is the middle of September. When I breathe, it hurts, but not for reasons of weather.

It is, as Brian would say, a great day for tennis.

There, I recognize the house. Geography restores itself.

Phenomena assume their reality again. I am a woman for whom phenomena have sufficed.

Does this house mean anything, except in the empirical sense?

Brick Colonial, white shutters, black trim, gutters sagging a bit, slate roof, the chimney screened over to prevent the nesting of birds.

We conceived Robin in this house, a month after we'd moved in. If I scraped off the wallpaper we hung, if I unplastered the cracks in the walls and the ceilings, took down the paneling in the study, if I stripped the coats of varnish off the planked floors and worked my fingers down to the rough grain, if I took it all back, layer by layer, year by year, to the way it was when we began, would I, in the process, discover anything important about any of us?

I know better.

A house sloughs off memory like cells of dead skin. The tissue disintegrates invisibly, in silence.

Think of chronology as an outmoded tool.

Think as a physicist: Time is a place where nothing changes, nothing achieves permanence.

If I knew more physics, would I be wandering these rooms, trying to remember what no longer exists and has never been forgotten?

Yes.

I know better, but yes.

A limitation of the species. A stirring in the skull. The ancestral organ itches: you scratch.

The kitchen. The round oak table that we found in an antiques shop in the Maryland countryside. We tied the table to the top of the car. The carved claw feet stuck up in the air like those of a giant insect flipped over on its back, or the stiffened limbs of a dead animal, carried home from the hunt.

We liked old furniture. Primitive pieces. We had, as they say, things in common.

And we had Robin. We conceived her here, in the living room, before the sofa had arrived, the Stiffel lamp still resting on the floor, the paintings leaning in a stack against one wall. In front of the fire, on the Oriental rug, we made a bed of pillows. I loved the intricacies of the rug's design. I loved the structure of Brian's back, the shape of his forehead. I loved to put my palm against that fine plane, to feel the skin stretched taut across the rugged bone. He said my eyes were beautiful, that they changed color when I became aroused.

Alchemist.

He touched me alive, I him.

We thought that if our bodies could come together in such pleasure, it did not matter much that our minds, from the beginning, were estranged. We did not expect many connections. We did not come from families in which there had been many connections. We touched each other alive: at the beginning, that seemed more than enough.

We labeled our estrangement "a healthy balance."

We said we had "complementary natures."

We were not naïve.

We were simply wrong.

I take the whole world in with one eye. The microscopic squint. I am, you could say, a reductionist.

Brian sees through a wide-angle lens. From Fletcher's office on Capitol Hill, Brian sees the entire country, including Hawaii and Alaska. He sees, always, in the plural.

One way in which Brian and I are alike: we both hate to be wrong.

When Brian moved out, Robin said, "Is Daddy going to live in the White House when Fletcher gets to be president?"

She was eight years old. Already Fletcher was making plans, though it is not until now, this year, seven years later, that he is making those plans public. On the record. Brian and Fletcher are on a boat somewhere off the Florida Keys, planning a press conference at which Fletcher will make his announcement.

Robin did not make an announcement. How long has she been planning to run away?

I am in her room. I am sitting on the edge of her bed. The dotted Swiss coverlet is tucked neatly under the pillow just as she left it yesterday morning. She has always been an orderly child. I have not had to remind her to brush her teeth or hang up her jacket or put her books away or make her bed before school. In the maple dresser, the clothes she left behind are folded in neat piles. Under the beveled lid of the rolltop desk I bought her for her thirteenth birthday, her supplies are stored carefully in the bank of cubbyholes. From the start, she reveled in symmetry. She woke four hours to the minute from her last feeding. She took the bits of cheese I spread out for her on her high-chair tray and shoveled them with her tiny fingers into a perfect mound in the tray's center. She could spend an hour combing smooth her favorite doll's tangled yellow hair.

"Her mother's daughter," Brian would say, rue invading his face. Later the rue would harden into bitterness, the bitterness into indifference.

There were no more connections.

No, he could not take Robin for the entire weekend. He had to be in Cincinnati Saturday night, big speech for Fletcher. No, he would not be able to go to the sixth-grade play next Tuesday. He had a meeting with money men, didn't I understand how it was? He worked for a senator with presidential aspirations. Didn't I understand *yet*, after all these years?

I understood.

Robin said she understood. She has never gotten angry at Brian's absences. He is going to the White House with Fletcher McPherson: that is his dream. Robin dreamed herself into her father's dream and allowed him whatever privileges he required to make that dream real.

Her mother does not deal in dreams. Dreams require an expansion of the imagination that troubles the empiricist, a certain sloppiness of the mental processes. An abandonment of methodology.

I have abandoned methodology.

The bed is moving beneath me like a raft on a crazed river. Or is it my blood, changing its course in the middle of my life?

I stand up. Take deep breaths. Exhale. Self-resuscitation. You can drown in the turbulence of your own blood. I never knew before that there was so much danger in this room.

I would call this all a dream, but the note she left perched for me on the nightstand beside my bed was real. I gave it to the officer at the Bureau of Missing Persons. He took it in his hand and acknowledged its substance.

Mom,

I don't expect you to understand. This has nothing to do with love, but I'm leaving. I just had to get out of this house. Sometime soon I'll get in touch.

Robin

She is right: I do not understand. But she is wrong: this has everything to do with love.

I was naked when I found the note.

I'd come home from work at six. Next door, Mr. Henski, pulling weeds that sprouted between the bricks of his front walk, rose from his knees to give me his archaic gentlemanly salute. In the front hallway, I sorted through the mail—bills, advertisements, *Newsweek*, *Scientific American*. I called for Robin, who did not answer. I knew where she was. (This was yesterday, when old assumptions about my daughter still commanded my faith.) She was at Laura's house, or Ruth's, or the library, studying for the chemistry test she was to have taken today. I was glad she was not back yet. I was tired. My experiment was not going well. I had eaten eggplant for lunch, and my stomach had been sour all afternoon. (I am still, at forty years old, unable to strike a balance between my appetites and my limitations. In most cases, I lean toward the limitations. But my passion for eggplant is boundless.) I wanted to get undressed and soak in a hot tub and not have to talk to anyone until my stomach settled, my muscles relaxed, and the headache I'd been fighting since noon evaporated with the steam.

I took off my clothes in my bedroom. After Brian and I

separated, it had taken me a good year to think of it as "my" bedroom, and only after I'd painted it blue, taken down the curtains and put up shutters instead, moved every piece of furniture to a different wall. In the door-length mirror, my body neither alarmed nor pleased me: it was simply my own, and I did not think to give it more accord than one gives to any familiar object. I have always been startled when a man finds my small breast or the curve of my hip or the ordinary line of my calf *moving*.

I bent down to retrieve the slippers I'd kicked under the bed that morning, and then I saw the note leaning against the digital clock, obscuring its dependable precision.

I will tell you what I felt when I read that note: contractions.

As if my womb were remembering its loss.

As if it were understanding for the first time in fifteen years how far from its dark comfort its child had traveled.

I began to shake, and then to shiver, the film of moisture on my skin chilled by the air conditioning seeping out of the silent vents in the ceiling. I saw my mother dying again in a spasm of fever and chills, and in that instant birth and death closed around me like hands forming a circle and I could not have told you, that moment, the difference between being born and dying.

Do not assume a mystical experience. I had hyperventilated. It affects perception. A certain disorientation occurs. You can believe that the saints had visions, or you can deduce a metabolic imbalance. Perhaps a brain tumor. Some scholars suspect drugs.

I put my hands on the nightstand and the wood gradually made its impression on my numbed fingers. I counted out loud, attached myself again to order.

The contractions weakened.

My mother's image weakened.

"ELEVEN . . . twelve . . . thirteen . . . fourteen . . . fifteen . . ."

I dressed again in the same clothes I had removed—how long ago? I looked at the clock. Six-fourteen. In less than a quarter of an hour, the earth had slipped out of its axis. I had been sucked into the vacuum. The entire universe had witnessed my terror.

No.

Robin Sorokin, fifteen years old, had run away and left her mother a note which said, in part, "This has nothing to do with love." Her mother, unobserved in her bedroom, experienced a short interval of shock, then recovered her equilibrium and told herself: *Talk to Laura and Ruth. They'll know where she's gone.*

Laura Mathis insisted she did not know where Robin had gone.

I could not read her face. An impassive cameo. A face camouflaged by its own perfection. Her flecked green eyes gazed at me with a directness that neither revealed nor took in. The directness of objects in space. Small pebbles in the street, marbles in a bowl. This hardening had occurred gradually, over the years, so slowly that I had not noticed how much like chiseled stone the face of Robin's best friend had become. I had carried to the Mathis house my old image of a more pliant and expressive Laura, little girl Laura, and not until yesterday did I realize how inaccurate that image was. It shocked me.

Not Laura's face.

I mean the faultiness of my perceptions, the distortions and evasions of my overrated eye.

Laura sat between her parents at the wrought-iron table on the Mathises' flagstone patio. She chewed on the end of one pale-blond braid. Eve Mathis, her mother, drank scotch on the rocks. Laura's father, Phil Mathis, combed his manicured beard over and over with his fingers.

"Seems to me," Phil said to Eve, looking over Laura's head as if she were not there beside him, "that we have to believe the girl."

Laura smirked. "Your faith overwhelms me."

"Don't get fresh," Eve snapped. To Phil, she said, "And don't call her 'the girl.'" To me, she said, "I'm sorry, Janet."

She was not speaking about Robin's disappearance. She meant the discord. I have known Eve for twelve years, and she has been apologizing for the discord all that time.

Brian used to say, "If we fought like Eve and Phil—I mean, if we were always *at it*, Janet—it would be easier to deal with."

17

When the fighting began between us, he said, "I can't deal with this, Janet. I'll have an ulcer before I'm forty."

The year Brian turned thirty-three, our divorce became final, his mistress had to have an abortion, and he spent two weeks in the hospital with a bleeding ulcer.

In politics, the ability to predict trends is an asset.

The trends of each life are inscribed in the genes. Hieroglyphs.

I deciphered Robin the best that I could, but the translation was inadequate.

"Laura," I said, "maybe if you and I could talk privately—"

She moved toward me, almost imperceptibly. Phil felt the flicker of movement in his daughter and he put his hand on her arm.

"There's nothing she can tell you, Janet, that she can't discuss in front of her mother and me."

Phil Mathis works for the State Department. His assignments have included South Vietnam, Chile, and Rhodesia. He provides, he says, "technical assistance." I wanted to say: *Stop playing games. Be my ally. Teach me everything you know about espionage. I need technical assistance.* His eyes refused my request. They are the kind of eyes that require some gesture of submission before they will negotiate: a tremor, or a humble bow, or, in Eve's case, scotch on the rocks.

I gave him nothing and he kept his hand on Laura's arm.

Eve said, "What do you think Janet is going to do to Laura? Brainwash her?"

Phil said, "Eve, shut up."

Laura said, "If you both don't stop it, I'll have an attack."

Laura has asthma. When the atmosphere, inside or out, gets too rancid, Laura cannot breathe. Laura's brother, Zane, is troubled with skin rashes that no ointment is able to soothe for long. Laura has been to many allergists and pulmonary specialists, and Zane has seen a number of dermatologists.

Why didn't I notice when her face began to harden?

Once Laura said to me—she was eleven, maybe twelve—"I wish you were my mother. I wish Robin and I were sisters, and you were our mother, and I lived here instead of in my house."

Robin wrote, *I just had to get out of this house.*

I said, "Laura, didn't she say *anything* to you in the last few

18

days? Maybe it didn't seem important then, but now it might—"

The words swelled in my throat, lost their form. I stared into the Mathises' yard. It is rich with perennials: phlox, iris, day lily, rose. Eve once said, "I don't do a damn thing. Every year they just come up. If they depended on me, they'd have been dead a long time ago."

I have approached my own garden scientifically, testing the soil to determine nutrient levels, fertilizing, mulching, plucking out the smallest wisp of weed.

My garden does not do much better than theirs.

The secret must be in the bloom itself. In the tenacity of its instinct to survive. Either it will bloom or it won't, depending less on the care it receives than on the message carried in its pistils, in the tunnel of its stem, in the twisted strands of its roots.

I am not sure if I believe that.

I said, "Laura, are you sure?"

"I don't know anything," she said.

I did not believe that at all. But it was clear to me that her denial was impenetrable. Defeated, I said, "If you remember something, please get in touch."

Robin had written, *Sometime soon I'll get in touch.*

I stood up. Underneath her gauze blouse, Laura's chest began to move in little heaving spasms. She made a circle of her mouth and sucked on an imagined tube of oxygen. Eve took a last gulp of scotch, set down the glass, and massaged Laura's back.

"C'mon, sweetie," Eve pleaded. "It's okay, baby, in and out, in and out."

Laura wheezed like a wounded animal.

Phil Mathis took my elbow and guided me out of the yard, down the black-topped driveway to my car.

He said, "She can't be upset."

I took with me the sound of Laura's jagged rasp, that discord, a static I have not been able to clear out of my mind.

The sociologists lament the breakdown of the family, but the scientist knows: everything breaks down. Cells divide. The entwined strands of DNA separate. Life sunders itself again and again.

———

Ruth's mother came to the door with flour all over her hands. "I'm baking bread," Carol Hemming said. "Come talk to me in the kitchen."

She assumed I'd come for a visit, though I am not one to drop in on people. Carol is a woman of anachronistic faith. She believes in all the passé rituals: coffee klatches, bridge clubs, Tupperware parties, and recipe exchanges. For the three years that she has been in Washington, she has not been able to find women with whom to organize these rites, but she grows hopeful each time the doorbell rings, or the phone. Eagerness emanates from her like a sweet-smelling incense from which you draw back or which you decide to inhale, growing drowsy and complacent in its presence. I have learned to be vigilant. It passes for aloofness, but be aware: the organism marshals its defenses against that to which it is most susceptible.

I followed Carol to her kitchen. She poured me a cup of coffee, sliced me a piece of bread just out of the oven. I sat on a stool at the counter while she punched down another swollen mass of dough.

"The girls aren't back yet," she said.

I shuddered with hope. *"Back from where?"*

"From the library. Ruthie said this morning she'd be home late, they were going to the library to study, she'd get dinner at Roy Rogers. I don't like it when she comes home this late, even though it's still light out. I like her home earlier, especially when Mike works late, but no one else around here seems—"

The Hemmings came to Washington from Indianapolis when Mike Hemming got a good job at the Federal Trade Commission. They moved their Early American furniture into their Tudor house, and Carol has been lost ever since.

I am lost now.

I told her about Robin's note, and Carol Hemming covered her face with her hands. When she lowered them, her face was floured a deathly white.

"Oh my *God*," she whispered. "You don't think that my Ruthie . . . oh my God, Janet, I'm sorry to be so selfish, but you don't think that my Ruthie—"

I said, "I understand," but that was imprecise.

20

I meant, *I feel the same about Robin.*

Robin wrote, *I don't expect you to understand.*

I do not.

When Ruth Hemming slammed the front door and yelled a greeting, her mother began to cry.

Ruth materialized in the kitchen. She put her arms around her mother and spoke to her soothingly. She patted her mother's head, smoothed the hair back from her mother's brow. She was focused on her mother's pain with such complete attention that I was not sure Ruth even knew I was in the room. There was about the scene a ritualistic familiarity, an ease with which daughter comforted mother, and the mother allowed herself to be solaced. I realized then that Carol cried often, and Ruth comforted often.

A confusion of roles, perhaps: a neurotic syndrome.

But how I envied them that embrace.

The timer buzzed. Carol dried her eyes on her apron and took another browned loaf out of the oven.

She said, "I'll be back in a minute, Janet. I have to go wash my face."

Ruth said to me, "Was she upset when you got here, Mrs. Sorokin?"

The static.

I said, "No, she was fine, Ruth. She—"

"My mother is never fine. Sometimes she's less upset than other times, that's all. But she's never fine."

What I have valued in my work is the candor on both sides of the lens. The scientist admits: *I want to know everything.* The specimen submits: *I will not pretend to be other than I am simply because you are watching me.*

This was Brian's complaint: that I wanted marriage to have the clarity of an equation. That I did not have enough respect for coyness. That I failed to understand that life was more theater than laboratory, and masks were as vital as spleens.

Ruth's face looked old; she was not wearing a mask.

Think of chronology as an outmoded tool.

When I told her about Robin, Ruth said, "I know where she's gone, Mrs. Sorokin," and she spoke in the same tone that she'd used when she'd comforted her mother.

Isn't that what you croon to a child in pain? *I know, I know.*

Ruth crooned to Carol and now she crooned to me. "I know where she's gone." *I know, I know.*

It struck me then that a reason Robin had liked Ruth so much from the start was because Ruth crooned and comforted, while I had lost the skill, had judged it obsolete and allowed it to atrophy.

"Where?" I said, the word hanging like a net in the air.

"To Charlie's."

"Charlie who?"

"*Charlie,*" she said. "That poet. *You* know."

Of course I did not. My ignorance was the only fact of which I was certain, and even there I had doubts about its magnitude.

"I don't know any Charlie, Ruth. Is this a boy from school? I thought I knew all the boys that Robin—"

"This is the older one," she said. "I wouldn't call him a boy." She smiled. "I guess it's relative."

"What *older* one? Tell me his full name."

She stared at me out of the heart of her midwestern innocence. "You really don't know?"

I shook my head.

Her face closed itself off to me. Not a mask. A light, extinguished. "This is worse than I thought."

"What?" Carol said, coming back into the kitchen. "What's worse?"

"About Robin," Ruth said.

To me she said, "I never realized you didn't know about Charlie. I wouldn't have told . . . I just assumed—"

"Who is he? Where does he live?"

Ruth was silent. Her silence filled the room like dough rising in a bowl, taking up all the space, all the air in the space that contained it. My mouth grew very dry.

"Answer Mrs. Sorokin," Carol said to her daughter.

Ruth shook her head no.

I wanted to punch through that silence, to pummel it back to a short pause, a simple breath between sentences.

I persisted, but she shook her head *no* again and again. She had realized: I was not after information; what I wanted was intelligence.

If your child leaves you a note which says, in part, *I just had to get out of this house,* are you behaving like a spy if you decide to find her?

If you want to know Charlie's last name?

Charlie's address?

(Once, when Brian told me proudly that Eve Mathis had agreed to work as a "plant" in the congressional office of Fletcher's opponent in the senatorial primary, I said, "Brian, I don't know how you stand yourself."

"Ah," he said. "The lady who's been faking orgasms for the last two years is now on the Ethics Committee."

There are certain forms of coyness which Brian does not appreciate. Certain masks.)

Carol said, "Janet, I think it would be better if you went home and I'll call you there. I think Ruthie and I need to work this out alone."

I wanted to stay and watch. I wanted to know what it was in this particular household that enabled this mother and daughter to *work this out.* What were the variables for *working this out?*

But I could not stay. I was, to put it harshly, a contaminant.

I cannot think of a less harsh way to put it.

I rifled through Robin's drawers but found no trace of a poet named Charlie. No scrap of paper, no photograph, nothing, zero. I closed my eyes, no blinder than when they'd been open. I waited for compensatory powers: none came.

I had lost certain vital senses. I was not operating properly. Then I realized: I had been injured. Yes. There had been an accident of sorts, and I was smashed flat as the sheet of paper on which Robin had written her crushing message.

After the skeleton is formed, the genes that produce new bone tissue rest. But should a bone be crushed, these genes awaken to orchestrate the healing process. I waited to be healed. I waited for sleeping genes to recognize the emergency. I counted on internal compensations: none came.

What came was Carol's call, and it took me fourteen rings to answer it. Say that my reflexes were slow. Say that I am an electrical system, the circuitry wired before I was born, and I had blown a fuse.

Say that I was temporarily out of order.

Carol said, "When you didn't answer, I was afraid—"

"I was, too."

Say that I was afraid to answer my own telephone. And it could have been Robin. I knew that, vaguely, even as the ringing persisted. That is what fear does, it renders everything vague except its own formlessness. I can only deduce that I was, in part, afraid to hear from my daughter, afraid of that which I wanted the most. Afraid of what she would say, or would not say. Of what she had become in those short hours. Or of what she had been all along that I had failed to see.

For how long have I been blind? Out of order for how long?

Carol said, "I got Ruthie to talk to me."

Shaman.

"And?"

"His name is Charlie Frayne. He lives near Dupont Circle. Robin met him this fall when he ran a poetry-writing workshop in her English class. Ruthie says they got to be . . . close. Ruthie says that Robin went to his apartment lots of times after school."

"And she's with him?"

"Janet, Ruthie doesn't know that for sure. I know she *told* you she did, but she just . . . *assumed* . . ."

I wanted her assumptions to be correct. English class. Dupont Circle. An apartment less than two miles away. I found him in the phone book. Charles M. Frayne. 207 1/2 P Street.

(This is a city that pretends to run on logic. Naming streets by letter, in order, is one way in which the guise of logic is perpetuated. "As long as you know the alphabet," Brian would tell Robin when she was small, "you can't get lost.")

I could imagine the apartment. Mattress covered with faded madras spread, piles of dirty clothes on the bare floor, posters tacked to the wall, orange crates laden with candles and incense burners, prayer bells hanging from the ceiling. I could see the beaded curtains shimmering in the doorways and I could hear the music, a pulsating chant, some guru with electric guitar.

I could see Charlie himself: great mane of hair and beard, fine-boned face lost in a mass of tangles, laser-sharp eyes, tie-dyed T-shirt and frayed jeans, beach thongs, a copper bracelet on his thin wrist.

Stereotype or archetype, what does it matter? Say *poet*, and the mechanism in me which produces images yields the picture I have given you.

Say *Robin*, and this is what I see: Brian's long reed of a body, a fluidity of movement that implies the absence of joints; a Modigliani face of planes and angles; the cat eyes I gave her; the cat's stillness she carries with her as if there were a song, some private lyric, for which she listens, to which she might dance, which she would follow like a child of Hamelin.

A more concrete observation: I have just remembered that the obstetrician who delivered Robin used forceps to guide her resisting body out of my body, and the instrument left slight indentations beside each ear.

Those marks of her birth are still there and I am the only one who knows it.

What else have I forgotten that only I can remember?

A maze, where I had presumed order. Inside this labyrinth, the streets are not lettered consecutively, the alphabet is not a reliable guide.

What I need is a new cartography.

Charlie Frayne said, "What you need is a drink."

His bar was well-stocked. He fixed me a martini, poured himself some Dubonnet, and we sat on modular chairs in a room filled with lush plants and fine lithographs. He was a pleasant-faced man, fortyish, and he had been in the midst of folding his laundry when I rang his bell. A conservative wardrobe: cotton shirts, khakis, white handkerchiefs, black socks, a good supply of Jockey shorts, and a green plaid bathrobe.

Simply because he was folding his laundry, on evidence that skimpy, I deemed him decent. In the past, it has taken me hours of talk and observation to come to conclusions about character, and even then I have administered tests and verified my findings. Since yesterday evening, however, I have not had the time to examine and weigh, and I am beginning to understand what Brian means when he talks about playing his hunches.

"Her girlfriend said she . . . visited . . . you. Here. Often. After school."

"A few times," he said. "Uninvited. She would bring her

poems with her. I never let her in the door. We'd sit on a bench in the Circle while I read them." His chin lifted. "She's got some talent, I thought it was worth the time. I think she . . . I think she saw me as a *father*, that was my impression. I admit I felt uneasy when she came here, but I try—how can I say it?"—he fumbled with his fingers for words—"I try not to analyze too much, makes everything more complicated than it usually is. I haven't seen her in weeks, and I have no reason to lie to you, believe me."

I did. Truth has its own physiology. A certain alignment of the facial muscles. The steadiness of the gaze. The mouth's shaping of words more than the words themselves. Respiration patterns: whether the nostrils flare, whether the cheeks puff out or cave in, the jut or fall of the jaw.

Inherited characteristics, true. But what is inherited? The body's particular gestures, or the meaning underlying the gestures?

Is there a gene for honesty?

He had an honest face: what does that mean?

Eli would call my conclusion "unsubstantiated." Brian would applaud my willingness to "go with the gut."

Charlie leaned forward, and his gray-flecked hair fell across his brow. "Look," he said, thinking me still suspicious, "I have two kids of my own." He cupped his hands, as if a child were in the cradle of each palm. "They live with their mother in Virginia. My daughter's eleven. I *know*—at least I *think* I know—what you must be going through."

I know, I know.

I said, "Do you know what I wish? I wish you were a lecherous bastard. I wish I'd come here and found her with you in your bed and—"

"No, you don't."

"Yes I do! I do! You don't seem to understand that now I have no idea where she is!"

A cyclone was rising up around me: the funnel was my own rage. I looked through its swirling mass, and the distinct angles of the room shifted and blurred. Matter broke down. Formulations collapsed. What match was order for this sudden burst of anarchy? I could have killed him with my hands, but it was not for Charlie Frayne that I was consumed with such anger.

27

It was for Robin, that she could hurt me like this.

The triple helix: *Don't hurt me. I love you. Forgive me.* This is the secret the race passes to each new member, the code whispered into our collective ear.

The anger subsided. "I suppose I'll go back home," I said. "She might call." My voice was little, tired.

"I just thought of something." He leaped up as if the idea had taken root in him like a tree and grown to full height inside his body. "I've got all the kids' poems here, everything they wrote for me, I pick out the best ones for a book I—"

He cut himself off with a finger signaling for me to wait, and I heard file drawers slamming open and shut in one of the rooms off the long center hall. He returned with a sheaf of papers, and I recognized Robin's squared-off script before I could make out a single word. If I were looking into a crowd of people now, features indistinct, colors blurred, still I would know her by the way her head tilts a bit as she walks, by the rhythm of her gait, or, if she were standing still, by the way her shoulders lift slightly and stiffen with what I have taken to be the impatience of a precocious child, but could be—now that I have felt my own—fury.

I sat with Charlie Frayne and sifted like a sleuth through Robin's poems. A bloodhound sniffing for nuance.

I have devalued nuance in favor of fact, but consider this: I once wrote poems myself, once I believed that metaphors were more reliable than statistics and surely more true.

Some of Robin's metaphors: "She was like phosphorus, faint glow and cold to the touch." "A grin of moon flashes in the sky's sullen face." "Lightning roars and wires come down like dreams."

Tell me what truth those words hold, and how reliable that truth is.

Charlie had written in the margin: "These poems contain a lot of pain and anger. But a beauty, too. A delicacy in the diction. Look how often you use the idea of *shining*, even when the ultimate connotation is dark. It's as if you're hiding your own radiance, but it sneaks out in the very language you choose."

Her radiance. If you had asked me to describe my daughter before yesterday, I would not have used such a term. I would have used terms such as *intelligent*, *responsible*, *independent*, *perceptive, mature.* On the negative side, I would have mentioned *inflexible. Radiant* would not have occurred to me, but now, in memory's prism, she is so luminous that I have to close my eyes, the light makes them water.

"Well," he said, "there's nothing here."

I feigned agreement.

He walked with me down the stairs to the front lobby of his building. "I'm sorry I haven't been much help," he said.

"I'm sorry, too," I said, not telling him how much, in fact, he had.

As I drove home, the sky turned smoky and the red sun drifted away like a child's balloon. I passed the National Zoo, its iron gate locked. All those animals, wild and rare, safe and accounted for in their replicated jungles, their imitation deserts, the birds in their roofed-in aviary soaring as if the sky were still their dominion. What kept them there, content in their simulated environments, while my daughter had flown from her natural home?

L ike a fireman waiting for a siren, I slept all night in my clothes. There was no alarm. No bell, no pounding on the door, no horn honking me out of my sleep. I say *sleep*, but it was more that murky state in which the brain bobs back and forth between thought and dream.

A procession of images. An all-night movie, sounds muffled, some frames indistinct, others more vivid than I can believe.

In certain laboratories in America, people slept last night with electrodes taped to their eyes and head, having their dreams measured.

I am speaking of the sort of dreams you have at night, of course, as opposed to dreams like Brian's of press conferences in the Mayflower Hotel and staff parties on the White House lawn, or dreams like mine of "breakthrough discoveries" and Nobel prizes.

Measure this: In the living room of the three-room apartment where I grew up, my parents are preparing for sleep. It is 1951. My father removes the dark green cushions from the Hide-a-bed, and stacks them neatly in a corner of the room. He and my mother struggle to open the bed, as they will struggle to close it again in the morning. The folding mechanism does not work properly. A lemon. This is my father's term: he is not a scientist, but he has a gift for objectivity.

Outside, the Pittsburgh steel mills sully the air. I learn early that rest is an effort, breathing a dangerous act. In the morning, my father packs an extra white shirt into his Fuller Brush sample case and drives his old Plymouth up and down the grimy hills of the city.

Earlier. 1937. My father travels a tri-state route with a new line of hand tools. In the glove compartment of his car, he keeps the mustache comb that had belonged to his father (dead of influenza in his son's infancy) and a bobbin from his mother's sewing machine.

I hear the treadle clank, I see her late at night, bent over her work. On the day my father graduates from high school, she comes home from the ceremony, lies down for a nap, and never gets up again. Her power has finally failed.

Now (then) my father calls on Gutman's Hardware in Yellow Springs, Ohio. He discovers my mother, one of two clerks, sorting nuts and bolts in the rear of her father's shop. Her own mother died when she was eleven.

Do my parents recognize in each other the signs of irreparable loss?

Or do they just like one another's looks?

(Once I heard Phil Mathis ask Brian why he married me, and Brian said, "Because she had a nice ass." That was not, and was, the truth.)

My father stays in town a week instead of the single night he'd planned. In three months they marry, though I do not dream that scene. I have heard you cannot dream your own death. I cannot dream my own parents' wedding, but I am not suggesting a connection.

When my father is not on the road, they sleep together in my mother's childhood bed, eat their meals at Jacob Gutman's table. My father chafes at the arrangement. He wants to take his new wife back to Pittsburgh, find himself a dazzling product and a local route, come home nights to his own private place.

Fearful that he means it, my mother takes him for evening walks along the pristine Yellow Springs streets. She winds

31

him through the famous college campus, appeals to his respect for the intellectual climate.

(My father was always a reader. In his spare time, he hunted for epigrams, aphorisms, wise sayings he could underline in books. He kept Bartlett's *Familiar Quotations* beside the sofa bed on the end table that doubled as a nightstand. "If I didn't have to make a living," he'd say, "I'd get an education." Even now, past seventy, eyes failing, he sends me clippings from the *Miami Herald* and petitions the nursing home where he lives for more magazines in the sunroom.)

Jacob Gutman offers him work in the hardware store, ownership in time. My father considers the proposition, declines. He feels shrunken, scaled down to fit the limits of my mother's small clean world. He misses noise, grit, the sheer power of size. He and my mother drive out of Ohio, through West Virginia, across the Pennsylvania border, into what my mother calls "the smelly fog that never goes away."

Jacob Gutman writes my father a letter. "I lost my wife young. For me it was an eye plucked out. Now you have plucked out the other."

In two months my grandfather is dead.

In dreams, all deaths other than your own are possible.

He leaves his store to his only remaining clerk, Oscar Cloward, a Yellow Springs boy.

A year later, my mother wakes in the middle of the cold January night, struggles out from under the quilts, and waddles toward the bathroom. On the faded rag rug that had been her mother's, she feels a sudden pressure, then a pop, then a gush of water pouring down her swollen legs.

The rug is drenched.

My mother screams.

Always at his best when traveling is involved, my father calmly helps her peel off the wet nightgown and get into dry clothes. He remembers the packed suitcase under the bed. He wraps her up in a coat she can no longer button, and winds a long plaid wool scarf over her head and twice around her neck, then ties a bulky knot under her chin. He eases her trembling hands, finger by finger, into her gloves. She fidgets, tells him to hurry. He speaks to her firmly: "It's a bitter cold night. You want pneumonia? You want complications?" She moves her helmeted head stiffly from side to side. He puts on his own coat. He closes the door to 4C behind them. He gives her a little push, as if she were a stalled mechanical toy, then he takes her elbow and helps her walk along the dim hall, down the four flights of rubber-treaded steps. He holds open the building's heavy lead-glass front door and eases my mother out into the frigid night of my birth.

I ask her: "What was your labor like?"

"You know what happens if you boil an egg too long? All the water cooks out and finally the egg explodes, bursts apart like a bomb. A terrible, stinking mess."

The overcooked egg, or me? Her meanings are rarely clear. Whenever she speaks to me, she looks distracted, as if part of her is having a conversation I cannot hear with someone I have never met.

1944.

Beyond these rooms, people (my mother tells me) are having a war and my father has joined them. This is what my mother tells me. She talks to his photograph. I watch the picture's mouth, but it has nothing to say to us. She sits in the kitchen for hours, reading his letters over and over. She tells me, "Daddy sends kisses," but I do not feel his lips on my forehead, I can barely remember the rough texture of his cheek. When he finally comes home, I huddle behind the sofa bed until my mother drags my unyielding body out from its hiding place.

"You're hurting his feelings," she says. "You're making him sad."

He thrusts a stuffed giraffe at me. I refuse to accept it.

My mother says, "Please, I haven't been out-of-my-mind lonely all these months for a child and her father to look at each other like stones." Her eyes are blazing with anguish.

I put out my hands for the giraffe, my father's lips graze my hair, but a silence hangs between us that still, thirty-five years later, has not been broken.

My mother takes in ironing. She spends hours each day getting out the wrinkles in wealthy people's clothes, smoothing their percale sheets, their embroidered linen tablecloths and matching hand-hemmed napkins. She watches soap operas while she works. "When I'm watching my stories," she says, "I forget who I am."

I am remembering who I am.

I am in bed, with a bout of bronchitis.

"Every time I turn around she's home again." My mother is talking to my father, who is soaking his feet in the claw-footed tub.

He sighs. "She has a weak constitution."

Her voice rises. "It's the smoke, the dirt, if we had stayed in Yellow Springs—"

He tells her to talk softer, does she want me to hear their arguments?

"She can't hear a thing, she's in bed."

In our cramped quarters, privacy is one of the illusions my mother insists upon, despite the facts.

Later I join them in the living room. My father is on the sofa, reading from Bartlett's. My mother is ironing and watching *I Love Lucy*. Lucy and her friend Ethel, locked in a meat freezer, pound frantically on the thick wooden door. My mother begins to cry. The tears stream down her cheeks, drip on the iron, and sizzle. She cries nearly silently, except for a bumpiness in her breathing. A life preserver, deflating.

For me, crying has always been a relinquishment. As if I am losing something I need for strength.

My father speaks to her, but she seems unaware of his presence. I ask her what is wrong, but her eyes look beyond me. My father unplugs the iron, sits her down on the sofa, sends me to sleep. I watch from the small hallway. He brings her tissues which she does not use. He kneels beside her and pats her arms, taps at her shoulders, gives her wet face tiny, gentle smacks. He fiddles with her as if she were our television set which he is always trying to bring back into focus. He does not understand how either is put together, the set or my mother. Finally he slumps in the chair that faces his broken-down wife and watches her as she is. When I go to bed, she is still crying.

She cries all night. They never even open the sofa. In the morning she is the same.

My father makes hushed, nervous phone calls. He packs some of her things in the battered brown suitcase that she

34

might have used when she went to the hospital to deliver herself of me. Mrs. Stein, the old lady from down the hall, appears in our apartment, puts her arm around me, says, "We're going to have such a good time together." But her chin quivers, her eyes are glazed. My father helps my mother into her coat. She is so limp, so emptied.

"We're going to be okay," he tells me as they leave. "We're all going to be fine." He tries to smile but his face is frozen in pain.

Mrs. Stein sets me up on her faded brocade couch, turning it into a makeshift sickbed with two big feather pillows and a gray wool regulation Army blanket that her youngest son brought her from France. In a small enamel saucepan, she boils water, drops in a dollop of Vicks Vaporub, sets the pot on the bridge table she has opened next to the sofa, and tells me to lean over the steamy solution.

I inhale, and everything inside me dislodges, warms. I think my heart itself may melt.

After the treatments, Mrs. Stein takes away the pan. She brings out mugs of cocoa and a plate of graham crackers and settles in for a talk.

She is a great talker. In warm weather, she is always outside, on the front stoop, primed for conversation with anyone who cares to join her.

"Won't be long you'll be back in your own place," she tells me. My mother has been gone for three days. "I can imagine how boring it is for you here, cooped up with an old lady, no?"

"No," I say, "I like it here a lot."

She looks around the cluttered room. The walls are plastered with photographs of children and grandchildren, familial images are everywhere. On the tables are trinkets, figurines, candy dishes, crewel coasters, souvenir ashtrays from places such as Atlantic City, Coney Island, mountain resorts in the Poconos. In addition to the couch and rocker, there are three upholstered wing chairs. Six lamps here in Mrs. Stein's living room.

Radiant.

So luminous I have to close my eyes, the light makes them water.

Once she'd had a big house filled with people and furniture

that fit. Now the people are gone and she has jammed together as much as she can of that vanished household into her small apartment.

"I try to make it nice," she says. She stops rocking, rests her wrinkled face in her hands. "But an old lady lives alone, the place . . . I don't know . . . after a while, it *smells* lonely." She smiles apologetically. "Not so great for a little girl, sick or not."

I tell her that the place smells fine. I say, "I think you're lucky to live by yourself. You don't have fighting when you live by yourself."

Mrs. Stein draws back. She makes tiny, precise motions in the air with her fingers, as if she is knitting me a vital message. "Three nice people like your family got more than fights. Problems, who don't? But happiness, too, that I'm sure." She rocks hard, with certainty.

Happiness, too. Mrs. Stein goes to fix our lunch. I close my eyes and begin to weave a fragile tapestry in my mind's darkest room: my mother washing my hair for me over the bathroom basin, her fingers massaging away the tension in my scalp, her off-key version of "I'm Gonna Wash That Man Right Out of My Hair" reverberating off the tiles; my father taking me one Sunday afternoon to see the dinosaur skeletons at the museum, telling me after our tour, "Whenever I feel like a failure, I think, *If such huge powerful animals couldn't make it, why should I expect miracles from myself?*" and whisking me into the corner drugstore for a chocolate phosphate, his sallow face flushed and invigorated with self-forgiveness. One winter night the electricity goes off, my father searches in vain for a flashlight, and my mother, in a fit of silliness, sticks all sixty birthday candles from a box she finds in the cupboard into the applesauce cake she baked that afternoon, and sets the candles ablaze; we all huddle around the table, partying in the fast-burning light.

I weave together the brightest threads I can find. Happiness, too. Happiness, too. A beautiful picture to look at.

But I live in dingy rooms. I breathe sadness and fatigue.

My mother is crying in some unknown place, and my father is out on the road, knocking on door after door, lugging his heavy case across the city's exhausting terrain.

Who am I fooling?
I open my eyes.

My mother is gone for two weeks. All my father will tell me is, "She's having a rest." When she comes home, she is less sad than before, less tired, but more jittery. I ask her where she'd gone. She keeps her back to me, talks from the sink where she is peeling potatoes. "I visited Yellow Springs," she says. "I went home."

I do not know if she is telling the truth.

Is there a gene for honesty? For trust?

We never speak of her absence again.

But she has told me one thing I have always suspected: my mother does not feel that she belongs with us at all. In her own family, she feels like a hostage.

Robin wrote, *I just had to get out of this house.*

Interpret the REM pattern here: after my mother returns from her rest, my parents stop touching each other.

Brian and I: we touched each other alive. It seemed sufficient, more than enough.

My mother no longer offers her cheek for my father's peck when he comes home from work. He does not take her elbow anymore when they walk beside each other on the street. Even at busy intersections, they navigate unattached.

Cells divide. The entwined strands of DNA separate. Life sunders itself again and again.

Before, on some evenings, he'd stretch out on the sofa and she'd sit at one end, his feet on her lap. But this ends: if one is on the sofa, the other chooses the chair.

She is standing on a shaky stepladder, changing a light bulb in the kitchen. My father reaches up for her knees to hold her steady, but she arches away from him. "You'll make me fall!" she says, and he withdraws his hands, curling them into fists at his sides.

There are no more connections.

For days at a time, they stop talking to each other. I am the courier. They send me across that vast distance alone. Harsh geography. Cold. Uninhabited.

Nights. I lie awake and listen for the old creaks and thumps of the sofa bed, my mother's moans, my father's shuddering sighs. Now there is only his snoring, the lonely rattle of solitary sleep.

(After Brian moved out, it took me a year to think of it as "my" bedroom, and only after I'd painted it blue, taken down the curtains, put up shutters instead, moved every piece of furniture to a different wall.)

The landlord, on his rounds to pick up rent checks, tells us about the new tenant who will occupy the vacant rooms upstairs.

"She's a nice single workingwoman."

My mother replies, "I've always felt sorry for spinsters," withdrawing into herself as if to imagine the inner life of a person even more unhappy than she.

Now (then) she cleans the slats of the venetian blinds and peers down on two husky men unloading Selma's possessions from the back of a pickup truck. Selma stands on the sidewalk, directing. She wears a white uniform. Her peroxide-blond hair is stuffed into a net. Her lips are purple-pink, her eyelids iridescent green. I have just come in from school. I say to my mother, "She's either a waitress or a nurse, which do you think?"

My mother says, "She's nothing but a floozy."

"What's a floozy?"

"A no-good, that's what. A runaround."

She hands me the rag and tells me to finish the blinds. She resumes her ironing. Selma's men pound up and down the steps. My mother gets lost in *Search for Tomorrow*.

Above our heads, Selma vacuums while we eat. She has lived in the building for six months. My mother eyes the ceiling. She says, "Aha."

"Aha what?" my father says. The piece of meat loaf he is sliding from the serving platter to his plate falls on the checked vinyl tablecloth. Tomato sauce spatters across his undershirt.

My mother stares at the stain. "Look at that mess."

He shovels the food onto the plate, wipes up the tablecloth with his napkin, dabs at his undershirt. "Aha what?"

She blinks, recalling. "Her," she says, pointing upward

with her chin. "When she sweeps, you know she's . . ."

"You know she's what?" I ask.

"Expecting . . . company." She sends my father a trapped glance.

But he refuses to receive it. He no longer comes to her rescue. "The way you carry on," he says, "you'd think she ran a whorehouse up there!"

My mother gasps. She grabs at the air, as if she could get my father's words out of circulation.

My father continues: "If you don't want your daughter to *hear* so much about Selma, don't *talk* so much about her. The way you carry on, you'd think—"

"Don't tell me what I think anymore! From you it comes out dirty, and I *don't need that*!" She pounds out the last three words on the table.

His hands rise defensively. "I resign." He pushes back his chair with such force, it leaves black streaks on the just-waxed linoleum. "You ladies will excuse me, I'll go soak my feet."

Upstairs, Selma pushes her furniture over her clean rugs. "Go do your homework!" my mother snaps. She begins to stack the dishes in the sink so carelessly I know she wants them to break. This after collecting the set patiently, one piece at a time, from the A&P.

"You don't have to yell at *me*," I say, and flounce out of the room.

My father sits in the living-room chair beside the open window. An early-evening breeze flares up the fringe on the paisley slipcover. He is watching the seven-o'clock news.

(Tomorrow Walter Cronkite will inform America that Senator Fletcher McPherson, Democrat from Ohio, has announced his candidacy for the presidency. Fletcher and Brian are planning campaign strategy somewhere off the Florida Keys.

I do not know where Robin is, or what she is planning.)

"I thought you were going to soak your feet," I say to my father. That was his plan. He had made that announcement.

"I didn't know it was news time," he says, keeping his eyes on the set. "I never miss the news."

(Once Robin said, "Look! There's Daddy on the television!" and kissed the screen over and over. Brian and Fletcher were in the Soviet Union, fact-finding. For weeks, she would not miss the news, although Brian did not reappear during her vigil. She was nine years old.)

An Englishman is sitting on a long couch strewn with embroidered pillows. He talks about being held captive in a little African country. "I would say they are brutes," the Englishman says quietly. "I would say they have little grasp of civilization as we know it." He puffs on his pipe.

I say to my father, "Would you like me to bring the basin in here for you?"

He slaps his thighs. "All I want is thirty minutes alone in my own house. A lousy half hour. Is that too much to ask?"

I lock myself in my room. In the mirror, I watch myself weep. My face grows puffed and mottled. Above me, music materializes. An orchestra plays "Singin' in the Rain" and Selma sings along. Then laughter, Selma and a man. Outside my door, my mother yells at my father to take out the garbage and he screams, "I'm in the goddamn bathroom soaking my goddamn feet!"

My name is Janet and my lineage is conventional.

I raise my window. I stick out my head. The music floats down to me on the warm shifting air. "There's a smile on my face and I'm ready for love," sings Selma. The dirty sky goes orange and gold. The moon drifts in behind the clotheslines out back, where Mr. Roselli's undershorts flap like flags. I climb out onto the narrow fire escape that zigzags down our side of the building, listen to the sounds from Selma's place, and watch the night come in like a shining ship.

(Charlie Frayne wrote, "Look how often you use the idea of *shining*, even when the ultimate connotation is dark."

A grin of moon flashes in the sky's sullen face.)

My mother bangs on my door. "Open up right this minute! You have no reason to lock yourself away from your family!"

I bolt up the iron steps to Selma's landing. I hunker down beside her artificial palm tree in its green plastic pot. A stuffed monkey swings by an arm from a frond. The sheer curtains billow out over my head, and I see Selma in a black slip dancing on her bed, while a man in nothing but undershorts like Mr. Roselli's sprawls on his back on the fluffy white rug and grins at her performance. She does a clumsy pirouette and falls down on the mattress. They laugh and laugh. He gets up, weaves around to the nightstand, and

40

fills a glass of wine for each of them from a bottle beside a dainty lamp with a fluted shade. On the radio, an orchestra plays "Some Enchanted Evening" and Selma drapes herself dramatically around her friend. He kisses her on the mouth. Wine spills all over the rug. Selma says, "Oh shit," draws back, rubs at the spreading stain with her toe. "Forget that," he says, and massages her lace-covered breast with his free hand. But Selma says, "I'm sweating like a pig, you know that?" "Hell," he says, "I don't mind." "Well I do," she says. "Let me get fixed up, I need to feel pretty."

Does she think of it as seduction?

(I gave up trying to seduce Eli a long time ago. A long time ago I did not think of it as seduction.)

She twists herself free from his hug and settles herself on the pink velveteen seat of her dressing-table stool. He plops down on the bed and watches her. The table is skirted with pink accordion pleats and covered with bottles of toilet water, tubes of lipstick, mascara wands, compacts, jars of foundation, hair rollers, little brushes and sponges, and a canister filled with cotton balls.

Selma looks at herself in the mirror. The microscopic squint.

She pushes her wild hair back from either side of her face and cradles it in her hands.

She takes one cotton ball and wipes her skin with slow, careful strokes. She smooths on foundation, working in the makeup with the pads of her index fingers. She dusts her face and neck and the glistening top of her chest with a big powdered puff. She steadies an elbow in one hand and draws on thin precise brows with the other. She glazes each eyelid with metallic blue cream. I see her move her face closer to the mirror's glass to examine her handiwork. She flashes a smile at her friend's reflection; slowly he moistens his lips with his tongue. She thickens a brow with deft fast pencil strokes. She coats each eyelash with mascara, taking her time, moving the wand leisurely from hair to hair. I can tell: she loves her face. She paints her lips magenta, then kisses a tissue over and over until the kiss prints fade away. She brushes her hair into high, frothy waves, and turns her head from side to side to admire the upswept look. Then she swings around on her stool, pouts a little, sucks in her stomach, pulls the straps of her slip off her shoulders, hikes the hem up on her thighs, and says to her friend, "Now aren't I just the most gorgeous thing you ever have seen?"

He growls like a bear and lunges for her. She flings herself into his grasp and they roll together in a tangle of arms and legs all over her bed. From the single writhing creature they have become, I see Selma's hand reach up to turn out the light.

They breathe heavily, raggedly, the dark room itself seems to breathe.

(Brian and I touched each other alive.)

I rise out of my crouch. Moonlight falls on the filigreed iron and I climb down the black lace steps. I go through the open window like a ghost. My true self is still upstairs, in that exotic, flesh-filled room, in that music, in that breathing dark.

My true self. The audacity of dreams, the dogmatic insistence of memory. Mere impressions proclaiming themselves proof.

Give me better proof.

My mother has shoved a note under my door. "Your father and I never want to hurt you," she has written in her tight backhand-sloping style. "We love you. Why must it always be a battle?"

Does she think I have answers to a question like that?

I am on my bed. Selma's face dances across the ceiling.

Ask her, I think, sending my mother a silent, bitter reply. *Maybe she knows, maybe she can tell you what you ought to do.*

Months later. Our apartment has turned equatorial. My mother wakes up with chills, even though it has been in the low nineties and humid for days. She puts a sweater over her housedress and shivers. Her chest hurts. She says, "Feel my head." I do: it is clammy, yet beneath the cold damp skin, I feel flashes of heat. She drinks hot tea. In an hour, she says, "I'm burning up," strips off her sweater, and fans herself violently with last week's *Life*. She begins to cough. When the coughing fit ebbs, she whispers, "Call the doctor," and I do.

He comes quickly. While he examines her, I stand by the window. The shabby block shimmers weirdly beneath me, the other drab buildings and the parked sedans and the cracked, littered sidewalk and a few women walking slowly toward the market with their aluminum shopping carts—all those solid forms waver, I feel that everything has drowned, the whole neighborhood is under water, but only my mother is gasping and choking, while the rest of us, people and objects alike, bob in dreamy acquiescence.

The doctor taps me on the shoulder. I look into his serious face. "Your mother's a sick woman," he says.

I nod.

"She needs to go to the hospital. Can we get in touch with your father?"

"No," I say. "He's out on the road, he doesn't work in any one place, he travels all day."

(Eli says I should get in touch with Brian, but he is on a boat with Fletcher, somewhere off the Florida Keys.)

The doctor says, "Well then, a neighbor, a friend. Somebody who can go in the ambulance with her."

"I can," I say.

He starts to object, but my mother rasps from the sofa, "She can, she can. I don't need a stranger."

He shrugs. He probably finds peculiarities in every family he cares for. He calls the hospital and reserves a bed. Telephones for an ambulance. Meanwhile, I pack what my mother tells me to in that same brown suitcase: her one good nightgown with appliquéd daisies ringing the neckline and cascading down the sleeves, her cotton twill robe, her terry-cloth slippers, a bottle of roll-on deodorant, an emery board, the box of afterbath powder I bought her for her birthday, her hairbrush and comb, the new issue of the *Reader's Digest*.

Observe and record. Observe and record.

She does not seem frightened or upset about going. There is something accepting in her attitude, almost relief. I remember how she looked last year, standing in the doorway in that posture of drained resignation as my father buttoned her coat, and I see the same surrender in her now.

This time I'm going with you.

This time she will not leave me at home with nothing but questions and a dark hole of helplessness opening up in me like a bloodless wound.

The ambulance siren wails, but from inside it sounds

muted and remote. As if the crisis it announces were happening somewhere in the streets through which we speed, instead of here, in this narrow, cushioned space, my sedated mother lying quiet and distant-eyed beside me, me braced between the stretcher and the wall, her purse wedged safely between my knees. It is as if we have gone to an amusement park, my mother and me, and here we are on one of those swirling rides, taking the curves together, sharing the jolts, hardly conscious of the fear we feel, of how anxious we are for the trip to end.

Pneumonia. A hostile microbe has worked its way into her lungs, used up all her breath.

The telephone rings at two in the morning. My father rouses me from a restless sleep. "They want us to come," he says. He has never looked so old.

About half of the people in the building come to my mother's funeral. She has never been close to any of them. They come out of neighborliness, or for other reasons I do not understand. Even Selma comes, toned down, almost prim. My father's few relatives arrive: second cousins, a decrepit uncle, family we rarely see. From my mother's side there is no one. She is the end of her meager line, except for two aunts in Russia and a cousin in California who wires condolences and a basket of gleaming oranges, each one wrapped in crumpled green tissue. Before the casket is closed and the rabbi offers his ancient, mournful chant, I go to see my mother for the last time.

I am so shy.

I walk toward her quietly, my father's sobs receding behind me. She lies in utter repose. But her hair has been crimped and waved in a style not her own—she had worn it straight, turned up at the bottom in a straggly, unfashionable fluff, one of her tortoiseshell combs holding it out of her eyes. They have made up her face with more powder and rouge than she ever used, reddened her lips, given her darker brows than she ever had. All the wrinkles in her skin are gone, as if they had simply ironed them away. And she smells like gardenias. My mother never used cologne, never, but they have doused her with it.

Oh, it comes to me so hard!

They have tried to turn her into Selma, as if I ever wanted that at all, as if I meant it the night I wished my mother were the kind of woman who danced in her slip, drank wine, embraced my father in the dark.

The tears nearly come.

They have to pry my fingers loose from the coffin.

My father mourns her for months, his bereavement traditional.

He calls out to her in the middle of the night. He pummels the deserted side of the sofa bed. He paces off miles back and forth across the linoleum. He curses himself for having let her down. He curses her for having abandoned him. He cries loudly, he cries silently, in the midst of meals, at traffic lights, in the market, in the library where he searches out books for laymen on the meaning of death. He has a spurt of religious fervor. He catches colds. He loses weight.

I appear untouched by my mother's death.

You would not know I am grieving at all: there is no empirical evidence.

My father and teacher confer.

"Write poems," my teacher urges.

"Cry your heart out," my father instructs.

I fail them both.

He grows proud enough of my domestic proficiency. I take over all my mother's tasks and he tells me, "You'll make a good wife someday," his mind's eye fixed on my future wedding.

I say, "Maybe you'll be like Grandpa Gutman and never want me to leave at all."

He flushes. "That was unhealthy, that was an unnatural attachment." He pops two antacids into his mouth and retreats behind the newspaper.

In the kitchen, I plunge my hands into the dishpan suds and lift out a dinner plate. It is white, with a fake platinum rim and a gray rose painted in the center. I throw the wet dish to the floor. It shatters into fragments at my feet. I throw another. I would break them all, if my father did not rush in.

"An accident," I say, and go for the broom.

He kneels down and holds the dustpan. I sweep up the

ruins of my mother's china, imported from the Philippines, collected from the A&P, one piece free with every five-dollar purchase.

"I'm sorry," I say.

For what, or to whom, I have never been sure.

The *Post* thudded against the door. Mr. Henski's vintage Ford sputtered and groaned in his driveway. Birds yammered. A child's Big Wheel caromed over the concrete.

I awoke. Inside, the silence was more discordant than the cacophony outside. The house vibrated with absence. It was as if I were tuned in to a frequency usually out of my range. Think of it: dogs hear sirens long before humans recognize the wail; hungry bats listen for the sound of insect wings slicing the air; leeches tap out rhythms on leaves and other leeches respond. The world reverberates with messages we never receive.

I lay in my rumpled clothes and listened to the hollow tones of loss.

Brian is a blues aficionado. I have claimed a tin ear and even this morning, what I heard had no harmony. One note, playing itself over and over. *Gone, gone, gone.*

But I have never had much affinity for dirges.

In the shower, water pelted me clean and I forced myself to sing. I sang "Go Tell It On the Mountain." I sang "This Land Is Your Land." I sang "There's a Hole in the Bucket." Off-key as usual, but at least my own voice, familiar, bouncing off the tiles.

I dressed, put Robin's note (without reading it again) in my purse, drove to the police station and made myself hum right up to the door of the Bureau of Missing Persons.

A passerby might have thought me lighthearted, but a true observer would have understood: I was throwing out clues, leaving a trail, singing *Come find me* to the only person in earshot, myself.

The window beside Robin's bed overlooks the silver maple she helped me plant in the front yard six years ago.

It is after three now.

Through the grid of branches, I see Laura Mathis move across my shadow-cratered lawn. Although it is warm outside, she is huddled into herself as if chilled to the bone.

My mother was anemic. Often, regardless of the weather, she wore two sweaters, long johns, a pair of my father's socks over her own cotton stockings. At the onset of her final illness, nothing could warm her except sudden explosions of fever, and then nothing could cool her down. She blamed extremes of weather on fallout from Hiroshima. On what did she blame her own body's weather, its refusal to be temperate, its last fatal storm?

Laura says, "Please don't blame me for not telling you last night."

In remorse, her face softens for a moment, becomes the child I remember from the years when I looked closely enough to see her. I put an arm around her; the skin on her arm is cold to my touch.

"Not telling me what, Laura?" I am perspiring, the sweat trickles down my sides.

We are sets of programmed glands, each of us carries our own climate with us wherever we go.

"She's in Boston," Laura says. "She went to her grandmother's in Boston."

In the laboratory, the appropriate response to a major breakthrough is exhilaration.

I am not exhilarated.

The most I can say is that a certain inner turbulence subsides a bit.

"She went to her grandmother's." I repeat it like an oath I have been asked to take, or an axiom I must commit to memory. "She went to Boston."

Laura says, "I wasn't supposed to tell anybody." She is sagging under the weight of betrayal. She has been raised, after all, in a house which condemns betrayal above all other crimes, which values loyalty much more than love, which operates according to the principles of the simplest symbiosis.

In this house, symbiosis has broken down.

Robin is in Boston. She went to her grandmother's house, a drafty Victorian relic in Brighton.

Brian is on a boat with Fletcher, somewhere off the Florida Keys.

I have taken a leave of absence from the institute, stated my mission to Eli, and remained steadfast in the face of his skepticism; and now, facing Laura Mathis in the doorway to this house, receiving from her the knowledge I have been craving, I am further away from my daughter than I could have imagined.

T he first time I met Ada Sorokin, she set her hair on fire with the butane lighter she uses to ignite her perpetual cigarettes.

We were sitting out on the deck of the Sorokins' summer house at the Cape. I had arrived with Brian an hour before, and his mother had sent him to the supermarket in town. "I asked your father to bring some things out last night," she'd said in her Virginia drawl untempered by twenty years in Boston, "but he never . . ." Ada finished the sentence with a sneer which I'd thought, for an instant, had been directed at me. I'd flinched, as if struck.

When her hair caught, I lunged toward her. I flailed at the flame with my hand, burning it.

Ada doused her smoldering lock with lemonade. "I have never considered self-immolation," she said. "I've considered numerous strategies for doing away with myself, but never self-immolation." She examined the soaked, singed ends out of the corner of her eye. "I'll probably die of lung cancer, don't you think?"

I rubbed ice on my palm. I pretended not to hear her.

"Are you in cancer?" she said. She lit her cigarette. "Brian tells me you're in medical research. Does that mean you're in cancer?"

"Genetics," I said. "Reproduction."

From around her neck, she untied her orange silk scarf and wound it like a bandage over her damaged hair. "Like that Dr. Kinsey," she said.

I said, "I'm concerned with the reproductive mechanisms of lower forms of life."

Ada Sorokin closed her eyes. She smiled. "I didn't know," she said, "that you could get much lower than that Kinsey does. Passes it off for science, but it's just one more dirty book, don't you think so?"

Brian's car door slammed. He moved toward us through the rippling heat—it was August, we had come up from Washington's swelter to spend a week at the ocean, introduce me to his parents, tell them of our marriage plans. I heard the waves smashing on the private beach behind the house.

I thought, *He is connected to her*, reminding myself that families marry families. An egg and a sperm are each group affairs, reunions, each tribe turns out *en masse* at weddings.

Brian said, "No Cornish game hens, Mother. I got you a chicken." He set the bag of groceries down on the redwood table.

Ada gave him a mock grimace. "Oh God, you don't expect me to make you chicken *soup*, do you?" She looked at me. "He's been trying to turn me into a Jewish mother all his life. Doesn't believe how awful it would be for him if I obliged. Thinks he's *culturally deprived* to have been raised up by an assimilated Southern girl instead of some rabbi's daughter from Brooklyn, New York."

Brian reddened, picked up the groceries again. He did not seem to see me at all.

Pleased with her speech, Ada Sorokin lowered the back of her beach chair and raised her face to the sun, for its benediction.

I stood up. I said, "I'll help you put those things away, Brian," and followed him into his family's cottage, that ostensible retreat from the city's strains and stresses.

The first time I went out with Brian Sorokin, we walked through the gardens and groves of the National Arboretum

50

and traded family histories. In the midst of well-tended, labeled plantings, we talked in an orderly manner, in a reasonable way, even-toned, concise, influenced, no doubt, by the landscape's symmetry, its careful cultivation.

We had met the previous weekend at a fund-raising dinner party given by one of my graduate-school professors for Fletcher McPherson's congressional campaign. The professor liked Fletcher's attitude toward basic research. Fletcher's attitude was that basic research should exist. On such flimsy accords, humankind negotiates its contracts.

Brian and I negotiated a contract on the basis of these accords: I liked his voice, that Boston staccato, the way it summoned me out of my silence. I liked his eyes. Brian would later tell Phil Mathis that he decided to marry me "because she had a nice ass." At the dinner party for Fletcher, Brian said, "You've got beautiful hands, anyone ever tell you that? I mean, this is the first time in my life I have really *enjoyed* watching somebody cut up her food."

He called the next morning. We juggled our respective schedules to find a time we would both be free. The following Thursday, for lunch.

He suggested a restaurant near Capitol Hill. I suggested the Arboretum.

"You bringing your microscope?" he said. "Collecting bugs?"

I said, "Well, you could hand out leaflets. Then we'd both get something accomplished."

We met in the parking lot and walked together up the steep wood-chip path. When we reached the crest of the hill, the acres of growth lay before us, the azaleas in bud, the forsythia in blazing yellow conflagration. I heard Brian inhale. When I looked at him, his eyes were slits, his chin puckered as if he were about to cry.

"What?" I said.

"My dad used to have the most beautiful yard in Brighton," he said. "Before he started boozing. This reminds me."

We entered the formal gardens.

I said, "I've never had a yard."

"Just one more place where they can fence you in," he said, and I imagined him leaping over pickets, chain link, spans of

51

stockade and split rail, running and running, escaping forever from domestic confinements.

I said, "Tell me about your family."

I will tell you about family: an endless genetic campaign. Bonds formed and broken, formed and broken. Biological politics.

We came to a rise. A stream shimmered beneath us like a bright-green snake.

"My mother grew up in Norfolk, Virginia," Brian began. "She hates Boston, always has. 'People don't know how to live,' she says, 'they don't know how to relax.' She tried to get my father to move down there for years. He'd say, 'The South's no good for Jews.' And she'd say, 'That's another one of your myths, Walter. I've never encountered discrimination. Even back before the Civil War, Jews could have slaves like everyone else.' "

Walter Sorokin met Ada Marks at a canteen in Norfolk. It was 1938. Ada was ladling ginger ale punch into amber-colored cups. He watched her from the far side of the room. Her hair matched the goblets, and her features (he would tell her this later and she would laugh in his face) were as delicate, as precise, as the chiseled design of the cut-glass bowl from which she dipped out refreshments for the sailors and the local women with whom they danced. Walter and Ada danced to "My Blue Heaven." Another sailor cut in, and Walter seethed in the corner, nursed his punch. Already the sad tune to which they would dance for decades was playing itself out.

They both came from money. (This was my mother's expression. She talked about people "coming from money" as if it were another planet, as if "coming from money" meant you were not born like the rest of us, in spasms of pain and blood.) Walter's father was the founder of the Hathaway Brothers Shoe Company, a factory that made better ladies' shoes and whose name Abraham Sorokin had found in the phone directory, looking, he said, for "something refined." When Walter was just out of the Navy, his father died and Walter changed the name of the firm he inherited to Sorokin Shoes.

"That's how I know he had guts," Brian said. "Once."

Ada's family owned the biggest department store in Norfolk. Ada had been to Europe with her father, to buy an order of Italian leather purses that did not sell well in Norfolk. "I don't care," Samuel Marks said of the loss, "my little girl had the time of her life."

"Spoiled," Brian said matter-of-factly. "Spoiled from the very beginning." As if he were talking about improperly canned fruit, or meat left out in the sun.

Walter courted tenaciously. He wired her flowers. He sent her a dozen pair of shoes. He took her for rides in her father's Buick, parked among thick clumps of pine trees, necked with her until the car turned into a steaming hothouse, and finally, the night before he shipped out, convinced Ada Marks to take off her white piqué dress and her silk stockings and her imported lacy underwear and, twenty-three years later when Brian said, "Why in the hell did you *marry* him if you think he's so terrible?" Ada would tell him, "He knocked me up, dear, to use your generation's term for it. We told everybody we'd gotten married in Norfolk before he shipped out, but that was a lie. What would you have liked me to do, put you up for adoption?"

Afterward she would tell him, "I've always been surprised I got pregnant at all. I didn't even enjoy it. I always thought you had to enjoy it to get pregnant, but that isn't the case."

That is not the case. At the front end of the sperm head, a concentration of enzymes acts like a battering ram to break down any barriers which bar entry into the egg.

Some people call this process *fate*.

Ada would say, "Well, there's no sense in my complaining, this is my fate."

Brian does not believe in fate. He believes fatalism is a way of conceding defeat, and he refuses to concede. When Brian is on the verge of death, he will call for a recount.

And, in fact, Ada *has* complained. Example: each summer Walter Sorokin took his wife and son to a different beach —Miami, Honolulu, Bermuda, the Italian Riviera, Fire Island, Puerto Rico—and each summer Ada grew less enthusiastic until finally she said, "Walter, one damn sandbar is the same as another, why don't we just go down to the Cape like everybody else in Brighton?" Example: after eight years of marriage, Ada said she could not bear Walter's snoring or the fact that he slept with the pillow over his head ("I feel like you're trying to asphyxiate yourself all night long, I feel like I'm watching you die," she told him), and took the guest room as her own. Example: in the midst of a dinner party of "Walter's friends," as she termed all their social contacts, Ada Sorokin, having finished her third glass of wine and feeling, as she would later explain it to Walter, "whimsical," rose at her place at the table and announced, "I am sick of hearing you people put r's on the end of all your words, you don't know how to talk at all, you all sound like you've got a speech impediment."

In addition, she has not liked Walter's drinking, any of her lovers, any of her friends, Brian's "vulgarities" ("I do believe," she would tell him, "that people can disagree without resorting to the vulgarities"), and she certainly does not like me. In fact, the only person for whom I have ever seen Ada Sorokin demonstrate real affection is Robin.

When Robin was five months old, Ada came to visit us in Washington.

Brian brought her from the airport. Sleet lashed the window; through the frosted pane, I watched them struggle with her luggage up the slippery path. Ada linked her arm through Brian's; they moved awkwardly, as if each had just learned to walk, or were recovering, perhaps, from long confining illnesses. From my vantage point, it was difficult to tell if they were helping keep each other up, or contributing to one another's imbalance.

I opened the door.

"Oh," Ada said, setting down her suitcase, "look at that angel!"

Without taking off her coat—needles of ice clung to her shoulders and sleeves—she reached for Robin, who slept against my chest, her tiny heart beating like an extra pulse in my own body.

Humans are among the few animals who remain dependent on the mother long after the event we have carelessly labeled "birth." Gestation, in fact, has two phases: one in the womb, one in the world.

When Ada reached for Robin, I refused to give her up.

In all cultures, the first phase takes nine months. The

second phase is more difficult to calculate, it varies in length from culture to culture, tribe to tribe, family to family.

I would speculate, for example, that some of us die before ever having completed the second phase.

I would speculate, for example, that Brian is still stuck in the second phase.

He would speculate the same about me, if he had time for such speculations, which he does not.

"She just dozed off," I said to Ada. "I don't want to wake her."

As if responding to some cue from her grandmother, Robin opened her eyes, began to squirm in an effort, it seemed, to detach herself from me.

I gave her up.

Ada walked with Robin from room to room. Ada cooed, all harshness gone from her voice, its usual stridency mellowed, her tone musical and kind.

In the kitchen, Brian said, "I didn't know she had it in her."

I said, "Had what?"

"The maternal instinct," he said, warming his hands on his coffee cup. "Or do you think she took some kind of pill before she got here?"

"It's easier with a grandchild, Brian. There isn't the same *responsibility*."

He grinned. "Like a one-night stand," he said, "that goes on indefinitely?"

I said, "That's a lousy analogy."

Ada came into the room. I could smell the sour odor of excrement. Ada said, "She has a dirty diaper. I never have been able to stand it when they mess." And she gave Robin back to me.

Of course, Robin did not know that her grandmother could not deal with messes. What Robin knew, in the way that an infant experiences knowledge, was her grandmother's comforting voice, the welcoming bosom, twenty minutes of imprinted bliss.

Robin's third summer. The Cape. Brian had come begrudgingly, wanting to spend the summer recess analyzing recent data on voting patterns in key Ohio congressional districts: Fletcher was going to run for the Senate the following year. Brian could recite the names of every Democratic county chairman in the state, their wives, their children, the kind of liquor they preferred. He called this process "gearing up," and I imagined him on a motorcycle, racing back and forth across Ohio, shouting his memorized list into the air.

Walter preferred bourbon.

Recent research suggests a genetic component in alcoholism.

When I told Brian about this not long ago, he said, "We make *decisions*, Janet. You want me to believe that something in his genes tells him to buy Wild Turkey at umpteen dollars a fifth? Jesus. What do you think a human being *is*, a fucking chemical robot? He *decides*, sweetheart, every time he pours a lousy drink."

That afternoon Walter poured a half-dozen lousy drinks, slept through dinner, and would continue to sleep well into the next morning.

I cleared the dishes from the table.

Robin said, "Where Grampa go?"

"He went night-night," Ada said. She looked at the spiral staircase, its open slats twisting like a coarse vine through the heart of the house. "He went beddy-bye." A muscle in Ada's cheek contracted.

I said, "Speaking of bedtime—"

"Oh no!" Ada protested. "It's too early yet! I need some time with my baby." She pulled Robin onto her lap and they nuzzled each other. "We're going to go outside and find us some shells, aren't we, darling?"

Robin scrambled off her grandmother's legs, returned with a yellow plastic bucket, tugged at Ada's skirt.

Ada said, "Ask your mommy, angel. We can go if your mommy says so."

Robin raised her eyes to mine.

"For a little while," I said, abdicating, giving up power I was aware I possessed only in Ada's presence.

In Ada's presence, I have always felt like a person running for an office I did not want, enmeshed against my will in issues of strategy and calculation.

At the end of our marriage, I told Brian, "You wanted me to be like her. You don't want things clear and clean and out in

56

the open. You want one campaign after another, winners and losers, tactics. Living with you is practically *warfare*."

"I'm not ready for formaldehyde, sweetheart, if that's your alternative," he said.

So you see what we had come down to: irreconcilable differences. I felt strafed, he felt embalmed. What was life to one was death to the other: human beings are one of the few species, please remember, that murder their own. When two human beings marry, their contract carries the implicit provision that they will not die at one another's hand.

Ada took Robin's hand and led her out into the cool ocean air. I watched them from the deck, Ada's gaudy chartreuse sun dress fading to a wisp of green at the water's edge, her body bent into peasant-woman's posture, picking up shells as if they were potatoes or beans, her back making the arc of her ancestors as they dug for their livelihoods in the rocky soil of Russia. I watched Robin dance in the shimmering foam; she was as much the ocean's child as she was mine.

Finally, the claims we have on one another are no more binding—and no less—than water.

The enduring, unfathomable water.

When Brian moved out, Ada wrote me a letter on her monogrammed ivory parchment: "Janet, I know things have not been peaches and cream between us all these years. You are a career woman and I am not, and I have always felt that made for a great deal of tension between us. I am truly sorry if my son caused you unhappiness. I have never understood marriage myself. It's no secret that Walter and I have had our problems. Woman to woman, I can tell you *that*. What I am most worried about is Robin—you know how much I adore that child. I hope I won't have to fight you to keep close to my granddaughter, but I would if need be. Can we talk about this, woman to woman?"

I wrote her back on institute letterhead: "There is no need for you to worry about your relationship with Robin. It has been clear since her infancy that you love her very much, and she has responded to that affection. What has happened between Brian and me has nothing to do with you and Robin. I hope you will continue to be close to each other."

I should have shut the door in her face.

More evidence, though I am not sure for what. Appendicitis. An irrelevant appendage refuses to be consigned to oblivion. The body's anachronism makes its claim on the present. Take it as a warning (or a cause for celebration): in brain or bone or belly, each breathing cell maintains its hold on life.

In the ambulance, Robin murmured, "Am I going to die?"

She was ten years old. For an instant, I saw my dead mother's face in Robin's, saw my mother's eyes rise up in my daughter's like sediment floating to the surface of a pond.

"Of course not," I said, putting my cheek against her chalky face. "You're going to be fine."

After surgery, she *was* fine. Brian had flown back from California, where he had gone with Fletcher for a speech to farm workers in the San Joaquin valley; he brought Robin a picture of himself with Fletcher and Cesar Chavez.

"Is he a movie star?" Robin said. She was sipping apple juice through a bent straw.

Brian smiled at her naïveté. "No," he said, "Cesar Chavez is not a movie star."

When she fell asleep, we left her room, walked down the hall to the sunroom.

"My mother's coming," Brian said. "She wants to see Robin."

I had not seen Ada Sorokin for nearly two years, since the separation.

She arrived on time, swept out of the elevator like Loretta Young, her aromatic perfume colliding with the smell of disinfectant that pervaded the place.

"I just had to come," she said, apologizing for her presence as if I had voiced my displeasure.

We looked at each other, woman to woman. I saw her life—one long manipulation, a giant knot of lies and evasions and petty cruelties—I saw it coming undone, straightening out into a pure line of love that stretched from Boston to Washington, a line she had traveled as surely as her plane had traveled its own invisible route through the air.

"What I wrote you in that letter," I said, "still applies."

Ada's gaze shifted away from me. She had passed through Customs; now she could move on to her true destination.

In Robin's room, I watched Ada play it straight. *Play* is the wrong word. She was not *playing*, she was free of games and her usual posture of pretense. When she entered her granddaughter's room, Ada Sorokin's shoulders, usually lifted in a perpetual shrug, went soft; her fists fell open; the tension in her tight mouth gave way, and she said, "Hello, angel," in a voice resonant with care. I saw in her form, as I had that day years ago at the beach, an authenticity: when the heart is honest, the body finds its ease.

I watched Robin's arms—bruised from hypodermic needles taking her blood, feeding glucose into her veins—I watched them reach toward Ada. And I watched Brian flinch as his mother offered to his child the straight line of affection she had never been able to summon for him, for Walter's child, for the representative (to her) of her unfortunate "fate."

Ada held Robin. Brian flinched. I watched.

Reserve a Nobel Prize for the scientist who explains that particular chemistry.

Additional evidence: letters, gifts, love's customary indicators.

All letters closing with "Say hello to your mother."

All gifts expensive, frivolous, seemingly inappropriate for my sensible daughter. She basked, nonetheless, in Ada's generosity, the sheer expansiveness of her generosity. For instance: two dozen pair of designer-print bikini underpants, pre-teen size; three winter coats ("I picked these up at a fabulous sale. One for dress, one for play, one for school. Enjoy!"); a four-foot stuffed panda that came shipped in a box big enough to hold a washing machine; six sets of "The Wizard of Oz" sheets, after a phone conversation in which Robin had mentioned to her grandmother that she had watched the movie on television.

On plain blue notepaper, Robin would write: "Dear Grandma, Thank you very much for the gift. I really appreciate it. Love, Robin."

To me, Robin wrote: *This has nothing to do with love, but I'm leaving. I just had to get out of this house.*

She went to Boston. To her grandmother's. I have just found this out from Robin's best friend, Laura Mathis, who—raised in the tradition of her father's espionage career —believes herself an informer and sits on the floor of the foyer, crying into her small, guilty hands.

"Laura," I tell her, "you haven't done anything wrong. You've done the right thing."

The weeping ceases. She is dry as shale. "We'll see what Robin thinks," she says. "We'll see what Robin will say when she finds out."

What Robin will say. What Ada will say. Brian. Walter. My father. What I will say. It is all scripted. We have been rehearsing this scene all our lives. We began to memorize our parts *in utero*.

"Ada," I say, "this is Janet. I know Robin's with you. Let me speak to her, please."

"I don't know what you're talking about," Ada says, her voice obvious in its confirmation.

"I'm coming up on the first plane I can get out of National."

"Janet, dear, I don't think that would be wise."

"Ada," I say, "since when have you had the patent on wisdom?"

And then very gently, as if it were a baby, as if it were Robin herself returned to me as an infant, I lay the receiver back in its cradle.

There.

Then, a ring. I could nearly mistake it for a cry for food, or a colicky scream. I am expecting Robin's "Mom, it's me," expecting fifteen years to have replayed themselves in twenty seconds, expecting to tell her through the coiled yards of cable, *"I'm here, honey,"* sure she will hear me this time, sure I simply must have forgotten, all these years, to speak up loudly enough, and I say "Hello" in a tone as full and deep as hope itself.

And my father says, "So what's new in the nation's capital and when you coming down for a visit?"

O n the plane to Boston, the man in the seat beside me is sleeping with his mouth open.

My father used to sleep like that, his head bobbing against the back of the living-room chair. Sometimes I would come in from my bedroom retreat—after my mother died, I turned more and more into a reclusive scholar—and I would turn off the television that had been playing all evening to no one. He would wake immediately, jarred by the silencing, offended to have been caught in the depths of his fatigue.

"Leave it on!" he would say. "I was just taking a five-minute nap."

But I knew he had been sleeping since the end of the seven-o'clock news: it was as if reports from the world at large exhausted him with their stories of corruption and catastrophe, drove him, however fitfully, into the province of dream. Once I heard him cry out for my mother—she had been gone for a year—and there was such yearning in his voice that I felt malicious as I shook him awake into the reality of her death.

The plane bounces through an air pocket, and the man next to me bolts forward. His ruddy face furrows with confusion.

"Don't be upset," I tell him. "It's perfectly normal."

He peers at me through thick horn-rimmed glasses. "*What* is?" he says, defensive as my father at being observed in the private act of sleep.

"Turbulence."

He relaxes, relieved I am not judging the normalcy of his somnolent visions, glad he did not, perhaps, call out in his sleep to someone lost to him, did not, perhaps, articulate for all the passengers to hear his most intimate terrors. "That doesn't bother me," he says, "I fly all the time."

The stewardess brings us ginger ale and dry-roasted peanuts. He offers me his package, but I decline.

"You have kids?" he says.

"A daughter."

"Take them for her," he says. "Kids love surprises. Mine are grown, one's in L.A., trying to break into movies, living like a hippie if you want my opinion. Other one's in college, the boy, says he wants to drop out and take up carpentry." He shrugs, telling me with his body that he is beyond trying to comprehend his children's lives, telling me it is a fruitless effort.

When I told my father I was going to college to study biology, he said, "You mean nursing? You mean taking classes to be a nurse?"

"No," I said, "I'm going to be a scientist. I'm even going to get a Ph.D."

He looked up from the order forms he was filling out at the kitchen table. He said, "*Ph.D.*?" pronouncing the name of a new and deadly disease.

I was stricken. "I thought you might be proud," I said.

"What's it got to do with *proud*?" He smacked his hands down on the table. His order forms scattered. "I'm not talking about *proud*. I'm talking about *money*. Where's it going to come from, that kind of money?" His eyes flew around the room, as if he were searching for a secret cache.

"Scholarships," I said. "Loans. I'll work." My voice was calm, disembodied.

"I don't like it," he said. "What's the matter with nursing school? Two years and you got a good profession. I could scrape together something for two years, I could cash in a policy maybe, I—"

"I don't want to be a nurse," I told him.

"Of course not," he said. He shook his head in resignation. I thought he might cry. But then, with grudging respect, he added, "*You* want to be Madame Curie." For a moment, he looked deferential, meditative, moved to be in the presence of such aspiration.

I did not want to be Madame Curie. I wanted to disappear into the realm of research, a place I believed to be antiseptic as a hospital, serene as a church, orderly as the inner workings of a clock.

The first time I dissected a frog, my knife moved with ease through skin and muscle and bone, extracted the small pouch of a heart, each perfect eye, the brain that I pulled from its cavity as simply as a peach pit can be tugged from the fruit's soft meat. A collection of parts in the palm of my steady hand.

Now my hand is trembling. I accept the packet of nuts —unlikely amulet—and put it into my purse.

I do not tell the man about Robin.

He takes a sip of his ginger ale. "Too sweet," he says. "When I was a kid, we drank seltzer water. You ever have seltzer water?"

"My father used to drink it."

I did not tell my father about Robin, either.

Eli said I should have gotten in touch with Brian (Brian is incommunicado) *and* my father (my father is seventy-one years old, his heart beats irregularly, his eyes water and burn most of the time, and the one thing he depends on the most is his only child's "success," which includes his only grand-daughter's assumed well-being). Eli said, "This is a family emergency, and you're playing it like Joan of Arc."

Eli is right: this *is* a family problem. It is the doctor in him that believes it can be solved in the way that vaccines are developed: the cure created from the virus, the poison enlisted to battle the poison.

As for Joan of Arc: she did what she had to, and I am doing the same. Other than that, I do not sense any particular kinship.

Between my father and me, there are these indices of kinship: thick wavy black hair (what's left of his is white and mine straightens itself by its own weight, hanging to my shoulders in a deceptively smooth mass—but inside the follicles, our hair remembers its real identity); the same gray eyes, slanted upward in a vaguely Oriental manner, suggesting Mongolian ancestry, exotic and remote; good teeth; an erect bearing that leads people to describe my father as "dignified" and me as "stately"; long, narrow feet.

Shared gestures: scratching an ear that does not itch; covering our respective mouths in the midst of a smile; sitting with one leg wrapped around the other, like a vine clinging to a post; meshing and unmeshing our fingers as we speak.

In the plane to Boston, the man beside me, engrossed now in *Sports Illustrated*, runs his tongue over his teeth. Does his daughter do this while she waits to audition in a smoky Hollywood studio? Does his son do this as he sits in the library, a book opened in his lap, his eyes fixed on some vision of hard oak curving in accordance to the turn of his saw?

Robin and I pace the floor when we talk on the phone.

Robin and I cannot carry a tune.

Robin and I love big breakfasts; in the morning, Brian's stomach clenches itself shut against food.

My father liked his eggs soft-boiled and served in a Pyrex custard dish. He liked seedless rye toast, dark, a little butter, a thick glaze of grape jam. He liked weak coffee, half milk. He had no use for fruit juice, cereal, tea (my mother had loved tea, she had loved a good strong cup of tea), or strawberry preserves. "Jam," he insisted. "Next time remember, Welch's grape jam." Until my mother died, I had not realized how many habits, tastes, eccentricities my father had. Suddenly I was deluged with detail. Had he always cleaned his teeth with baking soda, leaving the toothpaste for my mother and me? When had he started wearing two pair of socks to cushion his feet from the miles of concrete he trekked each week on his Fuller Brush route? Every morning he gargled with hot salt water, and every night he took a plain glass of water to bed with him. "You never know," he'd say. "You could get thirsty, you could have a coughing jag, a person never knows."

It was as if for thirteen years, my mother, slight as she had been, had stood between my father and me, so that I had seen only his outline, the mere shape of the man, the sketch a painter makes before the brushwork begins.

I began to fill in the particulars. I tried to maintain a certain guardedness, a dispassionate eye, a clinical disposition.

"Life's for the living," he announced. We were driving to the cemetery after breakfast as we had every Sunday for three months since my mother's death. I sat in her place in the dusty sedan, bouncing over the pot-holed Pittsburgh hills to her grave, when suddenly my father swung the car into a violent U-turn and the flowers I'd been holding sailed from my hands into the backseat.

"What's wrong?" I said, striving for balance. "Did you forget something at home?"

His eyes glittered with tears. "Life," he repeated, slowing down for a red light. "Life's for the living."

The light flashed green. In front of us, a crowded trolley clanged its bell and we followed the travelers back to our neighborhood, back to our building, where my father and I climbed the steps to the fourth floor. In the living room, he dropped his coat on what had been my mother's side of the sofa bed. Then, as if she lay there sleeping and he had violated her rest, he grabbed up his coat and strode to the closet and flung open the door: my mother's clothes still hung inside, and he looked to me like a ghost-haunted man accosted at every turn.

He stared at her small wardrobe.

He whispered something I could not hear.

He touched the shoulder of each housedress and faded cardigan sweater with a shaking finger.

He took several deep breaths, then motioned for me to follow him into the kitchen. There he emptied the cardboard carton of new samples that had arrived for him the day before. He stacked the brushes, cleansers, and assorted household gadgets on the porcelain-topped table. He handed the empty box to me. "Pack up your mother's things," he said huskily. "Tomorrow you'll call Goodwill."

I took the carton and filled it with her garments and shoved it into a dark corner of the closet. I never called Goodwill.

Say that I was too detached to follow through on such an emotional mission.

Or say that, at thirteen, I was already one of those for whom love and grieving have no real end, and the final gesture did not exist that would free me once and for all from the memory of loss.

My father, though, plunged into the rituals of modern exorcism with a new convert's zest. These are the things he did during the last months of 1952 and the beginning of 1953: He traded in his Plymouth for a used Chevrolet. He grew a mustache. He bought a new gabardine suit. He subscribed to both *Time* and *Newsweek* and absorbed them as if he were a scholar. "TV's good," he told me, "but you can't beat the printed word." He did push-ups, ten in the morning and ten at night, and collapsed on the sofa after each session in the transported exhaustion of an athlete with his eye on the Olympics. He bought a reconditioned record player at a secondhand appliance store, and listened for hours to Mario Lanza, Ezio Pinza, The Great Caruso. "Oh," he said, "if I were young again, I'd take in so much culture." Sometimes I caught him staring in the mirror, as if he did not recognize himself anymore, or wished he knew the man at whom he gawked. One rainy evening in March, he came out of the bathroom, his trousers rolled up to his knees, his callused feet red as lobsters from their nightly soaking. "Starting tomorrow," he said, "I'm going to play cards one night a week."

I looked up from *Elementary Algebra*. "Cards?"

He nodded. "Gin rummy."

I said, "Ma hated cards."

"Ma's gone," my father said. He sat beside me, clenching and unclenching his toes. " 'All work and no play . . .' You know that one?"

He looked at me hard, with a clarity I had never seen in his eyes before, as if some overlay, like cellophane wrapping, had been removed from them at last, so that finally they were unprotected, opened to me, their true fragile crystalline depth offered, with tremulous hesitation, like a long-overdue gift.

I said softly, "I know that one," and though I did not move, the world wobbled, the perch from which I viewed my father, from which I classified the elements of his presence, from which I kept my distance and where I learned, early, the scientist's crucial skepticism—that perch swayed beneath me and I came closer than I have ever come in my life, until now, to falling down from that well-constructed platform.

He gave me a rare and tentative hug. I reached out for his hand and squeezed it. He squeezed back. From a broken gutter on the building's roof, water gushed down the window and I felt as safe that moment as if the world were being ravaged by floods and I had found refuge, here with my father, in our three-room ark, seventy dollars a month, including utilities.

"I have to do my books," he said, and we let go of each other. He meant he had to tally up the day's sales, send his orders in to the company, get his deliveries ready and prepare his route for the next day. "The supermarkets are killing me," he confided. "They sell everything I do. And not just that." He lowered his voice. "Women don't like to open their doors anymore. It's murder, the way things are getting. Even some that know me, they talk to me through the glass." He seemed suddenly ashamed of his naked legs, leaned over to roll down his pants.

"Maybe I could go with you someday. Maybe if they saw you with your own daughter, they wouldn't feel so . . . nervous."

"Don't talk crazy, you're a schoolgirl."

"Next Thursday I'm off. Teachers' meeting."

He sat still, weighing, considering. Finally he said, "What could it hurt?"

All week I drifted, neglecting my homework, forgetting to dust, buying milk when an unopened quart sat in the refrigerator, answering questions in class the teacher had not asked. "Where's your mind?" she said, and then her face went lax. "Oh," she said, "of course. Your mother." She thought some fit of grief was responsible for my confusion, but she was wrong: it was hope, expectation, the imminence of adventure. Inside me, ice jams were breaking up and Thursday looked like the open sea my father and I would navigate together.

Thursday morning. Slate sky, a drizzle streaking the windows.

"Stay home," my father said. "You'll catch a cold."

I poured Rice Krispies into a bowl. "I'll bundle up."

"You'll get bored. It's a long day."

"I want to go."

"Well," he said, cracking the shell of his soft-boiled egg, "don't say I didn't warn you."

On Filmore Avenue, all the small tidy frame houses on each side of the steeply inclined street were connected to each other, as if they were keeping one another from sliding off the mountain along which they'd been built. They were called "party walls," and I imagined a huge common cellar in which the lucky families that lived there congregated regularly for festive communal bashes.

"Usually," my father said, "this is a good area."

He had been silent up until now, sullen even, and I blamed his mood on the snarled traffic, the blaring horns, the front windshield that kept fogging over, so that he had to drive like an old man with failing sight—hunched over the steering wheel, nose almost touching the window. He parked the car near the corner; the engine sputtered and stopped. I started to open the door, but my father remained fastened to his seat, his hands still clutching the wheel. He pursed his lips and wrinkled his brow. Scanned the dark sky.

"On a day like this," he said, "you can't count on anything. You know what they say about weather? How it affects a person's behavior? Absolutely true." He glared at me as if I had contradicted him. "You take the same woman when the sun's out, she's all smiles, she's glad to see you, when it rains, she won't give you the right time of day."

"It's not raining now," I told him. "I think it's clearing up."

"It's a bad day for business," he snapped. "Don't I know? Aren't I the one who would know?"

"I didn't mean—"

"Nobody means," he said. "Nobody ever *means.*"

He sighed. He straightened his tie in the rearview mirror. I thought, *Now we're going,* but he drummed his fingers on the horn, wiped some dust from the dashboard. Cracked his knuckles. I began to understand: he did not want me here at all. I made him nervous. I had come as a confidante, an accomplice, a collaborator, but he saw me as a spy.

Bringing my knees up to my chest, I lied to him: "You know

what? I have a bad headache." I fingered my cheeks. "I think I have a fever."

He smacked his forehead with his palm. "Didn't I predict?"

"If you lock the doors," I went on, my voice quiet and reasonable, "I can rest on the backseat."

"Next time," he said, shaking an authoritative finger at me, "you'll listen to your father."

While he covered Filmore Avenue by himself, I lay alone in the car and saw my own breath cloud over each window until the houses disappeared, the sky vanished, the morning itself seemed to be obliterated. Somewhere a dog barked, like a sound from another world. I thought about my mother, lying under the earth in her own timeless void. Did she hear the same dog yelping, did she even remember dogs at all? Did she remember me? My eyes burned. I buried my face in the tufted seat and called her, I lay there calling and calling my mother, I wanted her home and I wanted to go home to her, I wanted to help her sprinkle her day's ironing and hang up the shirts for her as she finished each one, I even wanted to hear her tell me, "You should be outside with other children, you should be playing, I don't understand why you hide yourself away like a hermit, if you don't have fun now when will you ever?" Outside, a mill whistle blew, but it sounded to me like the voice of sorrow itself.

"You don't look good," my father said when he returned to the car. More than an hour had passed. "I'll take you home, you'll be much better off."

With his handkerchief, he wiped the windows clear again. Filmore Avenue looked exactly as it had when we'd arrived: modest, immaculate, undisturbed. As if we had never been here at all. Had women opened doors when he knocked? Had anyone given him the right time of day? Had a single person heard me calling my mother from inside the cloud of my own breath? We rode through the wet streets as we'd come, in silence.

"You take a couple aspirin," he said as we pulled up to our building. "Curl up with a book, watch a little TV."

"I'll be fine," I said.

"I'll tell you what," he said as I got out. "I'll bring home deli, you don't need to bother with cooking."

The Chevy rattled off. I went inside. In the downstairs hall, Mrs. Stein was at the mailboxes. Hers was stuffed with letters from children, grandchildren, and other assorted relatives all over America. They were always sending her snapshots, homemade cards, newspaper clippings about promotions and awards, long letters recording the details of births, engagements, holiday outings.

"My family," Mrs. Stein would say, "we keep the U.S. Postal Service in business, believe you me."

I reached into our box and removed a bill from Sears Roebuck.

"You got plans today?" she said as she sorted through her envelopes.

I shook my head no.

"Well," she said, "if it wouldn't be too boring for you, I'm making strudel, you mind helping me slice up the apples?"

I told her I would not mind. She fished in the pocket of her apron and handed me a tissue. "Here," she said, "it's clean." I wiped my eyes and all the way upstairs she read me "knock-knock" jokes from her grandson Eliot in Tucson, Arizona.

"Knock-knock."

"Who's there?"

"No one."

"No one who?"

"No wonder people think you're crazy, answering the door when no one's there."

My father brought home hot pastrami, sliced tongue, kimmel rye, two pickles from a barrel, and a pint of cole slaw. He fixed himself a fat sandwich, heaped slaw on his plate. I picked at a bowl of applesauce, a half-slice of bread. As we sat in the kitchen, daylight ebbed. My father wavered, his density seemed to diminish, he became more and more shadow to me, hazy, the way a slide specimen looks when the microscope is out of focus.

I had lost him again, and this time not because of my mother.

I am speaking of a family in which disappearance is a dominant trait.

———

The stewardess says, "Ladies and gentlemen, we are approaching Logan Airport. . . ."

Beneath us, the lights on the runway glitter like stars plucked from their various configurations in the sky and assembled on the ground in a pattern so regular, so clearly delineated, that it seems impossible not to follow the straightforward direction they provide.

But the plane's wheels could jam. An engine could fail at the crucial moment. Another plane, misguided, could explode our smooth descent. Someone could rise up from his seat with a gun and demand to be flown to Cuba.

None of these things happen.

We land smoothly, without incident, according to plan.

I want to scream: *Listen! Bring out the Rescue Squad! Sirens! Bulletins on the radio! Can't you see my life has gone out of control?*

The man beside me puts his magazine into his cowhide briefcase and unbuckles his seat belt. "Well," he says, smiling, unaware of my rising sense of emergency, "we made it safe and sound."

PART TWO
ROBIN

The way I got the money for the airplane ticket was by selling my wristwatch and the gold chain Grandma sent me this year for my birthday. Just from the box, I knew it was expensive: blue velvet lined with silk, and the little tag that said "14 K" attached to the clasp.

When I got to the airport in Boston, I called Grandma on the pay phone and hung up when she answered. I hadn't wanted to talk to her, just to be sure she was home. It would be hard enough to explain things to her in person. In the airport gift shop, I bought her a sachet with lace around the edges and her initial embroidered on the satiny cloth. It smelled like lilacs. I bought Grandpa one of those zippered pouches for pipe tobacco. Bringing them presents made it seem more like a visit, kept me from remembering what I really had done.

The only person I told at home was Laura. I'm not sure why I even told her, except that telling it changed it from a dream into a secret. Dreams (I don't mean the kind you have at night) can take over all the space inside you. Grandma told me once about a vine called kudzu that grows in the South, covers acres overnight. Dreams are like that. Secrets don't grow, they just live quietly between two people like a rose in a glass of water.

Laura didn't think I'd given her a rose, though. More like a weed. She said, "Your mother is the easiest person in the world to get along with," and I knew she was comparing my life to hers, which is never fair.

I said, "She's easy to get along with because she's never there."

"You mean when she's working?"

"I mean all the time. Sometimes we eat dinner and don't say a word to each other. I hate that."

"I guess you'd rather have the kind of scenes *we* have practically every night."

"I don't think she'd miss me very much."

"God, Robin, she's your *mother*."

"I still don't think she would."

"Wouldn't *you* miss *her*?" She was looking at me as if I were a stranger, even though we've been friends all our lives.

I said, "I miss her *now*, and we live in the same house." I had started to cry, and the words came out in a ragged stutter.

Laura tried to put her arms around me, but I wouldn't let her. "I think you're really mixed up, Rob, I think you should tell her how you feel and—"

"Oh sure!" I yelled. "Tell her how I *feel*! My mother doesn't *believe* in feelings, she thinks they're . . . *weak*, she thinks—"

"Hey, you're flipping out, you know? Calm down."

She can never let me be angry. I'm the calm one, Laura is the one with "bad nerves," her mother's name for how angry Laura is. The doctor's name for it is "asthma." She's angry that her mother drinks and her father screams a lot and slams out of the house (I was there one night when he did that, and Laura said, "Isn't it awful?" and I said, "At least they're still married"). She's angry that the girls in school are jealous of her because she's beautiful, and the boys are afraid of her because she's beautiful, and sometimes I think the main reason she's my friend is because I'm not jealous of or angry at her, instead of for reasons that have to do with who I am myself.

One thing I am is plain. My father's always telling me, "You're one gorgeous girl," but it isn't true, at least I don't see it myself. For one thing, I'm too thin. I don't have *shape*, I mean sometimes I feel more like an unraveled thread than a body, sometimes I have to put my hand on my heart to convince myself I'm *solid* enough to have organs at all. I think gravity must work overtime to keep me attached to the ground, like it knows I could just drift off, unnoticed, disappearing into the air someday. Once Mrs. Mathis said, "Robin, with your figure you could be a model," but I thought: *Because I wouldn't get in the way of the clothes, because no one would see me at all, that's why.*

My face is plain, too. People's eyes glide right over my face like it was a still pond or an empty sky, like the most interesting thing about it was its calm surface. Mrs. Mathis said I should learn about makeup and "Use those wonderful bones of yours, highlight those lovely eyes." But I told her I didn't believe in makeup. She said, "Robin, it's not a political platform. It isn't something you believe in, it's something you *use*." But I thought, *What if I started sweating and it runs off my skin and right in front of somebody I change from my beautiful made-up self into my natural plainness, wouldn't that be worse than just being who I am?* And I wouldn't trade with Laura. Other girls can't help staring at her, telling her with their eyes, *I want that complexion* or *Let me have that perfect nose*. For me, being watched like that would be as bad as not being seen: either way, your real self is trapped inside your body, and hardly anyone ever knows who you are.

When we were little, she was the one who was always getting into trouble. In her backyard, she'd rip out flowers by the roots, put dirt in the birdbath, throw handfuls of sand at me until I'd start to cry. Mrs. Mathis would shake Laura by the shoulders. "What's Robin's mother going to think! You bad girl!" The summer we were five our families went to Rehoboth for a week, stayed together in a big stucco house a block from the beach. One morning, before anyone was awake, Laura went out onto the screened-in porch on the second floor and slashed the screening over and over with the red metal shovel that matched her pail. Her mother's screaming woke up everybody, and then her father started hollering at her mother to "shut the hell up, Eve!" and then *my* mother said, in a careful voice that sounded like a radio announcer breaking in with a bulletin: "The child can't breathe, she's having an asthma attack." We all looked at Laura, and her baby brother started to giggle, thinking his sister was making funny faces at him, when really she was suffocating. After that, she didn't get in trouble anymore. I'm the only one at school (except for teachers) who knows about the asthma, and that she carries this special spray with her in case she has an attack when she isn't home, but she never has. I promised her I wouldn't tell anybody. "They'll think I'm like Penny Dodge," she said. I remembered the day Penny had an epileptic fit in the middle of recess, how she twitched and jerked on the blacktop like a squirrel I once saw dying in the street after it had been hit by a car.

When I told Laura I was going to Boston, I said, "*I* never told about *you*, so you can't tell anyone *this*."

"This is completely different. This is something you're *doing*, not something that you can't help. Something *wrong* that you're doing."

I said, "If you tell, I'll really hate you, Laura."

She folded up into herself the way you do when you think someone's going to hit you and you're afraid. She closed her eyes and said, "Okay, I promise."

When Grandma told me my mother was on her way up from Washington, I knew she must have found out I was here from Laura. I was furious that I hadn't had the guts to keep it all to myself, even if it was getting out of hand—keeping me up for hours at night, making me sleepy in school, ruining my appetite, and giving me stomach cramps—running wild inside me like kudzu, and my mother never even noticing that anything was wrong.

After she called, Grandma came to talk to me in the yard. I was lying on a big beach towel that had scenes from Italy printed on it. I made believe I was there, floating down a canal in Venice, and I could even feel the ripples under me, and the ground was hard as a gondola moving through the green water. Charlie Frayne says that's why my poems are good, because I can get inside of things and let them get inside of me. But I can't get inside of my mother, she's a locked-up house, nobody's ever home when I knock.

Grandma pulled a webbed lawn chair across the grass to where I was, back where marigolds and tomato plants had gotten tangled up with each other because Grandpa hadn't gotten around to putting in stakes. Tomatoes were rotting on the ground and I'd worked them into my Venice dream, making believe they'd fallen off a fruit peddler's cart he was pushing along the canal's edge and calling out for customers in Italian, which I don't know, but still I could imagine the sound of his voice. "I just talked to your mother," Grandma said, and there was nothing Italian about her.

My grandmother looks like Rita Hayworth, at least this is what Grandpa always says. "You should have been in the movies, Ada," he'll tell her, "you got a face like Rita Hayworth." Once I was writing a poem about that, and I went to the library and found pictures in the reference room—in old *Life* magazines, the pages getting yellow and curling up at the corners like leaves on a plant getting ready to die—and I could see that Rita Hayworth was very beautiful in an old-fashioned way (I mean, all that makeup and those shoulder pads), and probably Grandma looked a lot like that when she was young. When Grandpa met her, he must have taken a picture of her with his heart, and that's what he's been looking at ever since, not his *real* wife at all.

I sat up on the towel and the sun flashed off of Grandma's gold hoop earrings and bracelets and rings, blotting her out in its dazzle. All I could see of her in the glare was the edge of her skirt. I said, "I didn't hear you," when I really meant, *There's nothing left of you but your voice.*

She said it again, slowly: "I just talked to your mother."

I shut my eyes and even the skirt was gone. "Did you tell her I was here?"

"At first I didn't. But she knew. We would have had to call her anyhow, angel. We just would have had to do that eventually."

"I don't want to see her," I said. "I won't."

"Well," Grandma said, coming down from her chair to cradle me on the grass, "we'll just have to talk with her together. Robin and her gram will just have to be . . . a *team.*"

Hugging her made her real again; that, and the smell of her perfume and the sound of her bracelets clicking against each other in my ear.

"So don't you worry," she said, and I nodded into the soft pillow of her chest.

But when she got up to go inside and make a salmon mousse for supper—"It's one of the few nonmeat dishes your grandfather will eat, he's no sense of adventure when it comes to food. Or much else"—I knew that coming to Grandma's hadn't been running away at all. Running away means leaving one place, and not having any idea where you're headed; this had been more like a visit than I'd realized, but now I didn't have a choice anymore: I had to go off alone, not telling anyone where, not knowing where myself.

What I did was go up the back stairs, get my backpack and my raincoat, tiptoe down again—Grandma was in the kitchen and I could hear her beating egg whites in a bowl—and leave through the front door. Grandpa was just turning the corner, I saw the shining grille on his silver Oldsmobile growing bigger, like a huge metal mouth coming after me. So I stashed myself behind the shrubs that pressed against the front of the house and I waited in the hot prickly branches while he parked in the driveway and got out of the car and walked across the flagstone path to the porch steps. Grandpa walks slowly. He talks fast, gobbles his food, drinks a glassful of anything in what looks like a single swallow, but he always walks slowly. I have the feeling it's because he's never happy about where he's going. When I watched him drag from the car to the house, I thought, *He probably wants to run away, too,* and then I realized how sad and confusing it was that I had come for comfort to the very person he would like to leave. Grandma makes me feel safe, she always has, but Grandpa is never relaxed when she's around—"He's a very *pressured* person," Grandma explained to me once when I was visiting and Grandpa left the table in the middle of supper. "It's how men grow up here in the North, pressured and tense." I wanted to go to him right then and let him know how funny and patient and full of concern Grandma was, and I wanted to remind *her* that he thought she was as beautiful as Rita Hayworth, but I was past believing, even then, that you can make two people love each other just because you love each one of them yourself. Now I know that loving someone yourself isn't even enough of a reason to stay with them, which is what I told my mother in the note I wrote her, and if I could, I'd tell her one more thing: *I might be the one who left, but I've been looking for you all my life.*

I had fourteen dollars left in my wallet, and after I paid for the cab ride to Cambridge, I had less than six. At first I'd thought about hitchhiking, but I've never done that; I've always promised my mother I wouldn't, and it still felt like a promise I wanted to keep. That's another thing it's taken me a long time to understand: how people figure out which promises they can break and which ones they'll stay faithful to. When my father was packing up his things and moving to his apartment on Capitol Hill, I went into his study where he was putting his books into cartons and I said, "You're not allowed to go." His whole body went loose, like he was turning to water, and the books he was holding slid out of his hand and thumped on the rug. "I *have* to," he said, letting me know I was right to think he was breaking promises and letting me know, too, that sometimes you have to do that. What I think now is that the ones you keep *keep you*, they put down roots inside you like trees; the ones you can change your mind about never go as deep, they're more like garden flowers you plant and water and protect from weeds, but still you can pull them up anytime you want; their roots never burrow down into your bones.

"Let me out at the Coop," I told the driver, because Charlie Frayne said once that it was the best bookstore in the world and I wanted the driver to think that I had a definite destination. When I was on the sidewalk, I thought, *I don't even know where I'll sleep tonight*, but I wasn't scared about it. I *wanted* to be, but my nerves wouldn't work, I couldn't find the switch in my brain that would turn them on and send me right back to my grandparents, whether my mother was coming or not. The only parts of me that worked were my feet and my eyes, so I moved down Massachusetts Avenue, right through the middle of Cambridge, like a mounted movie camera, looking and looking, everything I saw coming in bright and strange and flat as pictures on film. A knot of Hare Krishnas on the corner, pale-orange gauze shirts shimmering, light glinting off the tambourines they rattled in the air. Marijuana smoke rising in spirals from smokers huddled in a stairwell, passing around the burning reefer. At home, a lot of kids smoke, but I never have. A girl in the group saw me staring, held out the stub to me, and I wanted to try it, I did, I wanted to be silly and loose like her, but my arm wouldn't work and I kept moving. Couples linked together, hands in one another's pockets, hands around waists, on shoulders, hands holding hands—so much touching! I ran my thumbs back and forth across my fingers, trying to remember the feel of it, trying to remember Grandma holding me against her on the grass, the smell of her perfume. "Watch where you're going!" somebody said, whose body I'd bumped, walked straight into, and I said, "Sorry," because I remembered that was what you said. Kept moving. The street seemed like a tunnel, like the dark cardboard tunnel of a kaleidoscope, except now I wasn't only *looking* down to the end where the colors swirled, the shapes kept changing, flowing in and out of each other, I was *in* the tunnel myself, inside the kaleidoscope, Daddy bought me one when I was little but I never got *inside* that one, dizzy, getting dizzy, camera running wild, and then there was an old toothless woman feeding the pigeons, her stockings were falling down and her sweater was full of holes and she made funny little noises that the birds seemed to understand. The birds were stepping on one another's feet, trying to get to the bread crusts she dropped, and it made me sad seeing the pigeons hurting each other—if they were, I don't really know if they were, maybe pigeons don't feel one another's jabs and pokes, but I did, as if I were a pigeon myself, one of those little birds, hungry and selfish and waiting every day for that crazy old lady to come with her stale bread, and I sat right down on the curb, in the middle of all those people, those lights, those cars roaming up and down the street like cows. I sat there in my sadness, sore all over, feeling trampled and kicked, and then somebody coming down to where I was, low to the ground where the pigeons were still scrapping for crumbs, somebody said, "Need some help?" "Oh!" I said, starting to cry, "I *do*, I don't have anywhere to go!" And I was bawling now, not caring who heard, and then I realized that my nerves were working again, and I was very scared, and also very relieved.

W here I am is Beacon House.

Terri, who works here, led me the seven blocks from where she'd found me crying on the curb to the narrow house, its front covered with ivy so dense that at first I couldn't see any bricks at all—just ivy and the windows, some of them already half-covered with vines. Lamps inside gleamed through the leaves. The sun was going down, and each leaf on the ivy glowed. Beacon House looked magical to me, a shining place in the middle of the dirty, hard city.

By the time I followed Terri through the front door, walked under the jangling brass prayer bells, and shook Gabriel Asher's hand, I felt lucky to be here, not suspicious and edgy the way you think you'd be with total strangers.

It was the way Terri said, "Need some help?" that started me trusting her right away. The words came out clean and simple, I didn't have the feeling she had lots of other words underneath the ones she spoke. When I turned my head up to look at her, even through my tears I could see that her face was solid and kind, and I thought, *I know her*, which just meant she wasn't hiding herself from me. I think that's why I was able to be afraid for myself: because I wasn't afraid of

Terri, she was something firm to lean against while the big waves of fear crashed around me and finally lost their force, like the tide going out after hours of battering the shore. She sat down beside me. She wore jeans and a yellow T-shirt and her long brown hair was piled on top of her head, but some stray ends wisped around her ordinary face. She looked like lots of college girls walking back and forth behind us on the sidewalk; I wondered if she'd ever wished she were beautiful, and I wanted to tell her about Laura, about how being beautiful brought you as much sorrow as being plain, but it didn't seem to me that Terri needed to hear that, she was so peaceful in her own body.

"I work at a place for kids who have . . . who needed to split from their folks. Is that your trouble?"

I nodded.

"We have a 'safe house,'" she went on. "Do you know what that is?"

I said no.

"It means you can come and stay with us for a while, and we won't call the cops or your family, we'll just try and help you figure out what you want to do. Help you get your head together. The man I work with, his name is Gabriel Asher, he's a real good listener, plus he's smart. He started Beacon House, that's the name of our place; actually, he *lives* there. You want to hear more?"

I nodded. My tears were drying up and everything looked soft and still, the way things do after a summer storm.

"We've got four kids with us now," she said. "So you'd be five. We eat our meals together, divide up chores. In the morning, you spend about an hour talking with me or Gabe. In the afternoon, everyone raps together in a group. The rest of the day and evening are yours—to think, write, paint, go for a walk, get some sun. No booze, no dope, no sex." She grinned. "But *great* food. Gabe thinks he was a famous French chef in a previous life."

I said, "My name is Robin Sorokin," for no reason I understood, but maybe to remind myself that I *had* a name, and a life that went with it, in the present, and I could never run away from *that*.

"Terri Shepard," she said, smiling, her whole ordinary face

lit up like the moon, pale and beautiful, that sailed in the sky now, even though the sun had not yet set.

So we stood up—I felt wobbly for a minute, as if I hadn't stood on my own legs for days—and then we started walking to Beacon House, her hand gently on my shoulder.

Gabriel Asher is very tall and thin, and when he talks, his voice sounds like it has traveled the whole long distance of his body. Some people talk just with their mouths and it seems that their words have nothing to do with the rest of them, but Gabriel's words are as much a part of him as his blood, or the muscles that twist through his arms and legs like strong, knotted ropes. When he said, "We're glad you've come, Robin," I felt like he'd been waiting for me for a long time, his greeting resting inside him until I'd arrived. Or maybe that's what I *wanted* to feel, that and trusting Terri enough to come here with her, but what other way is there to leap over all your confusion into a stranger's cool, quiet house?

In the kitchen, Alice was washing the dishes. Terri said, "Alice, meet Robin," and she looked at us over the shoulder on which she'd draped a dish towel. Her blond hair was cropped short and frizzy and some soap bubbles clung to it, they glittered like stars, like a strange halo around her pudgy face. "Y'all come to crash?" she said, and sounded like Grandma does when she "lays it on thick," which is my mother's description of how Grandma talks when she lets out her own true speech.

I was too shy to answer, but Terri said, "She'll be moving in with you."

Alice said, "Wow. Roomies. Isn't that just too sweet? Just like boarding school."

"This is not boarding school, Alice," Terri told her. "And if you don't like it, you can—"

"I know." She drew herself up very erect and spoke in a gravelly tone. "*I am always free to leave.*" She was mimicking Gabriel, and her sarcasm punctured my idea of Beacon House as a perfect refuge, a place apart, some kind of miraculous salvation to get me out of my trouble. Even here, I saw, people would be nasty, there would be arguments or terrible cold silences, I would start to feel lonely again, not trusting anybody, and then where would I go? I wanted the brick floor to open up and swallow me whole, but just that moment Gabriel walked in and said, "You'll feel a lot better once you've eaten. How about a cheese omelette?"

Terri said, "Alice, let's let Gabe and Robin talk."

Alice wiped her hands, finger by finger, on the towel and followed Terri out of the kitchen without giving me a single glance.

"Her father's in jail," Gabe said matter-of-factly, fishing in the refrigerator for eggs and milk and a big hunk of yellow butter. "Tax evasion. She's ashamed to go back to Atlanta. How about *your* father, what's he do?"

I tried to take in what he'd told me about Alice and answer his question at the same time, and Alice's story smashed into mine, they got tangled up together: "He's in jail with Senator . . . I mean, *not* in jail . . . he's Senator McPherson's administrative assistant."

"You proud of that?" He was beating up the eggs, and he didn't seem at all startled or impressed. I could have said, "He runs a gas station," or "He's a schoolteacher."

"Senator McPherson's going to run for president," I said. "That's a secret."

"You're proud," he said, smiling. "That's good. How about your mother?"

I traced the lines of the red-and-white-checked tablecloth with my finger. "I'm . . . proud of her, too."

"But angry." He brought me a plate and some silverware. "Milk or lemonade?"

"Milk, please," I said, sensing hunger for the first time since lunch. It was almost nine o'clock. He brought me a glass of milk and several slices of bread, and then I tore into my dinner. Charlie Frayne thought I was angry, too, and it had taken me a while to feel it, it had gone inside me, like Laura's asthma had gone inside her, except with me, it had just sat there for years, like the nail I swallowed when I was three, that seemed to disappear inside me, until days later it turned up in the toilet and my mother cried for a long time.

"She's a geneticist," I said. "My parents got divorced when I was eight."

"How old are you now?" He poured himself some milk and

came to sit with me at the big trestle table that filled up the center of the room.

"Fifteen."

"Seven years of anger," he said. "Half your life. That's a big load to carry. I guess it finally got too heavy."

He swigged down his milk, and I thought how remarkable it was that he should understand it so easily, with so little talking.

I said, "I feel like you know me better than I know myself."

"Never," Gabriel Asher said. "Another person can *never* know you better than you know yourself. When it comes to Robin, you are the world's number one expert. Got that?"

I nodded, feeling stupid and very intelligent at the same time.

Now it's morning. All night it rained, and I swam in and out of dreams of drowning and planes falling into the sea and terrible floods. Every time I woke up, Alice was thrashing around in her bed, and sometimes she called out for someone named Harry, so I knew she was having nightmares, too.

"At least you don't snore," she said as we both got dressed. "In boarding school, my last roommate snored and it was like sleeping with a train, I near about *died* from exhaustion."

I said, "Do you always have bad dreams, or just since you . . . left?"

She scowled. "I don't dream. Not since I was about five or six."

"But I heard you—"

"I *told* you," she said, "*I don't dream.*" She was fluffing her hair with her fingers, and what had looked like a halo to me last night changed in my imagination to singed wires around her angry face. I wondered what it was she dreamed about that scared her so much she had to forget it before she woke up, and who Harry was, and I was glad I knew *I* dreamed, because otherwise your day-life and your night-life would be so separate from each other, you would be like a person cut in two, neither part knowing what the other was doing, or that the other even existed.

Besides Alice, there's Beth, Malcolm, and Luis. When I came into the kitchen for breakfast, Beth got up from her place at the table and skittered to the corner, where she's still huddled. Gabriel is flipping pancakes on a griddle, and he doesn't say anything to Beth about the fact that she's on the floor. She's small and mousey and silent, and the way she looks at me makes me remember everything wrong I've ever done in my life, and I want to apologize to her for all of it. Alice says, "Oh shit, Beth's pulling her 'poor wallflower' routine, makes me want to puke, I swear."

"Don't swear," says Malcolm. "We don't need your 'dirtiest mouth in the South' routine, either."

"Clever," Alice says. "You are so clever, Malcolm." She's blushing, though, glad for his attention.

Malcolm: He's rocking on the back legs of his chair, and when he brings the chair down, he drums on the table with his thick, nervous hands, and his eyes are everywhere, they're like two birds trapped in the cage of his head, searching for the way back out to freedom. Some part of Malcolm is always moving. His hair is sun-bleached and his face and arms are very tan, and I bet he was one of those boys you see running down the beach, racing, it seems, from one end of the ocean to the other. Even his smile comes and goes like lightning, and sometimes his face gets stormy, all the smooth lines turning to shadow, to sudden formations of rumbling dark clouds.

Luis: He's lapping up his cereal, taking no notice of anything. His brown skin looks polished, his hair's sleek black, his eyes gleam like coal, but he's placid as a housecat, no threat of sudden cry or motion. Finally, he raises his head in a slow arc, smiles at me, and says, "*Encantado de conocerla*," the Spanish words rolling off his tongue.

"Talk English," Alice says. "It's not like you can't."

Gabriel brings a plate of steaming pancakes from the stove. "*Encantado de conocerla*," he repeats, winking at Luis. " 'Delighted to meet you.' Right, Luis?"

Luis grins.

"Thank you," I say. "I mean, *gracias*."

Gabriel says, "You know, Alice-in-Wonderland, you could see this as an opportunity to learn a little of another language, instead of laying into Luis every time he says something you don't understand."

"I didn't come here to *learn* things," she says. She looks disgusted. "This isn't *school*."

86

"What do you think, Luis?" Gabriel says. "Think you might offer a little crash course for us *gringos*?"

"Sure!" Luis says. Now he winks back at Gabriel. "If Robin will take it, I will teach it."

In the corner, Beth jerks at the mention of my name, and now I know why she hated me the minute I walked into the room: it was because of Luis, because he might pay attention to me. I'm only halfway through breakfast of my first morning at Beacon House, and already it's starting to feel as complicated as a family.

What I'm doing is writing my autobiography. It's Gabriel's idea; he said I didn't have to do it if I didn't want to, but I told him I *loved* to write, although most of what I write is poetry. We were in his "office," which is the attic of Beacon House. He's covered the sloped walls with brown cork panels, and there's a moss-green rug on the floor, so the room looks like a very tidy cave—not dank or full of cobwebs and fungi, or even dark (there's a round window on one of the walls, and the light pours through the glass)—the kind of cave you'd hope to find if you were lost in the woods and bad weather was rumbling in your ears.

Gabriel said, "Well, if you're a poet, then I don't have to tell you about letting one word lead to another, one memory to the next. Free flow."

And he gave me a yellow legal pad, the kind my father uses all the time for rough drafts of speeches and the charts he's always making of boxes and circles connected with lines, like the pictures that come with tinker-toy instructions. "Try to keep it to twenty pages," Gabriel said.

My mouth flew open. "Twenty pages!" I'd never written anything that long in my life.

He shrugged. "Well, if you have to go over, go over. I don't want you to feel like you're skipping things that are important to you."

Things that were important to me. I'd been living for fifteen years, so twenty pages was hardly more than a page a year. Thinking about my life that way made it seem easier. Maybe I *could* write twenty pages. Maybe more.

This is what I have so far:

WHAT I REMEMBER
by
Robin Sorokin

The first thing I remember is light. Maybe I've just been born, or it could be my mother switching on the lamp in my room for a 2 a.m. feeding. Or just an ordinary morning leaving its trace, for some reason, in my memory. I'll never be sure. But it must have been important to me, because I've always loved the way sun spills across the grass, or how snow shines on a starless winter night, or the patterns you can make by waving a flashlight on a blank wall. I used to make flashlight designs all the time when I was a little girl. Once my father came into my room and said, "Looks like you're stranded on an island and signaling for help." I knew he meant it as a joke, but the picture his words made in my head scared me, and I threw the flashlight across the room, breaking to bits a figurine of Bambi on my dresser. "What made you do that?" he wailed, and his eyes were wide and helpless. He looked even more frightened than I'd felt, as if I'd discovered something about him and punished him by smashing the glass deer. I had to hug him for a long time to help him stop shaking. "Have I hurt you that much?" he said. I was five years old.

When my parents were five, my father was rich and my mother was poor. Even if they'd grown up in the same city, they wouldn't have been neighbors, they'd have been different from each other from the beginning. When they would fight about my father's job, about his being away so much on trips, at weekend meetings, just working late in Senator McPherson's office, my father would say, "Christ, Janet, you'd think you'd have developed just a smidgen of political awareness after the way your parents had to struggle, but I swear to God you don't know the difference between John D. Rockefeller and Karl Marx, and don't give a damn." And my mother would say, "I didn't marry John D. Rockefeller or Karl Marx." I didn't under-

stand most of their arguments until I was older and my father was already living in his own place. But it isn't important to know what your parents are fighting about, just that they are, that their words are hitting each other like small sharp stones pitched through the air and piling up in opposite corners of the room.

I remember all the rooms of our house—it's the only house I've ever lived in—so leaving it was like leaving my own body. It's supposed to be a good thing to live in the same house all your life instead of moving from place to place and having to get used to strange new noises and the shapes of new rooms, but I would rather have started over a hundred times, if that would have kept my father at home and my mother from forgetting that just because things are organized doesn't mean that nothing's wrong.

If you would walk into the house right now, you'd think it was perfect—no clutter, all the furniture clean and polished, the bathroom sinks gleaming, fresh flowers from my mother's garden in pewter vases, the beds made, everything in order. When my parents bought the house, it was, my mother says, "a disaster." Sometimes I try to imagine what they were like, before I was born, "madly in love" (my mother says that sarcastically, but I don't think she felt sarcastic about it seventeen years ago) and making plans for the future.

I think they must have touched each other all the time, and smiled at one another, and kidded with each other about things they would argue over years later. I don't think I'll ever be madly in love, because part of me will always be standing aside, waiting for the touching to end and the smiles to stop and the jokes to turn into sharp stones we throw at one another from opposite corners of a room.

When I was two months old, my mother—who'd had me in the summer, between semesters—went back to school, and by the end of that year she had her Ph.D. and a job at the institute, where she still works. Her boss is Eli Bell, who my father calls "your mother's priest," and before I knew he was being sarcastic, I used to wonder if my mother was secretly Catholic and Eli—who's never gotten married and often folds his hands in his lap and closes his eyes, which could be either tiredness or prayer—I wondered if he had once given sermons every Sunday morning and sat behind a black curtain listening to confessions. My mother isn't Catholic, she isn't anything religious, she says "the idea of God is empirically suspect," *but I still think Eli would make a good priest, and I would make a good Catholic, coming to him week after week with my sins written out in a neat little list and afterward, sitting alone in the dark chapel, waiting for the angels to sing.*

The lady who took care of me until I was four was Catholic, too. Her name was Mrs. Stupowski and sometimes in dreams I still hear her high, sharp voice talking to me in Polish and I am telling her I don't understand you, but she keeps on speaking the strange words. She was very thin and I can remember how it felt when she carried me around: as if I were lying against bedsprings, as if there were no mattress at all. But on some days she would take me to church with her—I remember being strapped into the stroller and a hat tied too tightly under my chin and the wheels clicking over the sidewalk that whizzed by, square after concrete square. Inside, it was very quiet and the candles flickered beside the altar, and the stained-glass windows shone like giant jewels carved into the walls. After Mrs. Stupowski went to St. Andrew's in the middle of the afternoon, she felt softer when she held me, puffed up, more comfortable to lean against. Even the way she smelled would change, from her usual stale damp-basement odor to something not quite perfumey, but still nicer, like almonds maybe, or cinnamon toast. And sometimes I would watch her stroke her rosary beads; her pinched, worried face relaxed, she looked peaceful to me, almost pretty.

On some days, Mrs. Mathis would bring Laura over to our house, and Mrs. Stupowski would watch both of us. I mean, she'd leave both of us to entertain each other while she watched soap operas on television and ate Cheez Doodles from the big cellophane package she kept in her knitting bag, though all I ever saw her do was rewind the ball of blue yarn that kept unraveling at the bottom of the bag. I don't know if I loved her, but I did get used to her and when I started going to the Pre-School Learning Center at the institute, I missed Mrs. Stupowski the way you miss a picture on the wall you never thought you cared about that much, but once it's gone, the whole room looks out of whack, for a long time nothing seems to fit, you keep noticing that empty space and the longer you look at it, the more it seems like a hole you're falling into, even though you know it's nothing but ordinary plaster, nothing that could hurt you at all.

When I was about ten or eleven, I found a picture of Mrs. Stupowski pushing me in the backyard swing. I didn't recognize her,

I'd almost forgotten she'd ever taken care of me. When I asked my mother who the lady was, she said, "I was so lucky to find that woman. She was just like a grandmother to you."

"But you never talk about her," I said, trying to understand how somebody so close to me could disappear out of our lives for all these years. "What happened to her?"

"Oh," my mother said, "she died." She said it the way you'd talk about someone you'd never met, like a TV star you knew only as a small picture on glass, not a real lady who held you in her thin arms and took you to church and afterward—it was so strange to remember it all!—bought you Necco Wafers at the drugstore and you let them dissolve one by one on your tongue. I wanted to tell my mother that it was wrong to have let Mrs. Stupowski vanish like that, to let me forget her, to have her turn up again in the bottom of a drawer, bent and faded and buried under socks. But that night I found the place in my memory where I'd kept her all along, and when I opened it up, she was shining and real.

When my father moved out of our house, I began to understand about needing to forget. "Oh," I'd say, when someone would ask me where he was, "he moved," and my voice would be as casual as my mother's when she'd told me Mrs. Stupowski had died, or when she mentioned her own mother to me, which was hardly ever. I cried and vomited for two weeks after he left, and then I realized that the only way I'd ever get better would be to start forgetting that he'd lived with us. Every time I bumped into a reminder, I would have to knock it down, tear it to shreds, do whatever I could to destroy it. At meals, I started sitting in what had been his chair, so I wouldn't have to look at that empty place anymore. I threw away records he'd bought me that we used to listen to together in my room, and I ripped up my whole collection of campaign bumper stickers, and got rid of my playing cards because we'd always play gin rummy together on nights when he was home before I went to sleep. I changed around my bedroom (my mother did this, too, which was my only sign that she was hurting in the same way I was) and stopped wearing the clothes that he liked the best, or outfits he'd bought me when he'd been on a trip somewhere with Senator McPherson. It seemed that all my energy was going into forgetting. My mother said, "What you're feeling is perfectly normal," but it didn't feel normal to me, it felt like the things you have to do after tornadoes or typhoons, the broken mess you're left to clean up after a hurricane sweeps through one night and nothing's like it was before, not ever again.

They'd each had a little speech for me about why they had to get a divorce, and my father, who gives speeches all the time, stuttered through his, but my mother talked in her usual calm, sensible way about something that made no sense at all. I was eight years old. How could she expect me to understand her explanation? She could have been reading out of one of her genetics books, that's how much I was understanding. But I made believe the things she said were clear to me, and when she said "Everything's going to be fine, Robin," I smiled as if I believed her, hoping hard she'd know I was lying, but she didn't.

She thinks I love my father better, but that isn't true. It's just easier to love him because I never have to pretend I'm happy when I'm not, he doesn't expect me to "understand" very much at all. Once he told me, "Life's a bitch, sweetheart, I don't know much more than you do. Probably less." At first it shocked me that someone like my father, who's going to work in the White House, should be telling me he might know less than me, but then I realized he wasn't talking about facts and information, he meant the kind of things you know in your heart, things you're probably born knowing, which is maybe why everybody starts out life crying. That isn't scientific, but I think it's true.

My parents were both born in 1939. In baby pictures I've seen of my mother, her face is very round and serious, and she's bundled up in snowsuits and scarves and hats snug as helmets. She's always sitting somewhere, in a carriage or on someone's lap or on the front stoop of the apartment building where she grew up, and it's hard to believe, looking at those pictures, that she ever got up on her own and ran. Whenever I think of her early years, I picture her doing quiet things, in place, spending whole afternoons building block towers and knocking them down, or scribbling endless crayon designs, maybe doing the same puzzle over and over. I can't imagine her giddy or rambunctious, but how could she have been when her own mother was so sad? I've seen photos of her, too, and she always looks like she's ready to cry, her face bony and pale, her eyes blank, not noticing anything in particular, not expecting anything to turn up that's worth noticing. How could my mother have felt like giggling in the midst of all those sighs? And Grandpa Lesser: even when he was young, he was stiff as a pole, his body was always saying: Keep still; don't bump me, I might break; can't you see how hard it is for me to get through the day?

In snapshots of my father as a little boy, you hardly ever see his face. He's moved just as the shutter clicks, so his features are one big blur; or else he's running or swimming or lunging after a ball. If he's being held, he's squirming to get loose. In one picture of him sleeping in his crib, he's burrowed his head into the crook of his arm, as if he's saying, "You think you've got me now, but you don't!" He doesn't think Grandma loved him, but I wonder if he ever stayed still long enough to be hugged.

So there they are as babies—my mother deep in serious concentration, my father jumpy as a rabbit—and here they are grown up: my mother bent over her microscope for hours; my father rushing from one meeting to the next, hopping planes, forgetting to eat, and hardly sleeping. From the beginning, they were completely different from each other, but maybe that's what they fell in love with, maybe they each felt that being with the other gave them what they didn't have in themselves. My father could watch my mother working away at her formulas, giving all her attention to a tiny cell squirming like a worm across her slide, and he could pretend to be as patient as she is; and she could watch my father traveling all over the country, talking all day long to tons of people in his office, in restaurants, on the phone, always in the midst of one noisy group or another, and she could pretend to be as active as he is.

Plus she's pretty and he's handsome, and maybe that had as much to do with it as anything. I don't suppose I'll ever really know, and if I did, what would it change?

When my parents got divorced, I remember thinking, You can't depend on them anymore for anything, you're completely on your own. They were giving me their "speeches," and it seemed that they were each getting smaller and smaller, shrinking right in front of my eyes, turning into tiny midgets who would never be able to take care of me again. I felt dizzy, the same way I felt at the top of the Washington Monument, all those wide streets and huge cars and tall people turned into miniature toys, and I was the only thing left in the world that was big and heavy. When my parents finally stopped talking, everything in the house seemed shrunken and fragile, except for me. I walked out of the room very carefully because I knew how easy it would be for me to break everything to bits with just one swing of my giant arm.

I went to the screened-in porch, sat down on the wicker rocker, and stared at the cedar trees that towered over the house. At least the world outside was still the right size, at least here I could feel like a little child again. For eight years I'd thought of myself as their little child, as Brian and Janet Sorokin's daughter. But now I could see that in one short evening, my other life—Robin Sorokin by herself—had become the real one, the important one, the one in which I was smaller than trees, small enough to curl my whole body into the curve of the chair, small and watchful and alone.

You wouldn't have noticed the change. Except for the first weeks of forgetting I already wrote about, my outside life stayed the same. I still lived in the same house in the same neighborhood, the school bus picked me up on the usual corner, I took piano lessons and gymnastics and ballet on Fridays, I had gerbils and a goldfish named Nellie, I went to sleep-over parties, got good grades, kept my room clean and baked cookies with my mother, which was one of the few things she seemed to like to do with me, as opposed to most of the time when she'd be so busy with her reading that I got to feel, more and more, that I didn't have the right to interrupt her with my silly questions, my simple problems, my uninteresting ideas. I'd see my father on weekends, unless he was out of town or tied up with meetings. One time I told my mother she made me mad because she brought work home with her every night and her face got stony; she said, "Why is it that you don't resent your father's impossible schedule, which sometimes results in your not seeing him for weeks, while I'm here with you every day and wind up getting all the flak?" She was there every day, but not with me; and my father was gone sometimes for weeks at a time, but when I finally did spend time with him, he was there, I had all his attention, it was like I was running for president, that's how important he made me feel.

But I couldn't let myself depend on him all over again, the way I did when we all lived in the same house. Otherwise, the missing would start again, and the crying, and needing to forget him after each visit, it would be like he was leaving and leaving and leaving, and finally I wouldn't be able to see him anymore at all. So I made sure I left part of myself at home every time he came to pick me up. On my twelfth birthday, a Wednesday, he called me long-distance, person-to-person, from Columbus, Ohio. "I wish I were with you," he said. "I'm eating rubber chicken and cold peas, and some guy's talking about electoral reform. How 'bout you?"

My mother had taken me out to dinner with Laura, to a fancy French restaurant in Georgetown where the waiters talked with French accents and the butter came on a sterling silver dish, instead of those little pats with paper on the top. But I didn't tell him any of that, I said, "I'm doing my homework," because I didn't want him to feel left out, but also I didn't want to give my mother credit for having given me such a nice time.

"Well," he said, and I could hear the dishes clattering in the VFW hall where he was calling me from, "this weekend we'll have a celebration. I've got something real special planned for the two of us. You available?"

I could tell from his voice, all the cheer he was pumping into his words, that he thought my mother had forgotten my birthday completely, but I didn't correct him. I had gotten to the point where I wanted them to think badly of one another. I didn't want to give myself any reason for hoping they would find a way back to one another, it was better to get used to their sarcastic remarks about each other, their flashes of anger at something the other did or didn't do, the way they'd come to refer to each other as "your mother" or "your father," as if they didn't think of each other as Brian and Janet anymore, as if the only reason they had to think about each other at all was me.

The celebration he'd planned was a weekend in a cabin on Skyline Drive.

On Saturday morning he picked me up before eight, and we rode out of the city into the hazy Virginia hills. In the car, we sang songs and told each other riddles and played word games that made us sillier and sillier. Our laughter and the mountain highway we were climbing made me feel light-headed and when I said, "This must be what it's like to be drunk," his smile disappeared and he told me, "Being drunk's no fun at all, it's bad news all the way," and I realized he was talking about his own father, about how much pain Grandpa's drinking had brought to his son's life. I've known about Grandpa Sorokin's "problem" for as long as I can remember, but I always thought of it as something he had to bear, like a bad tooth that keeps flaring up, or a shoulder that aches whenever it rains. I don't think I wanted to know that my father carried bitterness in him all the time, that it had grown inside him like the cells my mother studies in her laboratory, creatures with their own lives, a whole world you can't even see, but that's as real as the world you look at every day with your eyes.

By the time we got to the cabin, we'd gone back to joking and laughing, and the world we could see was the only one we cared about. The sun glittered in the trees, purple thistles and Queen Anne's lace and wild daisies edged the road like a beautiful embroidered hem, the sky was soft blue, cloud-puffs floated in the blueness. I heard what sounded like thousands of birds, and a chorus of crickets. Once my father had told me, "They don't have crickets in New York anymore. Isn't that disgusting? They've killed nature." The cabin was set back from the road, and behind the cabin, hiking trails twisted through the woods, and we walked together for most of the afternoon, side by side through the cool forest, twigs and pine needles crackling under our feet. Later, we made supper together on the wood-burning stove, hamburgers and fried potatoes and fresh corn we'd bought at the farmer's stand on the drive from Washington. We ate on the small deck by the side of the cabin, and we could look at the valley beneath us, its surface reflecting the red sun glowing now over the cabin's roof. After we ate, we lit the oil-burning lamp and played Monopoly and then we went to sleep on the cots we put our sleeping bags on, and I woke up to the same cricket song I'd listened to the night before, except now the birds were back, and the cabin was filled with morning light.

Everything seemed so simple there, and that's why I said what I said, because I forgot how complicated and confusing life was in Washington, I forgot about not depending on my parents anymore and learning to live with their dislike for one another and keeping a piece of myself behind whenever I left to spend time with my father, and I said, "I want you to come back home," like he'd gone a few days ago instead of almost four whole years.

His head tilted a little to the side, the way you do when you haven't quite heard what someone's said to you, and then he put his hands on his head, as if he had heard and the words were beating like drums behind his eyes, and he said, "That's not possible, Robin. Why are you asking me for something that isn't possible, instead of making the most of what is?" He swept his arm from one side of the room to the other, and I realized that I'd ruined his birthday gift for me, I'd wiped out the cabin and the woods and the beautiful view from the mountain, and just the two of us playing Monopoly and listening to the crickets sing us to sleep, I'd ruined it because it wasn't enough, I didn't want visits with my father, I wanted a family, one I think we had before my memories start—I wanted that back, and I guess I still do, and maybe that's why I've run away. Because I can't have it, and because I'm still searching for it.

Does this make any sense?

This is my fourth day at Beacon House, but it feels like my fourth month or year. Not because time is moving slowly, it isn't. But because everything that happened before I got here has turned into *memory*, a bright haze like the moon's corona, or the streak a shooting star leaves behind after it's disappeared into the darkness. Gabriel says these flashes I'm having are *insights*, that my life is starting to rearrange itself into patterns, and each time I discover a pattern, it is like finding a new constellation of stars in what I thought had been an empty place in the sky. Maybe he's right. Maybe I was already turning into an astronomer when I decided to run away, instead of a fifteen-year-old girl who knew where she lived and what was true. Now I live at Beacon House, the only place I'm sure is still anchored to the earth. When I try to imagine the future—What-will-I-do-when-I-leave-here?—it looks a lot like the past, all shifting lights and stretches of fluorescent vapor and nothing hard to stand on, nothing solid I can touch or name.

But here I can say *Alice, Luis, Beth, Malcolm, Terri, Gabriel*. Here I can sit in the kitchen in the late afternoon and watch the sunlight spill across the same section of floor each day, here I can lie on my bed at night and listen to the voices of Alice's dreams, listen to the soft chimes of the antique wall clock that hangs in the front hall. My mother would love that clock.

This morning Gabriel said, "I think tomorrow we'll talk about making some contact with your family, about how you want to handle that. If you do."

A terrible crackling raced from temple to temple. *My family.* I'd almost forgotten they were out there, alive in the present, worrying about me, angry and frantic. What was going on in my head? It sounded like paper burning, letters I'd thrown into a fire, years of messages turning to ash. Maybe that's part of the glow I see when I remember, maybe I'm burning up memories as well as discovering the patterns they make.

I said, "Well, we can *talk* about it," but I knew what I really meant was, *I don't want to leave here now; this feels more like a family to me than my old one ever did.*

Alice, Luis, Beth, Malcolm.

Alice finally admits that she must dream, because I asked her who Harry was and she got very pale and sputtered, "How do *you* know about Harry?" I said I didn't know *about* him, just that she called out his name in the night, and she said, "Then I must be having nightmares," and told me, in a big rush of words, that Harry was the man her mother had gone to live with when her father was sent to jail, how Harry would come home drunk and angry at nothing in particular, angry that her mother had left a skillet soaking in the sink instead of scouring it clean, angry that Alice, who was back in Atlanta during Spring Break from Ivy Simpson's School for Girls in Mobile, had her record player turned up "too damn loud," angry that he'd drunk the last bottle of Pabst's the night before and Alice's mother hadn't thought to buy more when she'd been out shopping anyhow. "You're a lousy inconsiderate bitch!" he yelled, and Alice said his eyes were red as burning coals. "Like he was a furnace inside," she said. "Like he was nothing but hot fire and smoke." Sometimes, she said, Harry hit her mother, she could hear her whimpering late into the night. I asked her if her mother still lived with Harry, and she said, "No, he left her. Women like my mother always get left. I mean, my father left twice before he got himself busted, which is just another way of cutting out on her. She'd never *think* of leaving a man. It's not *ladylike*. It's not in the Southern *tradition*. You know what I think of ladylike Southern traditions?" We were in our room. She flopped from her back to her stomach, buried her face in her pillow, and when she sat up, there was a wet stain in the middle of her pillowcase, and her eyes were puffy, and her mascara ran like scratches down her cheeks. "I'm never going back there," she said. "Even if they let him out of the can. The whole scene sucks."

Luis *wants* to go back to his house, which is in New York City, Bedford-Stuyvesant, a place my father went with Senator McPherson, who gave a speech about it later and said it was "America's burnt-out soul crying for redemption." He wants to go back home but he can't, because his mother lost her job cleaning rooms in a hotel and when she didn't pay the rent for two months, the landlord came from his house on Long Island, smoking, Luis says, "a cigar as big as a salami," and said, between puffs, that he'd rented their rooms to "working people. You got ten days to get out, I don't want welfares in my building." Luis's mother and his five-year-old sister, Carlotta, went to live with their grandmother in her two-room apartment over a take-out restaurant where, Luis says, "all day and all night you hear the sizzling and the smoke, it stings your eyes," and Luis's brother, Ramon, who's twelve, stayed with his mother's Cousin Maria and her six children, all under eight. Luis was supposed to stay there, too, but after three days, he says, "I was being a sardine, you see what I mean? I am so squashed in and missing my mother and sister, and my mother's sick now in the stomach so she can't find more work for a long time. So I say, *Luis, get out before you start breaking up windows,* and I come this far because I'm thinking I'll go to Nova Scotia and be, you know, a fisherman, but all of a sudden I'm feeling so much homesickness I can't keep no food down, nothing, I'm thinking I'll have to go to the Free Clinic, and right there Terri finds me, you know, takes me out here. So that's it. Luis's story." He looked like he was going to cry, then suddenly a smile took over his face. " 'Then he meets Señorita Robin Sorokin, and they live happily ever after. The end.' " We had walked to the corner, and now we were on our way back to Beacon House.

It was almost dinnertime, and the pavement was hot from the day's heat. Warmth rose up my legs, up to my waist, all the way up to my ears: I was trembling with warmth and I smiled at Luis and said, "I really like you a lot," and his black eyes flashed in his smiling face.

Beth hasn't smiled at me once, or said a single word. She doesn't hide in the corners of rooms anymore, but she takes her own corner *with* her, she curls up inside herself, her eyes dull, sometimes staring at me in a way that says, *Why did you have to come here at all?*; sometimes looking totally blank, like my mother's mother, or pictures I've seen of civilians after a bomb's been dropped on their village. Terri told me, "Beth's a very troubled girl, Robin. We are trying to get her the kind of help she needs, but while she's here, I don't want you to think you're the cause of her unhappiness." All I know about her is that her father is a famous eye surgeon, Alice says, her mother is an heiress, and they have homes in Connecticut and Martha's Vineyard and St. Petersburg, Florida. I can imagine Beth just getting settled in one place, when suddenly it's time to pack and leave for another. I can hear her saying *Good-bye, good-bye*, until she begins to believe it's the only important word, the one word you can count on hearing and speaking for the rest of your lonely life. I can see her father, clean and sleek and dangerous as a scalpel, and her mother: I imagine she's very beautiful and probably subscribes to *Vogue* and buys clothes in shops that smell like expensive perfume. What would a mother like that think of Beth, who never puts makeup on her sallow skin, and bites her nails to the quick, and eats with her elbows on the table? Terri's right, it's not my fault Beth's shut up like a clam, all of us came here unhappy and lost, but I can't forget that first morning four long days ago when she crouched in the corner and watched me with those hurt, empty eyes. "Does she . . . like you?" I asked Luis, and he said, "Oh sure. Once she said, 'Luis, please pass the sugar,' and another time she said, 'I've been to Puerto Rico twice.' She's not, you know, too *friendly*." But probably at night, in her bed upstairs, she dreams of Luis and they have long conversations and he smiles at her the way he did that time we talked about his life, and he tells her, *And then I met Señorita Beth Warren and we lived happily ever after.* So what I've done is smash right into her dream, and a dream is like crystal, fragile, in need of delicate handling; something special you can take down from a shelf in the messy house of your real life, hold up to the light, and say, *At least I have this, at least I have one beautiful thing left.*

Malcolm teases me about Luis. He teases everybody about something all the time, his wisecracks are like nettles. *Back off*, they say, *nobody gets too close to Malcolm.* Luis told me that one day when Malcolm was six, his father left Kansas City for a weekend in Las Vegas and never came back. Malcolm carries a deck of cards in his pocket and right in the middle of Group, or during meals, or when he's sitting somewhere by himself after his time with Gabriel, he'll take out the cards and shuffle them over and over, as if he expects to find his father inside the shiny pack. His mother left, too, when Malcolm was ten. He talked about her yesterday in Group. She met another kind of gambler—"Mafia," Malcolm says. "Straight out of *The Godfather*"—and told Malcolm, "*I* need a life, too, I'm no chicken anymore, you'll be better off with your grandparents anyhow, I've known that for years, I never was the mother type," and for a while she'd send him letters from Chicago or Baltimore or Freeport in the Bahamas, and then the letters stopped. He says his grandparents always looked at him like they were surprised to find him in their house, like he was only staying with them "until Vi comes back for you," but they all knew she wouldn't. "It wasn't a big thing, my taking off," he says. "I could've stayed there till they died and they would still be calling it 'a temporary arrangement.'" He throws back his head and laughs; you can see the fillings in his teeth, the dark cave at the back of his tongue. "That's what life is, right? A temporary arrangement, right? Pardon me, I'm just passing through. Right?" Then, for a moment, his face goes hard, all his hurt locked in place, stiff and permanent as a plaster mask.

So it isn't that I don't see the problems here. I do. I can just imagine what they say about *me*, what stories they tell about Robin. *Little Miss Perfect*, Alice probably calls me. *Miss High and Mighty. Someday they'll get that daddy dear of hers for having his hand in somebody's till and then we'll have to see what she has to say about her precious old man, her hot-shot politician.* Malcolm would say, *Shove it, Alice, you're no bargain yourself.* But Luis would be the one to really defend me: *She takes care of herself, what's wrong with that? She has—how you say it?—dignity. I think it's a good thing she loves her father, I think—* Alice would barge in, *You think what? When it comes to Robin, you don't think one bit. You just moon away like some silly lovesick cow.* Beth: *The thing I hate about her is the way she pretends to be everybody's friend. If she can get along with people so well, how come she had to run away from home? I don't trust her at all.*

Still, in spite of all the problems, I feel like we're *related*, like our winding up here lost gives us a chance to find what we've never really had. I mean a *family*. Maybe blood is thicker than water, but we all have loneliness in our veins; we're all the same type; we could give each other transfusions if we had to, we could save one another's life.

Beth didn't show up for Group today. Terri looked for her all over the house, out in the yard, up and down the block, but there was no sign of her. Gabriel said, "Well, let's get started. She'll turn up soon." But I could see his pulse fluttering in his throat and he kept watching the door, the window, like he'd miss her if he didn't look hard, like she'd turned into a ghost who could come and go in a blink. We were all nervous. It was strange to realize how much space her absence took up in the room, how lopsided things looked without her silence to balance off our talk, without her eyes saying to someone's joke, *I'm the other side of your laughter, I'm the pain you're trying to giggle away.*

Gabriel was gone all afternoon. He didn't come back in time to cook dinner, so I helped Terri fix hamburgers and salad, but nobody was hungry, we all picked at our food. It was raining outside, and the windows were clouded over with mist. The street lamps had come on early, and the headlights of cars moved like animal eyes through the fog. When Gabriel finally returned, we were clearing the dishes off the table, all of us staying close to one another in the bright kitchen. His thick blond hair was wet, plastered down

104

in jagged swatches, his skin looked like soggy bread, his denim jacket was damp and rumpled. He'd brought the bad weather right into the house, and I wanted to tell him to go back outside, this place was safe and dry, he wasn't allowed to barge in, dripping on the floor, tracking in mud and tattered leaves and something else I couldn't name, but whatever it was, I was afraid of it.

As soon as he started to speak, his eyes shimmered with tears. "I have bad news," he said. Standing in front of the window, his outline was blurred in the street lamp's milky light, even his voice sounded fuzzy and weak. "Beth's— OD'd. She'd already messed around with hard drugs before she came here, she—"

"Well, how *is* she?" Alice demanded. "What hospi—"

"She's dead," Gabriel said. He closed his eyes. "Beth's dead."

"Those goddam fucking pushers!" Alice bellowed. "Those—"

Her words were pummeling me, each one a fist. "Shut up, Alice," I said quietly. I covered my ears with my hands, but they barely muffled the sound of her voice.

"Asshole! Rotten pricks!" On and on, a litany of curses.

"*Shut up!*" I yelled, but she kept up the violent chant. She'd turned into one of those crazy faith healers you see on television who try to scream disease out of the bodies of dying patients, except Beth was already dead, Gabriel had just said that—"Beth's dead," it was plastered like a slogan all over the walls, I heard it on loudspeakers, his short speech played and replayed itself, over and over, while Alice raged. There was nothing to heal, it was too late for a healing, soon my own head would burst, blood and bone exploding into the noise-filled air. I lunged for her. Gabriel grabbed me around the waist, his arm was a hook I couldn't escape. I twisted and yanked and he tightened his grip. Finally I couldn't struggle anymore and the hook went lax. Even Alice's words withered, and she kept touching her mouth and throat, like she couldn't believe she'd done all that terrible screaming.

"Stop fighting," Luis whispered. "Please." He was crumpled at the table, his smooth face folded up like a fan. Gabriel let me go and knelt beside Luis, told him, "It's okay, *amigo*, I know how you feel." He cradled Luis's head, and Luis cried like a baby. *How about me?* I thought. *Do you know how I feel? Do you know that I'm to blame?*

When Luis started crying, Alice did, too. Terri put her arms around her and they cried together, rocked together back and forth. *Do you know that I'm to blame?*

Malcolm didn't cry at all. He lay on the floor, his arms folded across his chest, his face frozen and gray, like he was a corpse himself. *Listen to me, Malcolm. Do you know that I'm to blame?*

I said, "It's my fault." They thought I was talking to them. Everyone except Malcolm turned to look at me, but I *wasn't* talking to them. They were small and distant, everything in the room had backed away from me. I was talking to Beth. I saw her dead eyes staring at me from the corner where she'd crouched, except now she was pressed up against the ceiling, and I told her again, "It's my fault. I didn't mean to—"

Gabriel came toward me, and it seemed he was traveling miles instead of the few feet between us. He put his hands on my shoulders. Tears were dripping off my nose and chin, and I let them fall on his fingers. "It's *not* your fault," he said.

She was hovering over the refrigerator now, now she was wedged between the sink and stove, now she was crawling under the table. "Yes it is," I said. "I was spending time with Luis, and that hurt her, it—*killed* her."

Gabriel's hands dropped away, and my neck went rigid at the loss of his touch. "Do you know what?" he said. "That's very arrogant of you."

I stared at him.

"To assume," he said, "that you were the center of her life. The center of her trouble. Someone you hardly knew. To make yourself so important."

She went through the window then, she passed straight through the pane. He was chasing her away. *Come back, Beth, I need to apologize, I need you to forgive me.* But she was gone.

"I hate you!" I screamed at Gabriel, and I picked up a glass from the dish drainer, I flung it to the floor, I smashed it into smithereens at Gabriel Asher's rain-spattered feet.

Three in the morning. Still raining. In the black sky, a few persistent stars flicker like a code someone's sending, but I can't figure out what it means, or if it means anything. In the window, I can see my face floating like a dumb fish. *Beth's dead.* What does *that* mean? Every thought I have turns into a question, and every question mark sticks like a fishhook in my flesh.

Gabriel's awake, too. In the living room he's built a fire even though the humid night air hangs thick in the house. He must have been cold, like I am, from the inside out. The fire's reflection dances over his face, changes it into shifting planes of light. His hands look translucent as the stained-glass windows I remember from the church Mrs. Stupowski took me to when I was little. When Gabriel realizes I'm in the doorway, he turns to look at me and his eyes are candles.

He says, "I'm sorry if I hurt you, Robin."

"I'm sorry I broke that glass," I mumble. I'm still pressed against the doorpost in the darkened end of the room. "You remember what we decided this morning?"

He nods. "About contacting your mother."

"I don't want you to."

He doesn't look surprised. "Come sit with me and we'll talk," he says. He gestures to the floor beside him, to the circle of light the flames make on the polished oak planks.

"I don't *want* to sit with you," I snap, when I mean, *I'm afraid to come out of the shadows, I'm all covered with scales, I'm not who I was before and it scares me.*

"Okay," he says. "Talk to me from where you are."

I don't know where I am.

"Tell me why you've changed your mind about your mother."

"I just don't want to go home," I say. *I don't have a home, even my own skin has deserted me, I don't belong anywhere, not even inside my own body.*

"We didn't talk about your going home. Only about letting your family know you're okay, seeing if your mother's willing to—"

She's a locked-up house, nobody's ever home when I knock. I tell him, "I wanted *this* . . . to . . . be my . . . family." The words pile up in my throat. "I . . . thought . . . we could . . . could all—"

"Could all what?"

"Take . . . *care* . . . of each . . . other."

He stretches out his arms to me like beacons.

No, I'm covered with scales.

"Please," he says.

I shake my head no, but something stronger than fear is pushing me out of the darkness, sending me swimming miles toward the warmth across the room. In front of the fire, I shiver, I feel naked and cold.

"Robin," he says and touches my hair with his luminous hand.

"Don't!" I tell him, flinching, pulling away. *Your light will burn me, it will make me blind.*

"I won't hurt you," he says, and wipes away my tears with the tips of his fingers. I'm not even singed. All my pain pours out into the palm of his tenderness.

"Why did she have to die?" I sob. *"You were right, I didn't know her at all, I didn't—"*

"You knew her as well as you could. As well as any of us can know each other here."

"That . . . isn't . . . *good* . . . enough," I rasp.

"It isn't meant to be," he says, holding me the way he held Luis, holding me until my sobbing ebbs, saying then, "I want to share something with you, Robin, something about my own life."

A log falls apart into fragments, one shard sizzles to ash. He watches it for a while before he speaks again.

"I was born in Poland, in Crakow. My father was Jewish, a professor of psychology. When I was nine years old, Nazis knocked on our apartment door. They put my mother and sister in one wagon, my father and me in another. That was the end of my family. On the way to the train that would take us to the concentration camp, the wagon broke down, there was a lot of commotion, and somehow my father managed to push me into a drainage ditch on the side of the road. Don't ask me how I knew, a nine-year-old child, that I was better off alone in that ditch than in the wagon with my father, but I knew. I stayed in that filthy water until it was dark. For the next three years—well, that's another story. Let's just say I managed to survive. Finally I was smuggled out of the country—the war was almost over by now—and I wound up in a DP—that's 'displaced persons'—camp in England.

"That camp was full of strangers, but within hours I'd been 'adopted.' Everyone behaved as if they'd known each other all their lives. We *became* each other's lives. Overnight I had a family again—aunts, uncles, brothers, sisters—an enormous family. We ate together, slept together, played together —what more *was* a family? A lot more. We had no personal history together, except the war. We shared *suffering*, that was our cement, that was what we knew about each other. We shared a common plight. We were organized around the most severe crisis imaginable, but we *needed* that crisis to exist. We were a *temporary* family. If we had wanted to stay together in that camp, we would have had to sustain the crisis, to remain displaced. Lost. Homeless. Do you understand what I'm saying?"

My throat is so parched. "You never saw them again?" I whisper. "Your parents or your sister?"

He's staring deep into the flames. "Never."

In my throat, pain's rising and I swallow hard, my muscles like a tourniquet tying off a wound. "I know what you're trying to do," I say, and the words come out like little hisses through my teeth. "It isn't the same. You all—*loved* each other. You weren't—*they*—weren't divorced or anything."

"My parents argued all the time," Gabriel says. "My mother and I were never close." There's no anger in his voice, he sounds like he's telling me ordinary things, like what they all ate for breakfast, or where they went on vacations, or how old he was when he had the measles.

"Mostly," he goes on, "I look like my mother. But"—and he taps a finger against his forehead—"I have my father's mind. *His* father was a rabbi, quite a scholar from what I understand, but I never had the chance to know him. He died when I was a baby."

It's like they're right here in the house with him, like they didn't really die. I study my hands. They begin to look familiar again, they look like the hands I've had all my life, the hands I was born with. My mother's bones. My father's olive skin. There are whole generations of relatives still alive in the patterns my fingerprints make.

We sit together for a while, not saying anything. A log glows from the inside out. I feel calmer. Finally I say to Gabriel, "You can call my mother," and my voice is very soft, like there are others in the room, sleeping, who I am trying not to disturb.

PART THREE
JANET

At the front door, Ada raised her hands, fingers spread like sieves.

"She's gone," she announced. She looked bewildered by her own utterance, by the irrefutable simplicity of her statement.

Robin's Law: *She's gone.*

I said, "Gone where?" knowing there would be no corollary.

There was not. Ada shook her head. She opened her mouth, but nothing came out. *She's gone:* QED. The truth maintains itself against all our wishes.

Brian would say, "We believe what we want to believe."

I did not want to believe Ada, but she had spoken with axiomatic compression. In the cab, I had silently rehearsed a dozen different speeches I would give my daughter. I walked from street to porch with all those words flapping in my chest like the wings of a hundred sparrows, but as soon as Ada spoke, the flock cleared out, deserted, in their wake I hammered in a simple sign, the kind that designates landmarks, sites of battles, places where important scientific discoveries were made: *She's gone*, it said, and I staked it in my heart.

Slouched against the cushions of the crushed-velvet love-seat in the room Ada refers to as "the front parlor," Walter said, "Oh hell, she'll be back by midnight. You know kids."

Ada rattled glasses at the marble-topped table that held decanters on a silver tray. She handed me sherry. I felt the warm liquid travel through all the emptiness from throat to stomach. *No*, I thought, I do not know kids.

"What *happened?*" Ada said. "What brought it to *this?*" Meaning: *Why have you failed so badly as a mother?*

"An evolutionary process," I said, tight-lipped. Meaning: *Do not look for the garden and the snake and the single bad apple here. Do not look here for an easy myth to explain a long and difficult history.*

"*Something* must have happened in Washington," she shot back. "A child like Robin doesn't pick up and leave her home unless *something*—"

"There was no one thing." Each word walked a tightrope. "She's been holding a lot in, for years."

I had not acknowledged that until I said it aloud.

For years. I saw flashes of one cross section after another, scene after scene opened to me like those first frogs I had dissected in high school, in fleeting frames I saw beyond the surface of my daughter's days, under the thin skin of politeness, good grades, fastidiousness, compromise, into the complex substance of her life.

For years. Walter and Ada, too, were riveted by visions. We stared at one another. The fleshy sacks under Walter's eyes seemed to grow heavier, as if they were storing tears he could not cry. Ada sucked on her cigarette with the need of an infant at the breast, her whole face straining for succor she could not find in tobacco. In my own face, a nervous tic raced from synapse to synapse, setting off small shocks in eye, cheek, jaw.

Finally Ada said, "Oh God, I wish Brian were back."

"He'll be back in a couple of days," I said. "But I don't see what good that will do."

"Well, of course you wouldn't." She rubbed out her butt in

a bronze ashtray. "And that's why you're not married to him anymore."

I undressed in the guest room, where Robin had spent the previous night. She had not made the bed. The pillow sagged in the middle where her head had rested and I put my hand into that ridge, as if she had simply fallen into the down and I could retrieve her with my touch. "Robin," I whispered, speaking her name as if she were a lover for whom I yearned.

Of course, she did not answer. No one answered. I lay in silence deep as any grave.

Think of despair as the dissolution of gravity. Nothing adheres. All attachments fail. The mortar between the bricks loses its power to bind. Rooted trees drift from the earth like feathers. Everything you cared about or counted on becomes debris.

You, yourself, become debris.

I could have lifted the screen and swirled into the cluttered air like a speck of dust.

In college, a boy I cared for killed himself. I had not thought of him in years. Paul Lamm. He was going to be an archaeologist, in search of ancient bones and teeth. He took me to museums, the way my father had when I had been younger. Paul and I: winding past the glass cases full of relics dug up from tombs, remnants of whole cities buried in a sudden quake or lava spill. "Isn't it wonderful?" he would say, his face shadowed in the dim galleries. "So much is still intact." *But not alive,* I'd think. *Not alive.*

Being alive did not interest him that much. As a child, his mother would beat him with her hairbrush. "I never wanted you!" she would scream between blows. "I wish you'd never been born!"

Curse becomes principle.

He would devote himself to death in one way or another. He would work with skeletons, last vestiges, extinct cultures.

The first time we made love, Paul Lamm said, "When I die, let me die like this."

Each time I lay in his bed with him, I feared he would stop breathing in my arms.

At twenty-one, he took an entire bottle of sleeping pills

113

which a doctor had given him for insomnia. "I'm a night person," he had told me often. "The world and I operate on totally different schedules."

He died at night, on his own time.

As I lay alone in the Sorokin house—my daughter vanished again, Ada and Walter asleep in other rooms lonely as crypts, Brian unreachable, my father far in every way, my mother dead, Eli preserving his distance from me with a rationalist's cold dedication—I understood for the first time how Paul Lamm must have felt the night he killed himself.

Untethered.

All cords cut.

Newton's apple rotting slowly in the air.

Yet it was Paul Lamm's face I summoned as I dropped a hand between my legs and anchored myself to the world again.

Afterward, I heard him say in his dry voice, "What were you trying to do, Janet, seduce me back to life?"

Only myself, I answered, my fingers still wet with my own secretions. *Only myself.*

For the few hours left until morning, I slept.

In the kitchen, Walter was ripping the tough skin from an orange, collecting the peelings in a napkin beside his plate. "Ada's in the shower," he said when I walked into the sunny room. As if it were important to have us all accounted for. As if he needed to demonstrate to me his ability to keep track of the people under his roof.

I poured myself a cup of coffee from the glass pot.

"I'd like to stay here a few more days," I said softly. "Maybe by then she'll come back."

"*Sure* she'll be back." Juice dribbled down Walter's chin and he wiped it away with the edge of his bathrobe sleeve. "Hell, I ran off six, seven times when I was a kid. Came back every time."

"Why?"

"Why'd I come back?"

"Why did you leave."

He held a piece of fruit in midair, brought it to his lips, returned it to the plate. His face puckered. "That's a long story," he said. He got up, filled a glass with water, swallowed several pills. His hands quivered and he thrust them into his pockets, to still the trembling or to hide it from me. He did not look like a man standing in his own kitchen. He looked like patient in a hospital making his required daily visit to the sunroom. The hesitant shuffle. The hunched shoulders. The blank look in the eyes.

"I'd like to hear about it," I said. "Maybe it will help me understand Robin better."

As soon as I spoke, I regretted the implication. *Give me your memories, share your pain, I am collecting case studies, I am accumulating pertinent examples of a particular mode of behavior.*

In sixteen years, I had never talked with this man about anything more personal than the insult to the foot's physiology of certain styles of shoes.

I said, "And maybe it will help me understand *you*."

Embarrassed, Walter smiled. "Nothing complicated here," he said. "Pretty dull stuff."

("What do you get from watching a few primitive cells swim around for hours on end?" Brian would say. "Doesn't it get dull?")

I said to Walter, "Life isn't dull."

On the contrary: a bombardment of stimuli, unceasing motion.

Matter *is* motion: the physicists have established this fact. Behind the static appearance, unceasing flux.

Beneath the anesthetic of alcohol, a frenzy.

Walter said, "Ada thinks I'm as interesting as"—he surveyed the kitchen for an appropriate object—"as a dishrag."

"Did it ever occur to you that Ada might be wrong?"

"I heard my name," she said, appearing in the room with the suddenness of apparition. "Anything I should know?"

You should know your husband. You live together in the same house and you are strangers.

After the first rush of superior wisdom, the leveling: *And I should know my daughter, who is still fleeing the insult of my ignorance.*

"I was asking Walter about his boyhood," I told her. "He said he ran away from home half a dozen times."

"You did?" Ada said. "You never told me *that*."

The first crack in an old definition. She cringed at the possibility of larger fissures.

"I never told you a *lot*," he said. "You didn't seem interested, Ada."

She trained her eyes on his. "I don't think we should be getting into *personal* issues. Not at this *time*, Walter."

She smoothed her brows. Pushed back each finger's cuticle with a practiced thumb. In the midst of an earthquake Ada Sorokin would flex her vaginal muscles, making use, as the women's magazines instructed, of "those extra moments during the day" to improve body tone.

In the midst of an earthquake Walter Sorokin would pour himself a drink, making use, as the men's magazines instructed, of "those special moments during the day" to soothe the palate.

He did that now. A half-tumbler of Wild Turkey, a handful of ice.

Ada ignored him. "I'm going to make some scrambled eggs," she said. "Would anyone else like some eggs?"

I shook my head, and heard the bones creak in my neck. Walter's ice cubes slammed against the glass. The refrigerator growled. In a funnel of sunlight, dust motes crashed into each other like cars in a chain collision.

"We mustn't be squabbling," Ada said. She took out two eggs from the refrigerator. "We . . . have a *crisis* here." She was slightly hoarse, as if she had been screaming for a long time. "We need to be a . . . a *team*." An egg tumbled from her hand to the floor. For a moment, she stared at the fractured shell, the puddled yoke. Then Ada Sorokin began to weep, very quietly, as if that egg contained a lifetime's ruptured dreams, as if she were looking at the miscarriage of hope itself.

I remembered my mother, weeping at the ironing board, weeping all night, weeping even as my father led her from our house. I looked at Walter, but he made no move to comfort his wife. He did not seem to recognize her.

I recognized her.

"It's all right," I said, moving to her side. I forced myself to embrace her. "We're all going to be fine," I told her, my father's words to me from that other morning nearly thirty years ago forming again in my mouth.

The knowledge of his cells in mine.

A long evolution of sorrow and love.

An undocumented genealogy, stored in the archives of my brain.

Ada spent the morning "resting" in her bedroom. Walter did not go to the office. He worked until noon in his overgrown backyard. From the dining room's French doors, I could see him struggle with the tangled weeds, shake his head at the shambles his garden had become. He came inside bearing overripe vegetables and flowers going to seed. He lay the neglected bounty on the counter beside the sink.

"Well," I said from the doorway, "you put in an ambitious morning."

"Better than drinking," Walter muttered.

In sixteen years, I had not heard him mention drinking before. In the Sorokin house, Walter's drinking resided like a relative to whom no one in the family spoke, who kept his own hours, used a separate rear entrance, had his own shelf in the kitchen and was not permitted to take his meals with the others.

Now, for the first time in sixteen years, Walter introduced me to the family outcast. His own ghost. His silent double.

I said, "Brian worries about your—"

"Brian hates my guts," Walter said. He was washing the bruised tomatoes and peppers, laying them out on paper towels to drain.

"*I've* worried," I said, realizing that I had.

"I appreciate that," he said.

"A man I work with at the institute has been doing research on alcoholism."

"You setting your ex-father-in-law up as a guinea pig?"

"No. I was just—"

"I appreciate your concern," he said. "My son thinks I'm a coward, my wife thinks I'm a bore, it's good to know there's someone in the—well, *almost* in—the family who talks to me like a *person*."

The phone rang. Walter wiped his hands quickly on his trousers, grabbed for the receiver. All my muscles tightened into a single taut spring.

Volunteers of America. Yes, Walter told them, he would tell his wife their truck would be by on Tuesday.

I came apart, coil by coil.

"Here," he said. "Sit down here," and pulled a chair out for me. I sank to the caned seat. "There's nothing more nerve-racking than waiting, is there?" he continued. "I mean, it sets you on *edge*, if you know what I mean."

I looked into his creviced face. In that mass of wrinkles and shattered vessels, I saw the smooth-skinned boy he had once been. "Talk with me for a while," I said. "Tell me why you ran away all those times."

Tell me a story.

(When Robin was little, she would say, "Tell me a story, Mommy," and I would hold her in the nest of my lap, recalling Grimm, Aesop, Mrs. Stein's Yiddish tales.

Until I grew too busy.

Until I began to answer, "What about all those books you took out from the library? Or the records Daddy bought you? Try those, honey. Mommy has work to do."

She *would* read. She *would* play and replay "Peter and the Wolf."

She was a self-sufficient child, resourceful, undemanding.

The only thing she had lost was the nest of my lap.

Gestation, in fact, has two phases: one in the womb, one in the world.)

Walter Sorokin sat down across the table from me. "I don't remember a whole lot, to tell you the truth." He rotated an empty tumbler in his palm, as if his past were embedded in the smoky glass. "My parents were immigrants, they came from Russia with nothing, not even a suitcase. By the time I was ten, we had a nice house, good clothes. We had a Studebaker that my father polished every Sunday afternoon like it was a piece of sculpture. My mother and father worked twelve hours a day, six days a week in the shoe factory. I would go there after school and sweep up the scrap leather with a push broom wider than I was tall. Or sometimes I would help my mother with the books and call off figures to her that she'd write down in a thick ledger book. My sister, Bess, she didn't have to work in the factory after school. She would go home and do the housework, cook the supper. She wasn't any more free than me, but I resented her then." He stood, walked to the window. A sparrow perched on the outside sill, witness to whatever sadness Walter hid from me.

"Like I said, I ran away maybe a half-dozen times. First

118

time to the beach, Nantasket, I slept outside, got bitten up by sand crabs. I went home with one foot swelled up like a basketball. Another time I went down to the wharf and snuck onto a fishing boat. I was going to sea, this was my big plan. I was hiding under a tarp, it stank to high heaven from bait. I thought I'd suffocate from the smell. Then I hear one sailor threaten another with a knife. I was home in two hours. That's what happens," Walter said, turning back to me. "You think you *must* get away from your horrible family, you can't stand it there one more minute. Then you find out it's worse outside. You put your tail between your legs and crawl back."

"And your mother," I said. "What would she say to you then?"

"My mother? She would say, 'Why couldn't I have been blessed with two daughters? Who sent me this selfish boy?'" For a moment, he went rigid at the memory of that epithet. Then his shoulders jerked, as if he were throwing off his hurt. "*All* parents say things they shouldn't. Sometimes I think about fights I had with Brian. . . ."

Walter looked at the glass in his hand. He opened the cabinet over the sink and reached for a bottle.

I said, "Don't."

He ignored me.

("He *decides*, sweetheart," Brian had said, "every time he pours a lousy drink.")

Above us, floorboards creaked.

"She's up," he said and swigged down his bourbon. "End of story. Think I'll take a nap myself. You wake me if anything—"

I said, "Brian loves you, Walter."

Walter Sorokin grasped the counter. I saw his back heave. Finally he said, "Robin loves you, too."

This has nothing to do with love, but I'm leaving.

"I'm so afraid I'll never—" I covered my face with my hands, as if to keep myself from seeing my own worst fears.

The universal gesture for sorrow, and shame.

"Now, Janet," Walter said, kneeling beside me to pat my bowed head. For the first time since I had found Robin's note, in the unlikely haven of Walter Sorokin's flabby arms, in the cocoon of his liquored breath, in that unexpected shelter, at last I cried.

119

———

Two weeks after Brian and I were divorced, I had gone to visit my father in Miami. I had come after a week in Gainesville, at a university conference on fertility at which I had delivered a paper. I had found my father in his room, where he was recovering from the flu. He was propped against a mound of pillows, his white hair matted from days in bed, his skin robbed of its usual Florida color. He had hoisted himself up on his elbows; his arms looked thin and brittle as twigs. I had said, "I had no idea you've been so sick," and my father had said, in a voice so strong he seemed to have stolen it from another body, "I'm not worried about *me*. What I want to know is: have you *cried* this time?" I had looked at him blankly. "You couldn't cry over your mother," he had said. "That wasn't healthy. Over your divorce I want you to be able to *cry*."

"Is it bad news?" Ada said, rushing into the room. "What's *happened?*"

Do not look for the garden and the snake and the single bad apple here. Do not look here for an easy myth to explain a long and difficult history.

I pulled back from Walter, splashed cold water on my swollen face.

"No news," I heard him tell Ada. "She had to cry, that's all. I'm going to lie down for a while."

When he was gone, Ada came to stand beside me at the sink. "Now why did he bring all that rotten stuff into the house?" she said.

"You could make a good soup from it. Just cut away the bad parts."

"I don't fix soup in the summertime," she said and began to stuff a mottled green pepper into the garbage disposal.

I grabbed her hand before it could flick on the switch. "Don't do that," I told her. "It *means* something to him."

She shook her wrist free, but moved away from Walter's half-ruined harvest. "Let *him* make the soup, then," she said.

"I'm going for a walk," I said. "I need some air."

As I passed the window, a sparrow tapped his beak on the glass.

Observe and record. Observe and record.

What would he conclude, that tiny scientist, from the data he had gathered here?

As soon as I met his eyes, he flew. I watched him take his knowledge to the top of an ancient elm. Then, farther, into the vast brilliance of the sky.

You could mistake us for reuniting lovers.

The way Brian rushes toward me from the gate where his plane has landed minutes before. The mist in my eyes. The embrace so longed for, we appear to be both in pain as we clasp each other close.

We are both in pain.

Still it surprises me: this spontaneous and mutual reach across years of folded arms, pocketed hands. Then I realize: we are not embracing *each other* so much as extensions of Robin.

Surely.

Surely *her mother* and *her father* embrace in Logan's crowded terminal, while Brian and Janet remain outside the circle of their own arms.

This refined awareness is called *consciousness*, a state experienced only in higher forms of life.

By the time we reach Ada's car, which I borrowed to pick Brian up, we have remembered our practiced antagonisms. Like beached turtles heading back to the water, creatures seeking our required element, we move resolutely toward anger.

In even the highest form of life, certain primitive responses survive. Certain vestiges.

His accusations: that I should have known Robin was unhappy; that I had never told him enough about her problems; that I had been selfish to "rush right up here like some FBI agent" instead of "giving the kid some time to get her head together."

My accusations: that he never spent enough time with her; that he always tried to turn misfortune into blame; that "I wasn't planning campaign strategy, I reacted like a *human being*, which is what you've always claimed I've never been much of."

After that exchange, we ride the rest of the way to the Sorokins' in silence. Our inevitable milieu. That familiar environment in which love disappeared like the webs between the toes of our biological ancestors.

An evolutionary process.

Do not look for the garden and the snake and the single bad apple here.

Do not look here for an easy myth to explain a long and difficult history.

We got married in 1962. Early April, the cherry trees in high color, the entire city a stunning bouquet of spring flowers.

Brian called me at the university from Fletcher's office. "How about lunch?" he said. "I have seventy-three unscheduled minutes."

We met at a small Chinese restaurant we liked. Brian found me at a bamboo-framed table under a watercolor of a serene lagoon, a single boat drifting on the blue water. "Fifty-eight minutes," he said. "If we eat fast, we can get married before my two-o'clock meeting."

"Right. And then we can have our first child on Thursday, before you fly out to Ohio for the weekend."

"Janet," he said. "I'm not completely *kidding*."

In fact he was completely serious. About getting married on a lunch hour. We jettisoned plans for a party for fifty, canceled the room we'd reserved at The Shoreham. I withdrew my order for invitations on parchment. Ten days later, I waited for Brian in front of the university library. I wore a simple white linen dress, no hint of lace or mother-of-pearl. In the car, Brian tucked a sprig of white blossoms into my hair, another into the lapel of his glen-plaid suit. On that drive, too, we were silent, but out of shyness. We took the highway toward a state park where we had picnicked and hiked; Brian remembered having passed a justice of the peace.

Benjamin C. Doyle: his name was carved into a shingle that swung from the mailbox post at the edge of the road.

We turned into the graveled drive. Slowly the house, a hundred feet back, came into clearer focus: the white wood siding was blistered, peeling in places; the screen door had a rip in it, as if some angry customer had put a fist through the fragile mesh.

We did not mention these marrings. From a distance, the house had looked quaint, picturesque. We pretended the image was still intact.

From a distance, marriage had looked equally appealing. A precise convergence of desires. A well-constructed and functional design.

Benjamin C. Doyle opened the door. He was squat, undistinguished. "Caught me before my nap," he said, checking the watch that hung at his waist.

We followed him down a long center hallway. On one wall, a montage of family photographs, in muted sepia tones. At the end of the corridor, a pine-paneled study, moose head and swordfish mounted over a black vinyl couch, a circular braided rug covering most of the floor.

"My grandmother made this rug," he said. "Many a people come into this room, wants to buy it right up, tells me it's an antique and they'll give me a good price for it. But I tells them right back, 'No indeed, it's not for sale, that's an *heirloom*.' That's why I like to *marry* folks. Family's a priceless thing, you know? Now 'scuse me a moment, I'll go get the Mrs."

The Mrs. looked a great deal like her husband. Both of them short, round-faced, features ordinary enough to seem like afterthoughts. Mr. and Mrs. An entity. As if they had transferred cells to each other over the years. Exchanged chromosomes. Shared genetic blueprints the way some couples share the morning paper.

I took Brian's hand.

"Repeat after me . . ."

———

124

Turning into the Sorokins' driveway, Brian says, "And I suppose the head of the household is soused."

"I think he wants to stop."

"Right," says Brian, getting out of Ada's canary-yellow Buick. "And Billy Graham's giving up religion."

When I told my father I was married, he said, "Did you have a religious ceremony?"

"We're not religious."

"Not for yourselves, then. For me. For Brian's parents. For . . . your mother."

"It's *our* marriage," I had said.

"Who says so? A *family* marries a *family*. Nobody comes separate."

A family marries a family. The egg and the sperm are each group affairs, reunions, each tribe turns out *en masse* at weddings.

"I got Brie for you, Brian," Ada says. "Ripe, just how you like it."

"I didn't come here for a banquet, Mother. My daughter is missing. I do not have much of an appetite."

We are sitting on the screened-in porch off the parlor. Wicker furniture, painted the same yellow as Ada's car, cushioned in bold geometric prints of yellow and pink and lime green.

She sets the tray she is carrying down on the glass-topped table.

"At least have some iced tea. Unless you find that inappropriate as well."

"God *damn* it!" Brian shoots up from his chair. "I've been here fifteen minutes and already the sarcasm's flying. Can't we have one single civil hour in this family?"

He pushes against the screen door. It whirs open, clicks shut behind him. He walks along the flagstone path into the dark backyard. As he passes the lamppost at the patio's edge, a swarm of gnats break from their position on the light, panic in the air like a squadron under surprise attack.

"Well," Walter says, "I guess I'll go talk to him," and I watch him move out into the darkness to negotiate a cease-fire with his son.

125

"All over a piece of cheese," Ada says. She lights one cigarette with the stub of another. "He's always been overly sensitive. Didn't you find him overly sensitive?"

"No," I say. "No, I did not."

I am trying to remember: at what moment did the tissue of marital love begin its deterioration? In the literature, immunologists stress the importance of learning to predict precisely when the cells will break rank. Computing the instant of cellular insurrection. Intervention *before* the fact.

In the absence of cure, we turn our energies toward prevention.

For love's failure, there is no cure.

Could we have intervened, Brian and I, before the fact?

We spent the first night of our marriage in Brian's efficiency apartment. His sofa opened into his bed, and I watched from the bathroom door as he removed the corduroy-covered cushions, pulled on the handle that released the mattress from its folded-up position. Usually, he did this easily, but this time the bearings would not roll in their tracks. "Give me a hand, Janet," he said, but I did not move. He asked again, assuming I had not heard.

I had heard. Heard my father's "One-two-three-pull!" heard my mother's "What I wouldn't give for a normal bed." Heard his sighs, her weeping, the muffled racket of argument, the slammed doors, Selma's vacuum cleaner rumbling like thunder, my mother's breathless cough, my father's wailing grief.

In Brian's simple request, a fatal cacophony.

Or perhaps later, sprawled on top of the sheets, our bodies gleaming with sweat. "Promise me you'll be faithful," he said. "Oh no," I teased, "didn't I *tell* you? I plan to have a different lover every month." I burrowed my face in his chest. "I am insatiable, I am—" He pushed me away, sat up. "Don't joke about that, Janet. That's a sensitive issue with me. My mother—"

We had been married for nine hours. How much earlier could we have intervened? I would like to run out into the yard and tell him: *It was not an experiment for which we were suited. The appropriate protocol did not exist. Given our histories, there was no real chance for success.*

But Robin's image rebukes me: *I need a better legacy than that, Mother. I need more of a reason than that to come home.*

Hypothesis: That Brian "cooled down" before Walter met him near the jungle of rosebushes in the yard's far corner; and that, therefore, Walter did not have to enter into his usual defense of Ada's "good intentions" to which Brian always listened with an expression midway between contempt and disbelief. ("He should have left her years ago," Brian told me once. "Then he might have had some chance for self-respect.")

Hypothesis: That Walter chose, for once, *not* to defend Ada to Brian, but rather to enter into a conversation with his son in which Ada's "good intentions" were not the issue "on the table," as Brian would say; in which Robin's disappearance was the issue on the table.

Hypothesis: That Walter asked Brian to forgive him for thirty years of drunkenness.

Hypothesis: That Brian asked Walter to forgive him for thirty years of bitterness.

Hypothesis: That neither man said a word.

Evidence for each hypothesis: When Brian and Walter return to the porch, it is clear that each has cried, or come close to crying, or might cry at any moment.

Conclusion for each hypothesis: I do not have conclusions. In terms of what passes between parents and children in the dark corners of their lives, I no longer have conclusions.

"Do you know what happens on Monday?" Brian says to me after Ada and Walter have gone to bed. "On Monday Fletcher announces his candidacy for the Democratic nomination for president of the United States. You know how long I've been working toward that announcement? Fifteen years. All of Robin's life."

"Tell me the truth," I say. "What are the chances?"

"That Fletcher'll make it?"

"I don't give a damn about Fletcher. I mean our chances for finding Robin."

"I don't know," he says, his eyes glazing over with true helplessness. "I haven't taken a poll."

A self-parodying remark, a barb meant to score his own

skin, not mine. I watch him flounder in his pain, unable to offer solace he might refuse.

Two smooth professionals, but what good now is all that hallowed expertise?

I am dreaming.

Lost loves convene in my dream, a convention of ghosts.

In the dream, I am lying in my childhood bed and they assemble around me as if I were very ill and they have come with solace, or simply to suggest that I am less alone than I feel.

My mother brings me tea with honey and milk and a plate of Uneeda Biscuits, her remedy for every variety of pain I have contracted or contrived. She has nothing else to give me. But she bears that cup and plate as if they are vessels for communion, as if her humble offering were a miracle I had never recognized during her life.

Transported from Florida, my father brings me books—*The Complete Works of William Shakespeare*, Sholem Aleichem's stories—and kneels down beside my bed and whispers, "You see? You see how she put the crackers on the plate in such a neat arrangement, you see how the tea's not too cold and not too hot? I *told* you she loved you, in her heart she was a loving woman."

The sad distracted boy from high school with whom I had gone on silent walks, or sat beside in the movies careful that my elbow did not graze his and arouse in each of us yearnings from which we each fled—he appears in the room, older, still awkward, but able to tell me finally, his cheeks ablaze, "I care about you, Janet," as if he had been meaning to let me know that for twenty-five years and now at last he has delivered himself of that small human message.

I say, "Daniel, you remember my parents, don't you?" and the three of them bow slightly to one another, as if in courtly dance.

Brian paces the floor, suddenly spins to face me. "You live in the goddamn past," he says. "You're still playing the motherless child."

Paul Lamm answers him: "She *is* motherless," he says, back from his own death to testify for her.

But my father says, "No, no, for thirteen years the woman

did everything she could. Who does more? Can you tell me? Who does more?"

Brian's eyes go bright with tears. "I did what *I* could," he says to me, and I nod in acceptance of what we had tried to be for each other, failed effort though it was.

In the Boston rocker, pipe smoke rising like the mist that lifts off the Potomac on gray October mornings, Eli says, "Well, you *could* call it love," his voice coming clear through the fog that billows around his head.

In certain laboratories in America, people are sleeping with electrodes taped to their eyes and head, having their dreams measured.

Measure this: Robin, herself, glides through the room like a hostess at a party. *Can I get you anything? I'm so glad you could come. I've been wanting to get you all together like this for years.*

I have been here for six days, manning the phone and the door.

Brian flew back to Washington last night, after spending two days talking to the police; taking Robin's picture to ticket counters at the airport, the train station, the bus depots; for an hour, he says, he sat on a bench in The Commons and watched the flow of people for some sight of her: nothing. As I sat waiting for some sign of her to cross my vision as an aberrant cell dances suddenly into the microscope's arena of vigilance, so Brian took *his* skills into the streets, looking for his lost child with the same attention to detail and organization he would use to advance a campaign visit for Fletcher. Making the contacts. Working the crowds. Assessing support. In the end, he had nothing to leave me but a list of social-service agencies that deal with "runaway youth."

I said, "It sounds like a disease."

"It is," he said. "An epidemic."

So: we are suddenly thrust into some vast community of suffering whose symptoms include panic, guilt, the deterioration of hope. Not since the day we had watched each other across the courtroom where our divorce had been granted had I felt for Brian, *with* Brian, that kinship of affliction, that shared wound for which there is no salve. I wanted to offer him comfort, to receive some myself, but we were both too raw and knew it, knew that even one's breath on the other's cheek, one's finger on the other's arm, might be an abrasion beyond endurance.

I took the piece of paper from him. "They would have called *us*," I said, scanning the names.

"No," he said. "They'd be on *her* side."

By now, I am not even jolted when the telephone rings. Inevitably, it is Walter's accountant, or Ada's hairdresser, or one charity or another soliciting contributions. I know when Ada's maid arrives at the front door. I have learned to expect the mailman at his appointed time, I am becoming part of the daily workings of this household; soon I will be completely absorbed into its logic, my waiting will become one more aspect of its routine.

After Brian left, I called Eli.

"You should have come home *with* him," he said. "If she were coming back there, she'd have done it already."

"I didn't know you were a psychologist," I said. "I didn't know you were such an expert in motivational theory."

"How much longer, Janet?"

"I'm going to stay here until Saturday. Five more days. If I don't have word from her by then, I'll—"

"Come home?"

"Yes," I answered, because it was the expected response. But I knew the only home I had was in my lost child's keeping.

I have just taken a shower. Walter has left for work. Ada has gone to the supermarket and after that, she said, "I'm going to stop at the club for a massage, I am *so* cramped up with tension." I step out of the tub into the steam-filled room, its elegant flocked wallpaper, its coordinated lavender fixtures, its gilt-edged mirror—all obscured now in the swirling mist. Steam: that was my mother's treatment for tension. She would turn on the hot water in the tub where my father soaked his swollen feet, and wait until the room turned into the inside of a geyser. I hear her now, her voice seems to rise

131

out of the vapors: "I like it so hot you can hardly breathe. All the poisons float right out of your pores." How much she wanted to be rid of her pain. In another time, she might have tried bloodletting, opening her veins in hope of purification. In another culture, she might have tried herbs and wild dances and chants invoking the gods of healing. She might have spoken in tongues. She might have learned yoga, stood on her head in that cramped apartment, waited for the peace she craved.

For thirteen years the woman did everything she could. Who does more?

"Mama," I would call, "your show is on," and she would emerge from her chamber swathed in towels and her worn quilted robe. In front of the television, she would slowly unwrap herself, as if she were a patient removing the bandages after complicated surgery. "You have to be careful," she would say, "not to get a sudden chill." I remember how her face glowed after those treatments, how young and pink and smooth she looked. Then, inevitably, her skin would lose its temporary vigor, she would grow pallid again, drawn, I would watch her age before my eyes.

Can you tell me? Who does more?

I crack open the door, and the steam begins its slow evaporation.

I look in the mirror.

When Robin was born, I watched in the mirror mounted over the delivery table; I watched her emerge, whole and perfect, from my numbed loins. Inside my womb, it seemed I could feel again that small collision of two invisible cells, then one explosion after another: brain, lungs, heart, blood, the network of bones, skin, brows, the nail on each finger and toe. I watched the doctor snip the cord that bound her to me.

He handed me my daughter.

I held her slippery body to my own, moved my nipple against her cheek. Her tiny mouth opened in the rooting response. I smiled in triumph.

"You *should* be proud," a nurse said. "She's beautiful."

But it was not for Robin's beauty that I felt such a surge of victory. Not for my twelve hours of labor, my practiced breathing, my muscles working like the pistons of the powerful machine I had become.

132

No.

I smiled because we had found a way to attach ourselves to each other again.

I did not come from a family in which there had been many connections.

"You're crying," Brian said, and wiped my tears away with the sleeve of his hospital gown.

I am crying now.

Gradually my face reveals itself to me, feature by feature, one miracle after another: chin, mouth, nose, eyes, fringes of lash, forehead, wet mane of hair.

Is it that the glass is clearing, or am I witnessing my own birth?

Gestation, in fact, has two phases: one in the womb, one in the world.

The phone is ringing. Swaddled in towels, I flinch at the shock of the hallway's cool air.

"Hello?"

"Hello. My name is Gabriel Asher. I would like to speak to Janet Sorokin."

"Yes," I say. "Speaking."

RED CAMARO

"Y ou're so damn morose," David said, pounding his fist into his palm. "Your depressions are going to kill me." He could find no way to cheer me up and it was making him crazy. We had terrible scenes. Out of fear, I withdrew even further. Finally I packed up my clothes, my books, a few mementos from the happier times, and moved in with my friend Kate.

"You're so disoriented," Kate told me. "I think you should see a psychiatrist."

"No," I said, "I should see a lawyer."

She gave me a name. Kate is a woman of infinite resources. She works for a major philanthropic foundation. She grows bean sprouts in a mason jar and makes her own yogurt. She meets nice men who know how to compromise. She vacations in places like Yugoslavia and El Salvador. I have always wanted to be like Kate. But during the months I stayed with her, she kept talking about psychiatrists. The talks were making me crazy. When the divorce became final, I quit my job with the magazine and left New York. I drove to Boston in the red Camaro. I received it as my part of the settlement. I hadn't wanted red, but David had insisted. It was the reason

I left him. Not the red car. The insistence. About everything. He needed to prevail. It made me more and more unhappy.

Ben, the old lover I went to visit in Boston, said, "I never would have pictured you with a red Camaro."

I told him I'd changed quite a bit since my Cambridge days. I didn't tell him he was right about the car. I didn't tell him about David. About the terrible scenes. Ben and I made love exactly as we had seven years before. It was like dusting off an old vaudeville routine. Well choreographed, nostalgic, but ultimately anachronistic. It made me more and more unhappy.

Ben said, "Isn't it wonderful that we still mesh so well?"

By the third day of my visit, his exuberance was making me crazy. He went out for the paper. I drifted through the rooms of his apartment, waiting for some artifact to move me. Nothing. I could have been in a museum. I have never liked museums. They demand imaginative leaps of which I've never been capable. David explained this to me. His field is art history, with an emphasis on the surrealists.

I gathered together my things and left before Ben got back from the drugstore. On his bed was my note: "Called my parents while you were gone. Found out my father is sick. So I've taken off for Cleveland. Thanks for a lovely visit. Claudia."

Part of the note was true. I did take off for Cleveland. My name is Claudia. The rest were lies, which is proof to me that it was a less-than-ideal relationship. When a person means a lot to me, I tell the truth. Lies are easy, careless, and often malevolent. When David started to lie to me, I knew I would have to leave him.

My mother said, "At least the no-good let you keep the car."

I handed her a tissue from the box on the dashboard. The divorce had been a terrible ordeal for her. Among my mother's friends, divorce is still perceived as a failure. Nearly a tragedy. She was humiliated. Among my mother's friends, marriage is still perceived as a necessary refuge. An asylum from the world's cruelties and madnesses. She was terrified. What would become of me? While I stayed with my friend Kate, my mother called me incessantly. Her shame and fear were making me crazy. When the divorce became final, I quit

136

my job with the magazine and left New York. I drove to Boston in the red Camaro. There I spent three days with Ben, an old lover from Cambridge days. Ben had never left Cambridge, although he'd received his Ph.D. in literature six years ago from Harvard. He'd picked up a part-time job at B.U. and one at Emerson, and once in a while he published a poem in a literary magazine. He was nice enough, but his exuberance made me crazy. I left him a deceit-riddled note and drove to Cleveland, partly to let my parents see that I was okay, partly to make some truth out of the lies I'd written to Ben.

In the kitchen, my mother made me a chicken-salad sandwich and a cup of Sanka. "With your nerves," she said, "you don't need caffeine."

"How's Dad?" I said.

"Not well. You know where he is today? You think he's at the store? He's not. He's having tests."

She started to cry again.

"What kind of tests? What's wrong?" The note. The lies. The truth. "Tell me the truth, Ma."

"He doesn't feel right in his stomach. Pains. Gas. Probably gallbladder. My guess is gallbladder. But they test for everything. You know how they are."

"Why didn't you tell me about this before?"

"In your state?" she said. "The way you've been? You think your mother is crazy?"

I told her I needed to take a nap. I had driven straight through from Boston. I brought in my bags and took them upstairs to my old room. I told her to let me sleep until my father got home. I pulled down the opaque shades and lay down on my old bed. I felt more and more unhappy. I thought of calling Ben. But what would I say? "Everything in the note turns out to be true except the part about the lovely visit. It wasn't lovely, Ben. It was anachronistic. Your apartment reminds me of a museum. Why don't you grow up and get the hell out of Cambridge?" I didn't call. I fell asleep in my old dark room and dreamt about David. Terrible dreams. The dreams were making me crazy. But I was too tired to wake up. I had driven twelve hours straight in the red Camaro. I hadn't wanted red, but David had insisted. It was the reason I left him. Not the red car. The insistence. He needed to prevail. It made me more and more unhappy. My depressions made him crazy. When he started to lie to me, I knew I would have to leave him. I stayed with my friend Kate while I waited for the divorce to become final. My mother called me there incessantly.

"He's home," she said, and blinded me with light. I didn't even mind that much. At least the terrible dreams were over. I was still tired, even more tired than before my nap. In the bathroom I washed my face. I studied its reflection in the mirror. I could almost believe that I was looking at myself. Toward the end of my marriage, my face looked more and more to me like a picture in a museum. I couldn't connect with its reality. David explained to me that in order to fully perceive an image, one had to make imaginative leaps of which I was apparently incapable. This deficiency carried over into my perception of my own face in the mirror. My friend Kate said I seemed disoriented. She suggested I see a psychiatrist. I told her I'd be okay once the divorce became final.

"How's my girl?"

My father stood in the doorway. He recognized me. I was encouraged.

I kissed his stubbly cheek. "How are *you* is more like it," I said. "You should have told me you were sick."

"It's nothing." We walked together down the stairs. "It's nerves. A whole day. GI series. Upper, lower. I knew they wouldn't find anything. It's nothing."

In the kitchen my mother was crying.

"Don't," I said. "He's okay."

"Oh sure, sure. Just like you are. Two nervous wrecks I have. What did I ever do? Can you tell me that? What did I ever do?"

I said, "Stop it, you're making me crazy."

During dinner, I felt more and more unhappy. The meat loaf tasted old. After the dishes were washed, we called my sister, Toby, in Chicago. She's married to an orthodontist and they have two children, ages five and three. Toby is two years younger than I, but she has always been more organized. She drives a forest-green Buick station wagon, and her husband has a brown Saab. When it was my turn to talk to her, she invited me to come stay with them for a week. I immediately accepted. For Machiavellian reasons, I did not tell her about the red Camaro.

After the conversation with Toby, my father and I played Scrabble. My mother made seven more calls to her friends, informing them of my father's nervous condition and my surprise visit. Seven times I heard her say, "Not too bad, considering everything." And three times she mentioned bitterly that at least the no-good had left me the car. Sometime during the sixth call, I triple-scored with the word "conjugal," but that was not enough to lift my depression. David had said, "You're so damn morose. Your depressions are going to kill me." I told my father I was too tired to finish the game. He gave me one of his Nembutals. I slept for nine dreamless hours, and left Cleveland the next morning. In my red Camaro, I drove to Chicago.

As I came down my sister's street, Toby was pulling her station wagon into the driveway. She'd come from the other direction. I parked behind her. My niece and nephew jumped up on the Camaro's hood and pounded on the windshield. They seemed pleased to see me. My sister yanked them off the car. I knew she'd disapprove of it. The car. I was glad I hadn't mentioned it on the phone: she might have withdrawn her invitation. I hadn't even *wanted* red.

I carried in my luggage and she made three trips back and forth to the forest-green Buick for groceries. While she unpacked the bags, we chatted. Finally she said, "I hoped you and David would get back together."

"No," I said. "I became more and more unhappy. My depressions made him crazy. When he started to lie to me, I realized I would have to leave. I stayed with my friend Kate until the divorce became final. Then I quit my job at the magazine and drove to Cleveland."

I didn't tell her about Boston and my old lover Ben. Toby is two years younger than I, but she holds many of the ideas of my mother's generation. Toby perceives marriage as a necessary refuge, an asylum from the world's cruelties and madnesses. She doesn't relate well to divorces, lovers, or red Camaros. Our values are different. At least that's how I perceive her. We're not very close.

My niece and nephew dragged me off to their toyroom. I

played with them for an hour, until their father came home. Ian gave me a fierce hug. He kissed me on the lips. During dinner his leg bumped mine three times. I have never liked lamb. I felt more and more unhappy.

My sister said, "How is Dad really? Tell me the truth."

"All the tests were negative," I said. "We played Scrabble. I triple-scored with the word 'conjugal.' He gave me a Nembutal and I slept without dreaming. At least I don't remember dreaming, if I did."

My sister's face grew grave. Ian rose and put his arm around me. Into my ear he said, "Let me take you upstairs, Claudia."

"You prick!" I yelled. "I'm your wife's sister, for god's sake!" I wrenched myself away from him, ran to the guest room, and slammed the door. I could hear my niece and nephew crying. I could hear Ian and Toby arguing. So much commotion. It was making me crazy. I telephoned Ben in Cambridge.

"I think I'm going crazy," I said.

He said, "Come back."

He was restrained. I detected no trace of that maddening exuberance. "All right," I said. "I'll leave in the morning. Expect me in a couple of days."

"I'll be here." He sounded calm and gentle.

In the morning I told Toby that I was leaving. She was upset.

"You're wrong about Ian," she told me. "You couldn't be more wrong, Claudia."

"It was just too much domestic commotion," I said. "It made me feel disoriented. I'm driving to Boston to visit my old lover Ben. You should see his apartment. It's like a museum."

In silence we finished our cinnamon rolls and fresh-perked coffee. I kissed my sister. I gave her a fierce hug. She helped me carry my bags out to the red Camaro.

"It shows you how different we are, doesn't it?" she said.

"What does?"

"Our cars."

I started the engine. I said through the window, "I didn't want red. David insisted. It was the reason I left him."

She smiled ruefully. "Have a good trip," she told me. The

140

children perched on the hood of Toby's forest-green Buick station wagon and waved good-bye to me. Toby was crying. It made me more and more unhappy. Five blocks down, I parked the car and let my own tears come. They poured and poured. If I kept on crying, I would drown. I made myself stop. I fixed up my face. I looked at myself in the mirror and could find no evidence of my sobbing episode. Relieved, I headed for Boston. I was going back to my old lover Ben. We had been apart for seven years, but then we'd spent a few days together and discovered that we still meshed so well. His apartment was like a museum. I know quite a bit about museums. David, to whom I was married during the time that Ben and I were apart, is an art historian with an emphasis on the surrealists. Even though it was a less-than-ideal relationship, I learned quite a bit about art.

I drove all day. I did not have to go to the bathroom. I was neither hungry nor thirsty. I stopped only for gas. At six o'clock, outside of Erie, I pulled into a filling station and my car would not start again. The attendant tried the ignition. He lifted the hood of my red Camaro. He said it needed a new starter, but he wouldn't be able to replace it for me until morning. The mechanic was off duty. I told him I was in a rush to get to Boston. He insisted I would have to wait until morning.

I said, "Don't you know of any garages nearby that could do the work now?"

"Listen, lady," he said, "mechanics got lives too. They got families like everybody else."

I screamed at him, "There must be one mechanic in Erie who works on cars at night!"

The attendant could see that I needed to prevail. Out of fear, he motioned for me to follow him into the station. He took out an address book from the beat-up desk. The odor of gas fumes was making me dizzy. On a slip of paper, he wrote down a telephone number.

"Try them," he said. "Bruno and Frank. They keep crazy hours."

I used the phone on the beat-up desk. I leaned against its edge to keep my balance. I felt so dizzy. Bruno answered. I told him about my car, the gas station, the starter, the trip to Boston. I talked and talked, trying to explain my case.

Bruno said, "Pick you up in ten minutes."

"I'll be here," I said. I sounded calm and gentle.

The attendant said I could wait in the office. I sat down at the desk. He went outside to the pumps. A pale-blue Mustang had driven in while I was on the phone. I had wanted pale blue or tan. I hadn't wanted red. I hadn't even wanted a Camaro, but I could have been happier if it had been pale blue or tan. But David had insisted on red. Ben was surprised to see me with a red Camaro, and he was right. My sister, Toby, was not surprised, but she doesn't know me well. We're not very close. At least the no-good left me the car.

Bruno tapped on the window. I opened the door and the fresh air made me feel so much better.

"You Claudia?" he said. "The one with the Camaro?"

I nodded. He hooked up my broken-down car to his truck. He opened the door for me. The step was quite high and he gave me a boost. His hands were like clamps on my hips. "You prick!" I thought, but said nothing. I needed the starter. I needed to get to Boston. I can be very Machiavellian when I need to prevail.

He drove to his garage. He turned the volume on the radio up very loud. I hate loud rock. I hadn't eaten since breakfast. I still felt dizzy. I grew more and more unhappy. The music was making me crazy.

"Could you make it softer?" I said over the din.

He scowled, but obliged. He looked a lot like David to me. Not his features. His expression.

"Thank you," I said.

He said, "You got a lot of guts for a dame, you know that?"

I looked at him. He looked a lot like Ben to me. I said, "Do you think I need to see a psychiatrist?"

"How in the hell should I know?"

I started to cry. "I'm so damn morose. My depressions are going to kill me."

We were at a red light. Bruno put his hand on my leg. "You want something to relax you?"

"I'm a nervous wreck," I said.

"I got some good stuff under the seat," he said. "You want some?"

I had no idea what I wanted. I only knew what I didn't want: the red Camaro. I didn't want it.

"Forget the car," I told Bruno.

"What?"

"Don't fix the damn car! I never wanted it!"

He accelerated and we jolted forward. He withdrew his hand. "You're nuts," he said. "You're really crazy."

"Promise me you'll never lie to me, Bruno."

He didn't answer. I could see he was confused. He pulled the truck into the entrance to the garage. Bruno and Frank's. A ramshackle place on a grimy commercial block. I got out of the truck and stood in the doorway. He backed my hooked-up car into the garage. He got out. He unhooked my car from the truck. He opened the Camaro's hood. He put the car up on the rack. He took out the old starter. He found a new one among the automotive parts stored in cubbies along one wall. He fitted the new starter into the motor of the red Camaro. He turned on the ignition. The car sounded fine. He took the car down off the rack.

He said, "Okay. That's it," and told me the cost.

"I'd like to try some of your stuff," I said.

Bruno shook his head. "I made a mistake. I don't have none. I never. I."

"I told you never to lie to me," I said. I knew I would have to leave him. Lies are easy, careless and often malevolent. When David started to lie to me, I knew I would have to leave *him*.

I paid Bruno what I owed and drove off. The traffic was dense. Night driving is hard. I felt so disoriented. Kate thought I should see a psychiatrist. I found a motel and collapsed for the night. I dreamt about Bruno. Terrible dreams. When I woke up in the morning, I was more tired than when I'd gone to sleep. I washed my face. I did not recognize myself at all. It demanded an imaginative leap of which I was not in the least capable. I walked down the street and ordered some breakfast at a diner. The eggs piled up in my chest. The toast hurt my teeth. I thought about Ben. He had never left Cambridge, although he'd received his Ph.D. in literature six years ago from Harvard. His stupid poems. His museum of an apartment. His anachronistic routine in bed. Why was I going to see *him* again? He would make me crazy.

I drove to New York. I stopped only for gas. I drove to David's apartment. I rang his bell but no one answered. He was at work, I reasoned. He teaches art history at Columbia. He seduces his students. He is particularly interested in the surrealists. Our relationship was less than ideal. I wrote a note to David and shoved it under his door. I wrote, "I never wanted the red Camaro. At least it could have been pale blue or tan. Then I would have been a little happier. But you insisted on red. That's why I left you. That and the lies. You were making me crazy. The car is parked around the corner. The keys are under the seat. I don't want it. Claudia."

All of it was true. I never lied to David.

I took a taxi to Kate's office. She works for a major philanthropic foundation. I walked across the thick brown carpet, past the smoked-glass partitions, the large abstract canvases, the masses of plants. People kept asking if they could help me. I shook my head no. When I found Kate's cubicle, I nearly passed out with relief.

"What is it?" she said. "What's wrong, can you tell me?"

I told her, "It was the red Camaro. I finally gave it back to him." I talked and talked. I told her about Ben and my parents and Toby and Ian the Prick and the gas-station attendant and Bruno and the note I left for David.

She said, "Oh, Claudia, you're exhausted." She picked up her phone. "I'm going to call a doctor who—"

I ran out of the office. I ran like a gazelle. I was fine. I did not need a psychiatrist. It had been the car. It had made me crazy. I had never wanted it. In a phone booth I called Ben. Luckily, he was at home. He has two part-time jobs, one at B.U. and one at Emerson, and this leaves him time to work on his poems. I told him I had no car. I had given it back to David.

"What about your luggage?" he said. "Where are your suitcases?"

I said, "I gave it all back. I don't have anything left."

I started to cry. I cried and cried. The phone booth filled with my tears, water rose in the narrow compartment, I was drowning.

144

———

Ben came to see me in the hospital. David came. Kate. My parents. Toby and Ian. Bruno never came. Finally I stopped hoping.

When the doctors said I was better, I moved to Washington, D.C. I got a job with a major government agency. I found an airy apartment and furnished it with modest good taste. I used public transportation, and jogged in Rock Creek Park. I grew bean sprouts in a mason jar. I made my own yogurt. I spent ten days in El Salvador. I met Gregory, a nice man who knew how to compromise. I began to feel like a woman of infinite resources.

Gregory was the administrative assistant to a congressman from Minnesota. Gregory did not need to prevail. But he was overworked. So much pressure. As the months passed, he grew more and more morose. I was unable to cheer him up, and it was making me crazy. We had terrible scenes.

"Listen," I said, "let's take a vacation. How about Yugoslavia?"

He scowled at me. "I do not have time for a vacation, Claudia. But if I did, I do not think I would choose Yugoslavia."

He looked so sullen. It made me more and more unhappy. I said, "Gregory, your depressions are going to kill me. I think you should see a psychiatrist."

"No," he said, "I should see other women."

That was over a month ago. This weekend I'm going to visit Ben. He's moved to Ann Arbor.

RICHARD

There is a boy called Richard and he knows morning. He knows that the trees unfold their branches at dawn and the grass returns, silently, from its nest under the earth. He knows how the birds take the night sky, a great silk scarf the color of smoke, how they take it in their tiny beaks and fly with it to the forest where it lies all day in a gully, cool and dark as night itself. One thing else this Richard knows: he knows that people forget something about themselves when they wake, and spend all day trying to remember it.

Richard rises early. The iguana stirs, the gerbils chase each other through the plastic wheels, the parakeet flutters its green wings. Richard lifts the shade. He sees the blistered sky, weepy and pale, and Mr. Bone's dog out in the morning rain. *Mr. Bone, Mr. Bone.* But his porch is empty, the chintz-covered glider cushions wet-dark, the lavender flowers turned purple as ink, or peacock blood, or a bruise.

Richard's mother says, *Up with the crows again.*

She is making herself a woman, it is what she does in the morning. She draws delicate lines and streaks of singing color on a face that, really, in the honesty of sleep, is bulky and pallid. She is twisting her hair into the knot that only a woman is supposed to be able to tie, but Richard has tied the tail of Mr. Bone's dog, when it was sleeping, into that same secret knot. All day long she will pretend to be a woman, checking and rechecking herself in mirrors and storefronts and the eyes of men she meets in town, and it will never seem quite right. Tomorrow she will buy a new perfume, or shoes with thin black straps.

Eggs, Richard says, for she has asked him what he wants for breakfast. She cooks him his breakfast every morning. Sometimes while he eats, she gives him kisses on the neck. *My little man, my honey, my plum.* Sometimes her arms lock around him and Richard watches the hairs grow like beachgrass on the wide slope between her elbow and wrist.

She leaves first, telling him, *Lock the door behind you,* telling him this every morning, forgetting he knows, forgetting he never forgets what he knows.

All morning at school Richard worries about Mr. Bone. Richard worries about something every day. This is what happens when he worries: a mangy goat settles on Richard's desk and shreds his arithmetic paper; a hog crawls under his chair and snorts; an old woman, older even than Mr. Bone, a very old woman who is really a woman, whose face even in the morning's deceit is bulky and pallid, this woman hobbles up and down the aisles and swats at other children (never Richard) with her carved ivory cane. Because of worry—the goat, the hog, the old woman—Richard has no friends and his teacher believes that Richard has brought the creatures of worry into the room himself. He must sit in the hallway until lunch, and the creatures (he knows) will circle him all morning, doing their dance.

This banishment has happened before, often, but this is the first time that Richard understands that the hallway is not a hallway, but a tunnel, and that this tunnel ends at Mr. Bone's house, the only place in the world where worry—the mangy goat, the snorting hog, the old woman who is really a woman—cannot enter. When Richard discovers the tunnel, the clock stops ticking. In the tunnel, it is always the moment preceding the first hour, the instant of awakening, the sliver of time before time.

We're going out, he tells them as they dip and swish and hammer their hooves and heels. The old woman forgets to hobble when she dances: this is another thing that Richard has just discovered, and he knows he can use it against her.

Mr. Bone, Mr. Bone.

On the glistening steps, the creatures cower. Beyond Mr. Bone's rain-polished porch, everything hisses and wavers, an eye-wounding haze envelops trees and grass, pebbled streets, the tunnel's crystal span, the tar-fused shingles, everything sizzles and blurs. The sun impinges on everything, and Richard knows he has just escaped his own evaporation. On the glider, the solid dog sleeps, safe in his familiar mottled fur.

Mr. Bone, Mr. Bone.

Well, if it ain't . . . what in the hell . . . all right, come on.

There are three reasons why worry cannot enter Mr. Bone's house: whiskey, music, cards. The goat knows he would get drunk; the hog knows he would dance himself sick; the old woman knows she would lose herself forever in the riddles of diamonds and clubs. The creatures know these things, and never bother Mr. Bone.

Blackjack, Mr. Bone says, and takes another swallow of booze straight from the amber bottle. On the radio: wails and howls, stomping, prayers and hoots and spells. *Gimme that ol' time religion, gimme that . . .*

Mr. Bone says, *I'm tard, Richard, I'm needin' my nap.*

That's okay. I'll play with the dog. I'll do your dishes for you. I'll even scrub the floor.

Everything beyond this house wavers.

Do what you want, I jes know I'm tard.

When the dishes are done, and the floor scoured of its corrosion, Richard is tired, too. In the bedroom, Mr. Bone lies snoring in a rumple of sheets. Richard knows what snoring means. It means that the old man's heart has come loose and is rolling around in the great pit of his chest. The loosed heart rattles in the pit. It is the rattle of loneliness, and the one thing worse than worry (Richard knows) is loneliness, because there is no place in the world where it cannot enter. For the first time, Richard understands what Mr. Bone forgets about himself in the morning and what he spends all day trying to remember.

Oh, it is so apparent.

The boy called Richard feels his own small heart coming unhinged, and he crawls into the musty nest with Mr. Bone.

BALANCING ACT

They walked through the airport without intimacy or particular joy in each other's company, but also without hostility. In the huge concourse, it seemed they passed every imaginable permutation of the mating equation. Couples crazed by the imminence of separation clung like Siamese twins to one another. Other pairs of men and women strolled the terminal with easy affection, fingers brushing, strides matched. Still others tried to outpace their partners, one and then the other forced into an embarrassing trot, a whispered "Dammit, slow down." Some argued loudly, their words strafing each other on the zoneless battleground on which they fought out their lives. Trying to fit herself and her husband in somewhere between the lovers and haters, she speculated that they probably appeared much as they were: eleven years married, prospering, fond of each other, bonded by domestic ritual, speaking in familial civilities, enjoying well-regulated pleasures. She had a funny vision of the terminal as a laboratory for an earnest psychologist—days spent posing as a traveler, working in phone booths, gathering data, grinding out an article: "Coupling Variations in Transit." She smiled at her own joke, but did not share it with her husband, fearing it would take too much exposition to get him to adjust his sight to hers. They seldom stood at the same perceptual location.

"I think I'll buy a magazine," she said as they approached a newsstand.

"They've got plenty on the plane," he said.

"They might not have what I really want."

He shrugged. "That's entirely possible."

She caught his ironic smirk, the momentary despair of his retort, and turned away from it nervously. She studied the racks while he scanned headlines from all over the world.

Along with her magazine, he bought a pack of gum. He handed her a stick as they walked through the gate. "Here," he said, "for your ears."

"Thanks," she deadpanned. "Could I have a piece for my mouth, too?"

He gave a small smile, but he had no comeback and her appetite for banter reluctantly receded.

"Really, thanks," she said. "You're nice."

"Cub scout training. I've been nice since I was seven."

Now a uniformed man was taking down the chain that held them from the field; they headed for the plane.

She stood with one foot raised above, held aloof from, the field of their marriage, and she waited for the force of his personality to emerge, to pull her completely down into the circle of their relationship. She did what she could to invest him with the energy he would need to attract and hold her; she tired herself in the effort to create him, to make him believe in his own power. She closeted her own possibilities. Half asleep like a pelican on one foot, she waited for his transformation. She was very patient; but the patience seemed to infuse itself into her very veins, diluting her blood. She became too quiet; she did not laugh easily or deeply enough; she forgot to use body lotion; at parties she distanced herself from drinkers and flirts. She was waiting, in reserve.

She knew he was disheartened by her growing lackluster. It was as if, over the years, she were a photograph in the process of fading. He could not articulate it, but she could see his discouragement, even terror, when she moved like a shadow through the rooms of their house. She behaved more and more like a person unable to remember the most important fact of her life. He would ask her repeatedly, "What's wrong?" and she would reply, "Nothing. Just thinking," with a smile as tight as a fist and her brain shouting: *I am waiting for you to be able to read my mind.*

She knew by standing on one foot for so long that her other leg might atrophy, that she might never recover its use even if he were to manage to pull her from her strained position. She looked for exercises that she could do which would not jeopardize her crucial, painful balance. Half-hooked rugs she'd begun and abandoned were rolled up in the basement; oil paintings and acrylics sat unframed, unhung in the cluttered sunroom she had used for a time as a studio; overly large gardens choked all summer on weeds, and vegetables she forgot to harvest rotted in the untended furrows; a piano she snatched up eagerly at a house sale stood in the corner of the living room, newspapers stacking up on the bench.

Once he told her, "Your trouble is that you don't stay with anything long enough to know if you really like it."

While she felt like someone who'd been drinking the same glass of water for years.

The plane lifted and she clutched at the armrest during the moments of disconnection with the ground. She shut her eyes and worked on her chewing gum. She wondered how he could not feel brief uneasiness, some small pang of danger. He nudged her. "We've leveled out," he said, "relax."

She opened her eyes. It astounded her how her terror of takeoffs could dissipate once they were high enough and moving smoothly. She was always grateful for his apparent equanimity while she suffered through her short ordeal. But she felt guilty about using his strength while, at the same time, resenting it for its passivity. She looked out at the diminishing city.

"Sometimes I think we should fly on separate planes when we travel," she said. "Because of the kids. Reduce their chances of being orphaned by fifty percent."

He shook his head, as if at a child. "That's what I love about you."

"What?"

"My wife the optimist."

She wanted to tell him, *I need you to have a sense of doom; so we can laugh like mad hyenas every time we escape with our miraculous lives.*

Instead, she capitulated: "I have a morbid streak, don't I?"

For the rest of the fifty-minute flight, until the terrible descent, she lost herself in her magazine. He opened his briefcase on his lap and read the agenda for the impending week-long convention of the American Society of Architects.

They were waiting for the desk clerk to attend them. The hotel was old and sumptuous, and she was pleased that they would not be confined for five days to a stripped-down, thin-walled Holiday Inn. She often wished that environment did not mean so much to her mood, did not contribute so heavily to her frame of mind. She would have liked to have been as happy with him in a sterile motel as in this gracious building, but it was not the case and she allowed the atmosphere to work on her like a martini.

"One thing you can say about architects," she said, "they pick nice places to convene."

He smiled and nodded at her pleasure, accepting the compliment as if he, personally, had chosen their lodgings. "You really like old buildings, don't you?" he asked, as if just discovering something about her he had not known for years.

Breathe in the elegance, she wanted to tell him. *Absorb and retain it.*

He was not an architect of elegance; he designed schools, gas stations, supermarkets. "I'm really a technician," he would tell people when they asked about his work. "Some architects are artists, but I am more of a technician."

Afterward, she would tell him, with a kind of frantic confidence, "Don't demean yourself, don't underestimate your talent."

Their room was spacious and well appointed. They hung up their clothes and arranged their toiletries on a shelf above the marble sink in the gilded bathroom. When they were done with domestication, she took out the telephone book and began perusing the "Restaurants" section. "What are you in the mood for?"

"You," he said. He had taken off his shirt and shoes and

was lying on the bed; he was propped up on one elbow and a gentle lust washed over his features. She undressed quietly, with no effort at seductiveness. He watched her with wistful tolerance. They made efficient, kindly love. On the wallpaper behind the bed, seventeenth-century ladies and gentlemen touched only fingertips, but their eyes seared the air.

After a voluptuous breakfast—melon, eggs, Canadian bacon, English muffins, coffee in a silver urn—they separated. He went to register for the convention which was to begin at ten. She walked out onto Michigan Avenue and inserted herself into the flow of people. It was like being on a moving sidewalk, she thought, the way the crowds of a huge city like Chicago could move you along, block after block, allowing you to nearly forget your feet. She browsed in bookstores and little specialty shops, where scarves and bracelets and tiny bottles of perfume offered themselves up like gifts to her senses. By eleven-fifteen she was tired and slightly hungry, and she entered a coffee shop tucked into the lobby of a large office building. The place was nearly empty. Still, she wished she had bought something, that she could be carrying a package or a book and not look so much like a friendless wanderer. However, it did not keep her from settling into a booth and accepting a menu from the bored waitress. "A grilled-cheese sandwich and coffee, please." She relaxed as well as she could, fingering the icy rim of her water glass.

The only other customers in the shop were two young women and three small children; the women sat on one side of their table and the children on the other, so she could not tell to whom each belonged. The children, a boy and two girls, looked to be around six or seven years old, well-behaved but restless, held in line by the serious glances of the two mothers. The children sat on their hands and slurped Cokes through bent straws. The glasses wobbled dangerously on the table. "Hold on to your drinks," one of the women rebuked with a fair amount of gentleness. Little fingers rose reluctantly, and the woman who had given the order nodded approval. "Isn't that better?" she said. The other woman said, "All we need is three Coke-soaked kids." They all laughed at the inadvertent rhyme, and the boy sang out loud with delight, "Soaked by Coke! Soaked by Coke! Soaked by—"

"Enough, Jimmy, enough." The woman spoke with humor, but also with urgency. They all calmed down.

It made her think of her own children. Six and eight, their features beginning to be firmed and angled by their short lifetimes. She had chosen ether when her first was born, and it was hours later when she finally got to look at her daughter; it was as if someone had slashed her balloon of a belly and the child—a vital organ—had slid out. It took weeks to comprehend that the separate creature had grown inside of her. She read volumes on postpartum depression. Finally she accepted. It made her determined, however, to be awake for the next birth.

He agreed. He felt it would weld them all closer. He coached her in the necessary exercises of breathing and control, and she was touched by his enthusiasm. She began to hope that, just as the baby was growing inside of her, cells of awareness were multiplying within him—and soon he would give birth to his own new self which she had seeded. When the labor began, they rushed to the hospital. He attended her with nervous tenderness, and she accepted his help. But as the contractions intensified, she felt the pain suck her away from him; she did not honestly care if he was there or not. Although she held his hand tightly in the delivery room and turned her face to his kiss when their son burst from her body, the weight of distance from him bore down on her as surely as the doctor's hand urging the placenta from her abdomen. The baby looked just like his father.

She would call home tonight, she decided. She paid her bill and walked back to the hotel to take an afternoon nap.

The week moved on with his meetings, her trips to museums and galleries and the endless variety of stores. She bought a few things: a teak tray in a shop of Scandinavian imports, a silk blouse for her mother, a wooden puzzle and a book about clowns for the children. In the evenings they ate well, saw a play, went one night to the convention banquet. She began to relax, to feel acclimated. On Thursday night they made love again, this time at her initiation. Afterward, lying under the sheets, he told her, "When you want to, you can be so good." She knew that was true, and was happy for her courage to please him, to offer what she knew she owed.

He had a final meeting the next morning; she decided to pack after breakfast, in order to have the day and early evening free from the chore. They had an eight-o'clock flight home. When she finished, she decided to take a walk before meeting him for lunch—they were going to drive out to a little Greek restaurant in Evanston that a convention colleague had recommended for its wonderful salads. Leaving the elevator, she realized that the architects were having a midmorning break: they were fanned out in small, talkative groups all over the mirrored lobby.

She scanned faces and spotted him off in a corner, engaged in serious conversation with an urban planner from Philadelphia, an old schoolmate of his. She moved close enough to hear them, but out of his line of vision. He was deep into technical jargon, he was gesturing emphatically, he was —she realized it with a shock—in control of the discussion. The other man was listening to her husband with real concentration, the Philadelphian's brow wrinkled with respect. Her husband had *power* over the man, he had *dominance* over his friend. She listened to her husband make his points with assurance, with pride in his own intelligence. She had never encountered him before this moment as a separate entity from herself—or had she, and forgotten?—and his obvious poise startled her, confused her. He was with the Philadelphian the way she wanted him to be with her. She was unsteadied.

The architects were beginning to move back to their conference, and as he strode toward the ballroom, she called to him. He turned, and she looked at him with intense warmth, with something like desire; she could see that he'd received the curious, exciting signal. "See you at noon," he mouthed, and she nodded. He turned back toward the ballroom, she toward the street. She felt as if she had been entrusted with a fragile crystal of hope.

She studied herself in the glass caverns of Michigan Avenue. She tried to keep intact, like an engraving, the image of his animated force, so she could summon it when the deadly doubts moved in, when the distance re-emerged, when the isolation threatened to freeze her, render her immobile. She knew he would be thinking of the warmth he had seen in her eyes, the falling away of fear, the liveliness which he craved. Something had, at least for a moment, thawed her out, given her color again, energized her. How determined he would be to preserve it.

The drive to Evanston and the lunch in the tiny Greek restaurant were like a courtship, each of them striving to maintain faith in the other's possibilities. Each walked a tightrope of need. That single afternoon, she later decided, was what had kept them together for another three full years.

MEMOIRS
OF A
COLD CHILD

I never forgave them for naming me Maxine. It is not a name you give a child. They said it was after my grandfather whose name was Max and who would have loved me very much, but I could still not abide it. I took that name as a kind of message: Grow up quickly, be serious, avoid giggling and baby talk, learn to dress yourself at an early age. To chin-chucking and tickling I went stiff as a mannequin. I did not identify with Shirley Temple. When Aunt Rosie came for visits, I hid under the sofa, recoiling from her determination to plaster me with kisses. She'd slide quarters under the couch in an attempt to lure me out; I'd palm the coins and stay put. Ma told her time and again, "Of course she loves you, Rosie, she's just not an affectionate child." Afterward she'd plead with me, "Maxine, be a little warmer to your aunt." As if Maxines were able.

He barged in on me in the middle of the night.
"Get up, Maxine! Ma's ready!"
He had me by the shoulders, was shaking me like a can of shaving cream. I had done nothing wrong, not even in my

dreams, and he had no right to mishandle me. I bit him on the arm. He let go of me as if I were dangerous.

"We've got to go!" he said, trying to get through to me.

I looked at him dumbly, made no move to comply. He stuffed my feet into slippers and eased me from the bed. Still limp with sleep, whimpering, uncomprehending, I let him steer me out of the apartment and down the dim hall to 6B: Mrs. Green's. Old Lady Green, behind her back. Ma would coo, "Like having a grandmother right in the building," but I had no use for the woman. That night she came to the door in her ratty chenille robe, her pin-curled head (some of the bobby pins had come undone and random curls sprung up like coiled antennae from her scalp), and her face swathed in pink cream that had dried in places and looked like scales. The sight of her started me wailing; she put a hand over my mouth and another around my waist and pulled me like a hostage into her place.

"Don't worry, don't worry," she consoled my frantic-eyed father, "just take care of Fern!"

He must have felt I was in good hands: he disappeared.

Ungagged, I began to bawl. "What's the matter with my mother, what's wrong with—"

She gave me the kind of look reserved for imbeciles, cripples, and children. It is a look beyond pity. "Wrong, Maxine? You foolish girl. What could be wrong?"

My howls deteriorated into low, sniffling sick-dog moans. She set me down on the couch and whispered to me with the intimacy of shared gossip: "Do you know how many years your parents have prayed for this baby, Maxine? It's a *miracle!* Now, God willing, you'll be a real family."

She left the room to get me bedding. I collapsed onto the faded brocade upholstery and mouthed profanities over and over into the musty cushion. She came back with a pillow and blanket which I pulled completely over my head in the hope I might suffocate, but I didn't. She patted me on the rump and sang me off-key Brahms's Lullaby: I had no choice but to escape into sleep.

They named the baby Wendy; that told me a lot.

They put her in my room as if she were a birthday present—it is not polite to bad-mouth well-intentioned gifts so I had to pretend to a certain degree of gratitude. Friends and relatives paraded in and out of my quarters at all hours of the day and night: visits to the manger. After a few weeks, the novelty wore off, the adulation waned, the crowds diminished. I, who'd seen through the myth of Wendy-as-savior right from the start, was left to contend with the reality of her piercing colic cries, nasty-smelling spit-ups and urine-soaked sheets.

"Isn't she wonderful?" Ma crooned.

I knew she was feigning enthusiasm: she'd been dragging around the apartment for a month, she still couldn't sit flat-down on her bottom, her hair went uncombed and her eyes looked like they'd been underlined with charcoal.

Trying to appeal to her poorly disguised depression, I said, "I feel like I've been sleeping in a diaper pail."

But she jumped on me savagely: "Maxine, that is a cruel thing to say about your baby sister!"

I shrugged. "Truth's the truth."

"What a cold child you are, Maxine."

Truth's the truth.

She was three months old and hadn't turned over yet. Daddy pored over books on child development.

"How old was Maxine when she turned over?"

Ma scrunched up her forehead. "I can't remember back that far."

"Didn't we keep a little book on when she did things?"

"I don't remember it," Ma said.

I was shoving peas around on my plate. I wanted to tell them: *You don't keep baby books on a Maxine.* But I kept still. Let them live on illusions, I figured.

"Maxine, don't play with your food," Ma told me. "Saul, tell her not to play with her food."

"Don't play with your food," he said. "Maybe we should talk to the doctor about it."

I was outraged. "Just 'cause I play with my food?"

He looked at me in puzzlement. Then he realized. "No, no, about Wendy I meant, about her not turning over."

I was relieved that he wasn't nit-picking at my table manners, but I would have preferred it to being shelved for that baby's irrelevant gymnastics.

Ma brought out Jell-O for dessert, red Jell-O bulging with grapes, pears, and peaches from a can of fruit cocktail she'd mixed in when the gelatin was half-hard. I never liked my foods mixed up; I liked to taste each thing separately and I told her: "Ma, next time leave the Jell-O plain."

"There's no pleasing you, Maxine." She sighed. "Most children love it like this, this is the way almost all children love it."

"She's got a right to her opinion, Fern," Daddy said quietly, his eyes still in his child-development book.

That cheered me up enough to help clear the table without being asked. A person needs to be recognized for what she is, even if she isn't pleased with herself. I even hummed, which took me out of character. Made Ma think, I'm sure, that I'd be normal yet.

Still, they went on for days about the baby not turning over. I decided enough was enough. I figured it out one night while I was brushing my teeth. That's when I did my most serious thinking: standing in front of the bathroom mirror, my mouth wide with foam, me scrubbing away at each tooth as if it were a tarnished monument—it's the closest a child can come to mind-cleansing manual labor.

It was around eight-thirty. Daddy was at the kitchen table working on bills. Ma was watching TV.

"Guess I'll go to bed now," I said.

Ma looked up from her program. "You brush?"

I curled back my lips and showed her my shiny whites. She gave me a look of dispensation. I poked my head into the kitchen. "G'night, Daddy."

"'Night, Maxine."

They thought they were through with me until morning.

Wendy was asleep in her crib, on her stomach, which was how Ma said babies should always be put down. Ma said they shouldn't be on their backs because they would choke on their own vomit. Of which Wendy had more than her share. Very carefully, as if I were handling piecrust dough, I picked up my sleeping sister and turned her on her back. Her eyelids didn't even flutter. Then I put on my best look of excitement and strode into the living room.

"Ma!"

"Oh, what now?" she said.

"It's the baby!"

She came to life. "What's the matter, what's wrong?"

"Nothing," I said. Then I dropped the bombshell: "She turned over! Just when I walked into the room, she flipped right over onto her back!"

Daddy heard and darted in from the kitchen. Like the knowledgeable guide on an expedition, I led them to the site.

"See," I said, with the elation of the witness, "she's on her back!"

Ma and Daddy hugged each other. They smiled at me as if I were a saint. For the next two weeks I rotated Wendy from stomach to back, from back to stomach, about three times a day. Finally, to my relief, she started doing it herself. Maxines are good strategists; they need to be.

She heard me come in.

"Maxine?" she hollered from somewhere in the apartment.

"Where are you, Ma?"

"In the bathroom giving Wendy a bath. I thought you were out playing."

I was on the lam from hide-and-seek. I hated the game: full of threats and the fear of defeat. They'd made me It for the last time. I'd been hiding my face against the telephone pole we used for home base; all my enemies had dispersed to places I never would discover. Halfway to one hundred, sweating with the foreknowledge of my upcoming humiliation, I'd taken off like a rabbit and run home, tearing up the stairs like an escaped criminal.

I pushed open the bathroom door. Ma was on her knees, bent over the tub. Wendy grinned and held up a plastic boat.

"In or out," Ma ordered. "You're letting in a draft."

"I don't feel good," I told her.

She looked me over. I was trembling, perspiring. She wiped a lathered hand on her apron and motioned to me to come down to her level. She put her hand on my forehead.

"No fever, thank God. But you look like you're coming down with something."

"I feel really awful, Ma."

Wendy was flailing a washcloth in the water; droplets were

sailing out of the tub. Ma turned her eyes back and forth from me to the baby, from the baby to me, and shook her head at the immensity of her burdens.

"I got to finish the baby," she said. "Go lie down awhile. Then we'll see."

Her compassion did not wash over me like rain, but at least I'd communicated my failing health. Set up the pigeon, so to speak. Tightened up my alibi.

"Okay," I said. "And, Ma?"

"What?"

"If any of the kids come looking for me, just tell them I'm sick in bed."

Nobody came.

"So how you like being Big Sister?" Mrs. Green fished.

"It's okay." I was trying to finish my jigsaw puzzle, the Grand Canyon in 435 pieces, and just wanted her to leave me alone. She was in charge all afternoon while Ma and Daddy were at a wedding.

"Only *okay*?"

Her scorn could come down on you like a lash. She was a woman with set opinions that hid, like guerrillas, behind the camouflage of questions; the questions could trap you into believing that her mind was open to your answers, whatever they might be. But her opinions were waiting to pounce on you. I knew this about her and I was annoyed at myself for getting snared. I should have said, "Yes. Wonderful. Being a big sister is the most wonderful thing that has ever happened to me." And she would have gone back to her knitting. Instead she came at me with all her ammunition: "Only *okay*?"

I emerged from the Grand Canyon.

"Well," I said, "I don't have my own room anymore."

"Maxine, Maxine, Maxine."

Old Lady Green, Old Lady Green, Old Lady Green.

She sat down beside me on the floor and tried to cuddle me. I squirmed away.

"Little girl," she said sadly, "you should be so happy, *so* happy, to have someone to share your room *with*." She flapped her hands at my ignorance. Her eyes got teary.

"What I wouldn't give," she said, "to be in your position. You know what it is to hear yourself breathing?" She shook her head, no no no, as if she didn't understand her own words.

Then Wendy started crying from her crib and Mrs. Green ran to the bedroom. I could hear her gushing over the baby and the baby giggling back. I went back to the Grand Canyon.

One day I came home from school and Ma said, "Maxine, I have a treat for you."

"Is it a Hershey Bar?"

"Not *that* kind of treat," she said. "I mean a real big-girl responsibility." She made her eyes twinkle. I could tell it was artificial glee because she was also kneading her hands, which she did under stress and never in times of authentic pleasure.

"Maxine," she said, "here's what your mother is going to allow you to do. She's going to allow you to take Wendy for a walk in the stroller. And she's going to give you money for groceries, and a shopping list. You'll walk down to King's Market and you'll pick up what your mother needs—she'll write it all out for you. Then you'll cross over to the butcher and get a chicken, about four pounds. You'll put everything in the basket on the stroller and then you'll come straight home." She smiled. "See, a real big-girl responsibility."

She was turning me into a servant. I'd been warned it would happen. Amy Walters, a big-deal sixth-grader, had sidled up to me in school just weeks before and asked me quietly, out of the side of her mouth, "They using you to baby-sit yet?"

I'd looked at her with great surprise. "I'm just eight, Amy."

"Don't worry, they'll use you. Mine started using me at *seven*."

"Why didn't you say no?"

"Maxine, you're dumb. You can't refuse your own parents. Listen, they have it made."

"Mine won't do it," I'd told her. "Because they think I'd sell the baby." She'd given me a wait-and-see look.

"Ma," I said, "I don't want to."

"You have to!" she said, her eye-lights dying. "My corns are very bad today. I can't ask Mrs. Green, she went to Philly to visit her sister. So you have to."

"I'll go to the store but I won't take Wendy."

"Yes you will!" she screamed. "You will! My feet are in pain! I need a half hour alone in my own bed! I need—"

"Okay, Ma, okay! Don't yell! Get her ready!"

She climbed down from her hysterical peak. "It's always a battle, Maxine. Why must it always be a battle?"

Why did you name me Maxine?

She brought in Wendy and handed her to me. She stuffed dollar bills and a piece of paper into a change purse and shoved it into my pocket. "Money and list," she said.

"And baby."

She yelled down the stairs after me: "Be careful when you cross the streets, remember Wendy is your responsibility!"

"No, Ma," I hollered back. "I'm gonna stand in the traffic and wait for a bus to run us over!"

Actually, I was a bit nervous crossing the streets. The stroller was too tall for me—rather, I was too small for it—and it was a strain just holding on to the handle, let alone navigating properly up and down curbs. People looked at me like they do at blind men struggling through city traffic: they knew I could use some assistance, but they did not want to risk offending my sense of independence. By the time I got to King's Market, I had a terrific headache.

Mr. King was suspicious: "Your mama know you come down here by yourself, Maxine?"

"She sent me." I pulled out the change purse for proof. "She wants what's on the list."

He came out from behind the counter and bent down to fondle Wendy. He chucked her chin and she bounced with pleasure. She reached out for his head, hairless as a melon, and he thought her tremendously clever. "I'm expected home soon," I said, interrupting the love affair.

"Babies," he said. "Nothing like them."

I put the list in his hand. "This is what my mother wants."

"Maxine, you're a strictly-business kid, you know it? You're the most serious kid I ever known. You a genius or something?"

"I'm above average."

"Yeah," he said. "I could tell."

He got the order together and I paid him. He looked at me respectfully. "A kid like you, when you're twelve you'll be in college. And *that* one, she'll be a princess, the belle of the ball."

He had it all figured out.

Across the street, butcher Ben Grossman was slicing up liver. Ma was always trying to match him up with Mrs. Green. "Two lonely people," she'd say. "A left shoe and a right." A boot and a moccasin. Ma was a person who always tried to reduce people to their essential, dull similarities. But Mr. Grossman was not about to breathe the same air as Mrs. Green just because they both had noses: he held out.

When I walked in, he said, "Got the baby there, huh?"

"Yeah."

He did not coo, chuck, tickle, or otherwise show affection. I didn't know if it was because his hands were bloody or because he honestly felt no special attraction.

"She sleep in the same room with you?" he asked.

"Yes."

He looked glum, shook his head and clacked his tongue. "That's rough getting used to," he said. "That's why I had to move out from my sister's place after a few months. She puts me in with her boy, Robbie. Not that I don't love him, he's the closest I got to a son. But I been in my own room for seventeen years since Nelly passed. You get used to your privacy, you don't give it up so easy, know what I mean?"

He knew I did or he wouldn't have told me. So I didn't answer and he didn't mind.

"My ma wants a chicken, about four pounds," I said.

"A *chicken?*" (As if I'd ordered spaghetti in a Chinese restaurant.)

"Yeah. A chicken."

"A chicken," he said, in wonderment.

He put down his cleaver and walked to the front of the store. In the window, chickens—their neck stumps sheathed in brown paper bags secured with rubber bands—hung from a row of iron hooks. He picked out a cadaver and came back to the counter.

"This one's good and fresh, killed this morning."

"I'll tell Ma," I said.

He wrapped the bird up in butcher paper, tied it with a string.

"Maxine, there's more."

"She just wants one."

He grew agitated. "More to *tell*, I mean, more to *tell* about this chicken!" He held up the package as if it were a religious artifact; his eyes shone like a mystic's.

"This chicken died twice," he said. "Believe me, this is a chicken with a direct pipeline to God!"

"I don't under—"

"I'm explaining, I'm explaining!" He leaned over the counter and put his face so close to mine I could feel his breath. "We kill them right back in there, the rabbi comes in and gives the blessing and then the heads come off. Every day it happens, I don't give it a thought. On this particular chicken, the ax comes down and what happens? Head gone, no head at all, but it's moving around like it's a whole animal! Not twitching—I mean walking! *The chicken's still living!* I say to the rabbi, 'Rabbi, maybe this is some omen? Some sign we shouldn't eat meat?' But he says, 'Do it right this time, put the creature out of its suffering!' and starts up his prayers again. So this time it gets finished right, but I am feeling very uneasy. The rabbi says, 'Grossman, I'll tell you what it means. It doesn't mean you should close up the shop and go on vegetables, put that out of your head. It means this is a chicken what's directly blessed by God and whoever eats it will have a fortunate life, a *mazel*.' "

Then Ben Grossman put the sanctified chicken-who-died-twice in my hands. "I give it to you, Maxine, because you're a *good girl*, a real nice girl."

A girl who could use a little help from heaven getting through her days on earth. Strange he should have realized that about me. Still: a man who spends half his time slaughtering animals and the other half slicing them up has got to be a Maxine at heart. It's a line of work that requires a little distance.

"Thank you," I squeaked, my throat tight with stunned gratitude.

Don't think I was a religious child. It was Mr. Grossman who believed in the chicken. Which was why I was so grateful: he was giving me some of his faith without asking for anything in return, not even a kiss.

Wendy started to fuss the minute we got out of the door. It was as if she knew she'd been overlooked and sought to demonstrate her annoyance. As I eased the front wheels of the stroller into the street, she stood up, gave a war cry and flung herself out of her vehicle. The force landed me on my backside and tore the stroller out of my hands. It shot crazily into the traffic, spewing groceries as it went. Brakes screeched and horns started blowing like there was a wedding going on. A mob was forming.

Mr. Grossman raced from his store into the street and played policeman: arms raised against the cars, blood-stained apron for a uniform, he yelled, "Back it up! Hold it! Back it up!" He screamed to me, *"Maxine, where's the baby?"*

Dazed, I pulled myself up from the sidewalk.

A woman shrieked from a second-floor window, "She's going down the sewer!"

I took the twenty feet in what felt like one giant lunge through space. She was already half gone, down to her waist. I grabbed her by her ankles, held her up like a newborn. The crowd went crazy.

Mr. King came running into the melee.

"My God!" he screamed. "A seven-dollar order!"

He was out in the street gathering into his arms what he could of the ruined groceries like a man picking through the rubble of a war-torn village. He worked his way through the broken eggs, spilled milk, smashed tomatoes, dented cans, and two rolls of toilet paper that floated like ribbons over the concrete. What he could salvage he dumped into the basket on the stroller, which had crashed into a utility pole. Then he dragged the carriage back to me.

"Turn that poor baby over!" he ordered me. I realized I was holding Wendy upside down. She was howling. I righted her, put her in her seat, and she immediately stopped crying and fell asleep. (In even the most stressful situations, Wendys adapt beautifully; they were made for this world, they are never out of step. Maxines, on the other hand, have no sense of rhythm and do a very poor waltz through experience.)

"Did you see a chicken?" I asked Mr. King.

Before he could answer, the wide-eyed driver of a red Ford

which was trying to inch its way forward rolled down his window: "I think I just hit a dog! Did I just hit a dog?"

Mr. Grossman stooped down, looked under the wheels of the car and rose, stricken.

"Not a dog!" he shouted to the man in the Ford. "A chicken! Don't worry, it was dead before you ran over it!"

"Twice!" I yelled.

The driver shook his head as if he were hallucinating. Then he rolled up his window and streaked out of the intersection, nearly running down Mr. Grossman and leaving behind on the street the smashed remnants of my salvation.

"The way your mother tells it, you were a regular Florence Nightingale."

Mrs. Green was sitting on the front stoop when I came home from school several days after the Incident. She was cutting her cuticles, collecting the slivers of skin in her lap.

"I just got her before she went down the sewer."

I started up the stairs and she shifted her body sideways, blocking my way. "Sit awhile, Maxine."

"I have to go to the bathroom, Mrs. Green."

She closed her eyes and sighed. "Maxine, Maxine, Maxine, how you shy away from human companionship. Do you know I'm moving to Philadelphia to live with my sister Clara? I couldn't take this isolation no more."

"I didn't know."

She followed me inside, holding her skirt in front of her like a tray.

"Maxine, dear, that was a terrifying experience what you had. You having nightmares from it?"

I was at our apartment door. "No."

"I know, I know," she said. "But they'll pass. The important thing is, the baby's safe and sound. You should just stop hovering so much—"

"Who's hovering?"

"Don't worry, your ma told me everything. I told her, 'Fern, it's a blessing in disguise. Now they'll be close like sisters should be. It could change *everything*.'"

"My mother told you I hover over Wendy?"

"Don't worry, it's *normal*. Don't be ashamed you should feel a little warmth, it's nothing to be afraid of."

She patted me on the head with a smile and waddled off to 4C. She was still carrying her cuticles. I knew what she did with them: she put them in her plants. She did the same thing with her hair when she trimmed it. "Life is a precious thing," she told me once when I voiced skepticism over feeding a philodendron with her snipped gray curls. "It shouldn't be squandered."

I felt the same way, which is why, from my earliest years, I kept to myself. Stockpiling my resources. Call it hoarding. All I know is that from the very beginning I practiced the tough-minded stinginess of someone saving up for a future emotional emergency, some great distant crash of feeling.

When it happens, I'll be ready.

THANKSGIVING

Kessler crawls from his murky sleep. The pills he takes for his insomnia leave him groggy, battered, mired in the aftermath of uneasy dreams. Usually the alarm prods him awake, but this morning, light—too much light, at the wrong angle—pries at his lids. He squints against the unreasonable glare. He mutters to his wife, "What time is it?" but Grace doesn't answer. He turns his heavy head to face her: she's not in bed. Kessler growls. Paws at the nightstand for his clock. Reads it. Smashes it into the space where his wife's head had rested. Forty goddamn minutes late. Even if he rushes, he'll never make it to his class on time. Anger serves him like a rescue rope. He grabs on, rises in a fury from the swamp of sheets and quilts, speeds through the bathroom rituals, accosts Grace in the kitchen: "Why in the *hell* didn't you wake me?"

She sits like a mannequin at the table, her stiff back to the doorway from which he bellows. She flinches at his voice, pivots carefully on her chair, speaks to him in a flat voice which has in it the quality of rehearsal: "You snored right through the alarm, Louis. I was about to wake you—I had my hand on your shoulder—" (she fingers her own, as if to

171

demonstrate the authenticity of her touch)—"but I remembered all that yelling you did last night about how I try to make you something you're not—" (she moves up, center stage, to the edge of her seat)—"and I thought, On time or independent, which would he prefer? I decided you'd select tardiness on your own terms to punctuality on mine." (She smiles slightly, in appreciation of her own performance.)

He stares at her. He shakes his head as if he were in the presence of someone with an incurable disease. Grace's hands are trembling and she clenches them still, but otherwise remains motionless. Kessler sweats; a nerve twitches in his puffy cheek. To ease the burning in his stomach, he pours himself some milk, gulps it down, has to restrain himself from throwing the glass against the wall. In the eye of his rage, Grace barely blinks.

Kessler flees, grabs up his briefcase and old tweed overcoat in the front hall, slams out of the house. He wouldn't mind if the Victorian came down behind him in a ruined heap. He runs two red lights on the way to campus, but is still twenty minutes late by the time he arrives at the History Building. Beneath the graceful Gothic arches, the mild professor curses his wife.

Inside, he takes the massive marble steps two at a time, tears down the hallway to the lecture room. As he fears, the effort is futile: the students have flown. Kessler crumbles inside himself. Slinks down the rest of the hall's length. Forages in his pocket for his keys and lets himself into his shadowed office. Bolts the door. Drops into his chair without turning on the light or taking off his coat.

Weeps, silently, into his blotter.

In his youth, Louis Kessler had been an optimist, perhaps an idealist. In graduate school he worked in politics, and became engaged to a young woman who admired his convictions. "Some men only care about money," she said. "*You* have character." He believed that life would confirm his hopes, which, he believed, were reasonable and decent. In 1956 the country failed Adlai Stevenson for the second time. Kessler's dissertation adviser, denied tenure because of his socialist affiliations, threw himself under a bus. Kessler's fiancée ran off with a wealthy Chicago banker. Stunned and bitter, Kessler slunk back into the Middle Ages. He developed a scholar's reputation. He published articles in important history journals, wrote two highly praised books on the period. His students and colleagues found him deep and narrow. He had no apparent interests other than his work. He did not go to faculty parties. He lived in a style that resembled that of the cloistered, celibate, learned monks who peopled the era in which he was steeped.

In 1968 the McCarthy-for-President campaign roused Kessler from his long hibernation. The senator, he believed, had a medievalist's mind. Kessler felt a kinship, small stirrings of an abandoned faith. When he stepped into the grimy storefront headquarters on the fringe of the campus and offered to stuff envelopes for the cause, an age had come to an end in the thirty-four-year history of Louis Kessler. He reentered the modern world, found it noisy, smoky, exploding with a fierce energy he did not quite trust but could no longer deny.

He was greeted by an earnest young girl with troubled skin and a tall, bony body that reminded him of a Giacometti sculpture. The badge on her blouse said, "Hi! I'm Megan, Volunteer Coordinator!" Megan led him past crackling typewriters and ringing phones to the rear of the office. A mound of envelopes and fliers sat like a centerpiece in the middle of a long table, and a half-dozen seated workers folded, stuffed, sealed, and stacked. They chattered with each other like dinner party companions. Kessler felt weak. Megan pulled out a chair for him and spoke to the woman in the adjacent seat: "Would you please orient Mr. Kessler?" The woman smiled reassuringly. Megan disappeared. Kessler, the initiate, sat down nervously. "My name is Grace Jaffee," she said, and held out her small warm hand.

Kessler shook it limply. She continued to smile, as if in perpetual announcement of a good nature. She showed him how to fold, stuff, seal, and stack, and he allowed himself to be instructed in the rudimentary tasks. It could have been demeaning, but her voice had the soothing quality of a gentle instrument. A harp, perhaps. No: smaller, more delicate. A dulcimer. His stomach relaxed a little.

"What do you do, Mr. Kessler?"

"I'm a history professor."

"My goodness," she said, "you ought to be doing position papers."

He reddened. "I'm in the Middle Ages."

She beamed. "I collect antiques. I think one of our country's biggest problems is that we neglect the lessons of the past."

He blushed at her simple wisdom. She suggested they have a cup of coffee together when their work for the evening was finished. Dazed, he assented. It became a custom for the four remaining weeks of the campaign. Kessler talked little in the sandwich shop. Grace bubbled and oozed with stories about her life. She was thirty-six, a widow whose husband had died several years earlier of a rare blood disease. She had a twelve-year-old son named Scott who, she said, "is making a very good adjustment into adolescence." She lived in a Victorian house she'd bought and restored alone. "It was wonderful therapy after Franklin's death. I'm not a person to sit around and brood. Life's too short to feel sorry for yourself." She loved parties. She loved antiques, politics, Bogart movies, northern Italian food. She worked at a family-counseling center. "I started there as a volunteer when Scott went to school. Wound up with a master's degree and a full-time job."

She was a woman of so many balanced enthusiasms. Kessler immersed himself in them, hoping to be transformed into her counterpart. At last he would be rid of the bookish Kessler, the ascetic Kessler, the flesh-fearing Kessler. He had been miserable for so long without realizing it. He bought new clothes. He took up calisthenics. He subscribed to *Esquire*. Senator McCarthy was not nominated, but Kessler's campaign for Grace escalated. He envied her facility as a social being with a passion that imitated lust. It caused her to mistake him for a man of high sexual energy. In January, the day before Richard Nixon's inauguration, Louis Kessler and Grace Jaffee elected each other in the chambers of the Honorable Judge William McCracken.

Someone's knocking. Nose bubbling, red-eyed, Kessler, still coated against the cold, opens his office door. In the frame, Goldilocks.

"I'm sorry to disturb you, Dr. Kessler, I see you're on your way—"

"In," he says. And switches on the light, illuminating his despair.

Goldilocks shines. She's been trying to seduce him for the entire semester. To dazzle him with her undergraduate intelligence. To amuse him with her unseasoned wit. In the last few years, Kessler has developed a reputation for romance, but she hasn't been able to arouse his interest. Now she sees another, wiser strategy. She takes a tissue from her purse and wipes the moisture from his soggy cheeks, now somewhat green in the fluorescent glow. Kessler caves in to her comfort. She grabs him around the waist as if to keep him from falling over; he holds tightly on to her gently sloped shoulders.

"I'm parked right behind the building," she says. "Will you let me fix you a nice little lunch?" She moves her denim thigh against his. Hunger overwhelms him. "Oh, Dr. Kessler," she whispers into his damp, fleshy neck, "just wait until you see what a great cook I am." She giggles. He cringes, his appetite wanes, but still he follows her out of the building to her VW van, her blond hair swinging like a beacon in front of his bleary eyes.

Driving them to her apartment, she questions him gently about his distress. "You know you can confide in me, don't you?" He thinks of Grace and her famous empathy: *Don't tell me I misunderstand you, Louis. I'm a very empathetic person. I'm a family counselor, for God's sake. Do you think an insensitive person could have that kind of job?* He focuses on his student's feet, watches them move efficiently from gas to brake to clutch. He says nothing. She confidently swings the van into a black-topped lot beside a modest brick building. She turns off the ignition. He considers bolting and running, but he doesn't have the energy. He's not even sure what neighborhood they're in; he hasn't been paying attention to the route. She leans across the gear shift and kisses him sloppily on the mouth. Kessler notices that her eyebrows are plucked. Grace does not pluck her eyebrows. He's not sure if this is a significant difference or not, but it helps him separate them in his mind. He's begun, as usual, to think of this girl as a younger version of Grace. Indeed, there are times when all females seem to him heads on the same gorgon's body.

She leads him by the hand into the building and up two flights of steps. Babies yowl. Somewhere a radio blares and the rhythm of the bass sounds like his heart, misplaced in a stranger's apartment, or trapped inside the walls. Perhaps he's come to reclaim it. It seems as good a reason as any for this ludicrous episode. She takes out her key and opens her door. They cross the threshold and she locks the door behind them. The babies fade; the music recedes. The heart, however, continues its palpable thump.

Inside, everything is cheap contemporary. The living room is papered in shimmering foil that both reflects and distorts. Shag carpet, a garish green, seems to grow from the floor. The room is barely furnished: a canvas chair—not a chair, really, more like a sling, two pieces of cloth hung on a chrome frame; a black vinyl couch with no visible seams, as if human hands had not been involved in its construction; beside the couch, a Plexiglas table, nearly invisible so that the lamp on it—a white globe on a slab of wood—appears to float in the air like a mounted moon. He thinks of Grace's beautiful antiques. He thinks of Anselm, Bacon, Becket, and Chaucer. He thinks: *The past means nothing to me anymore.* Goldilocks takes off her clothes. He follows her into the bedroom: on the floor, a mattress covered with a batik-patterned spread. He hangs his overcoat on the door, sits down dejectedly on the edge of the bed. She undresses him; he feels like a wounded soldier being stripped, gently, by an attending medic. For half an hour, she administers treatment, but he can't summon enough spirit to respond. Thump, thump, thump: how it mocks him, that disembodied heart.

"It's not your fault," Kessler says finally.

"You're damn right it's not," she says. She sticks her chin on her knees and pouts.

He begins to dress. He can hardly breathe and starts to cough. It arouses her pity. She leaps from the bed, brings him a glass of water. Her eyes are bright with tears.

"I didn't mean to insult you," she says. "I love you, I really do."

She cries openly. He can see that she's honestly remorseful, and it touches him.

"I should never have come here," he says, buttoning his shirt. "You need a nice young man."

"Where have you been?" she says. "Most of the nice ones are celibate, impotent, or gay."

He laughs out loud. "How medieval."

She puts her arms around his neck. He tries to untangle himself. She says, "Listen, give me one more chance. I have an idea."

"I'm tired," he says. "I'm exhausted."

She lets go. "I'll drive you back to campus. You've got a two-o'clock class."

"I'd rather you didn't."

"I'll feel like a prostitute if you just walk out of here."

Kessler is not sure what his mode of departure has to do with her moral fiber, but he consents. He waits in the living room while she dresses.

She winds the van through the neighborhood he hadn't noticed on the drive to her place. A scrubbed, tidy, humble neighborhood. Kessler locates it in the historical matrix: working-class Lithuanian. Perhaps Hungarian. He'll be more certain once they pass stores, or a church. It's suddenly important to him that he know precisely where he is. Without asking *her*. He does not want to ask *her* for anything ever again. She turns onto a commercial block and he reads the names on the little shops: Grabowski's Bakery, Kosinski's Meats and Poultry, Stefanski's Variety Store. The best he can do is Eastern European; it will have to suffice. She continues to chatter; he scoops up her words listlessly, like stale peanuts.

At a red light, the small squat stores give way to a sprawling supermarket set back from the street in order to accommodate a parking lot for customers. In the pale November sun, icicles drip from the huge letters perched on the market's roof—VALUE FAIR. Banks of old snow puddle in the lot, and Kessler watches neighborhood women maneuver through the slush. The light flashes green. Without warning, Goldilocks right-angles into "Entrance," splashes a lady who screams a foreign epithet at them, and pulls into a space in the far south corner of the lot.

"You need something?" Kessler asks, wondering why she's picked such a remote spot to park.

"No," she says, "you do."

And then, before he can refute her, she springs out of her seat, crouches on the floor between his spattered shoes, wedges apart his knees with her gently sloped shoulders, and reaches for his belt buckle with her fragile fingers.

Kessler freezes. "Are you *crazy?*" he whispers, as if strangers might hear.

"Like a fox," she says huskily, and he knows it's cliché, he knows this is all terrible cliché, but nevertheless, there, at noon, in the pale November sun, in the slushy supermarket parking lot of an Eastern European working-class neighborhood, in the easy sight of good, simple, plain-faced women buying food for their families, the professor's own hunger builds and explodes.

Afterward, with some relief, he sees that the van's windows have been steamed over by their breath. She raises her flushed face and smiles at him. "Now you don't have to feel like a failure."

"My dear," he says, unable to look at her, "thanks to you I now see what a resounding success my life has become."

"I hope you're not being sarcastic." She climbs over his left leg and into the driver's seat.

"Sarcasm is a defense against pain. My wife told me that. My wife works in a family-counseling center, and she knows a great deal about pain and its defenses. She also collects antiques. I believe I am her only pre-Renaissance piece."

Goldilocks guns the engine. "You sound drunk."

"Self-pity," he says, "often has the same effect as alcohol."

For the last five minutes of their ride together, they do not exchange another word. As he gets out of the van, she looks straight ahead, pretends to a kind of detached, sullen anger, but he sees a tear roll like a jewel down her cheek. He feels the urge to touch her gleaming yellow hair in a gesture of reconciliation, but he restrains himself. She would mistake it for affection, and he does not intend that much. He shuffles across the campus in a daze, realizes he's had nothing to eat since his morning glass of milk, buys himself an egg-salad sandwich and a cup of cocoa in the room of food machines in the basement of the History Building. He eats his lunch alone in his office. Reads over his notes for his two-o'clock class. Delivers his lecture in the weak voice of someone coming down with the flu, or not fully recovered from a long, distressing siege.

Outwardly unmoved by her husband's morning fury, Grace runs her shaking fingers over the round oak kitchen table as if she were searching its surface for bullet holes. She bought it at an auction, stripped it back to its natural luster, sealed it with three coats of polyurethane finish (matte). Why can't she do the same restoration job on herself? She rests her cheek against the grain, remembers the work she did on this house a dozen years ago. Franklin's death left her stiff and aching; his loss seemed located in her bones, as if he'd kept her supple, been responsible for her pliancy in a way she hadn't understood during his life. For a month it was an effort to walk. She brooded—not about the pain, she'd known immediately that it was psychosomatic—but about her submission to suffering. When she heard about the house—"that old Victorian wreck on Lamberton Road, the one they rented out to students for years"—she went straight to the realtor, made a bid, used Franklin's insurance money for a down payment, and moved in five weeks later. Scott said, "We could go for days without even bumping into one another." For a few hours, he sulked. Other than that, he didn't seem to mind the change. Hadn't Grace and Franklin raised him to be resilient?

She lifts her face from the wood's impenetrable perfection. Above her head, antique copper pots dangle like religious artifacts from the iron hooks with which she spiked the ceiling beam. In this room, faith shrivels. Grace shudders. Abandons the kitchen, finds the front hall, leans on the carved mahogany banister, takes some comfort from its gleam, its graceful curves. She loves this house. After she and Scott moved in, she spent a year's spare time scraping off faded flowered wallpaper, taking up worn carpeting, stripping the floors and paint-layered woodwork, opening up sealed fireplaces. "I'll bring it back to its real self," she vowed, working evenings and weekends as if engaged in the excavation of an important ruin. Friends came and complimented her progress. The first time Louis saw the house, he toured it with awe. When they married and he moved in, he remained respectful. Gradually he grew disinterested in it, although she continued to lavish care on its spacious rooms. Last night Louis said, "I have had it with this fucking house."

Maintaining control, Grace said, "I love this house, Louis."

"What in the hell do two people need with an eleven-room, one-hundred-and-two-year-old museum? Can you explain that to me, Grace?"

Expired passion. As if his own wiring, faulty now for years, had finally fizzled. His complaints filled up the bedroom like puffs of acrid smoke. Her eyes reddened, burned. As they burn now.

Carefully, as if there were danger in the act, Grace mounts the steps. Pauses on the landing to wipe the dust with her bathrobe sleeve from the marble-topped table in the alcove. In their bedroom, she picks up the alarm clock and places it back on her nightstand. Stands very still for a moment, as if waiting for winds to die down. Then stretches the bed linens taut, pulls up the blankets, unfolds the heirloom spread and brings it up over the plumped pillows. Through the sheer white curtains, the November sun slashes across the solid brass headboard.

She drives the three miles to the Lighthouse Family-Counseling Center, and the scene shifts from stately residential to motley commercial strip. The Lighthouse occupies a portion of the second floor of the Westwood Medical Building. Grace parks with a sense of relieved accomplishment. Lately she finds it difficult to contend with the complex maze of signals that driving has come to entail. Or perhaps it was always this complicated, and once she was simply more able to navigate through the confusion.

She opens the car door, steps into a puddle, spatters the back of her stockings. Sullied. Panic rises, rests like a small stone under her heart. "Deep breathing," she instructs herself in the elevator and the relaxation exercise she teaches her clients forces the pebble, at least temporarily, from its lodging place.

In the waiting room, the receptionist is hanging up a new display of client artwork. Phoebe is a plump, gregarious, pleasant-faced woman who finds her front-desk job the first meaningful work she's done in fifteen years. She's been at the Lighthouse for seven months and is constantly thinking up new ways to incorporate herself into the therapeutic aspects of the center. The art display is her idea, though the counselors have to admit it's a good one.

"Pass me a push-pin," Phoebe says, balancing on the arm of a chair she's using as a step-stool.

Grace hands Phoebe a pin from the box by her foot.

"It never ceases to amaze me," Phoebe says, "what wonderful things *these people* can create." She says *these people* in a tone of simultaneous pity and terror (though she's undoubtedly unfamiliar with Aristotle's definition of tragedy). Grace scans the wall, focuses on a small acrylic; triangles of different sizes and colors fill the canvas, collide with each other in a random, unbalanced pattern. Fear flutters in Grace's throat. She thinks, *I could have painted that one myself.*

In her office, she calls Kent Harris at the furniture factory where he works as an upholsterer. He does extra jobs of his own on the side. Grace found his ad in the paper nine months ago when she needed professional help with an overstuffed chair. She knelt beside him in the sanctity of her own living room, marveled at the expertise of his hands as they treated the chair's innards. When he finished, she made them tea and asked him all the questions she could summon about furniture. Now she tells the skeptical switchboard operator, "*Yes*, this is an emergency. This is *definitely* an emergency."

"Je-sus!" Kent says when he hears Grace's voice. "Did Mitzi do something? Huh?"

Mitzi is Kent's wife; after years of withstanding dozens of his adulteries, she's threatened to kill the next mistress she identifies.

"Yes," Grace answers, "she married you fourteen years ago."

"You called me up at work to remind me how long I been married?"

"We need to talk, Kent. I've been having nightmares—"

"Grace! I'm at work!"

"When you get off." He works a seven-to-three shift.

Kent sighs. "You know I hate to talk, Grace."

"It's important. Verbal communication is—"

"Listen, you need it, we'll do it. Meet me like usual at the Pines."

She hangs up. Like a wheel-chaired patient, injured and

weak, she swivels from desk to window, looks down on the cars coursing through the glinting slush. Such a purposeful procession, an irrefutable sense of destination. How, she wonders, has she arrived at a point in her life where the only solutions seem to be in form of retreats, refusals, abandonments, and negations?

"Deep breathing," she demands of herself. Shakes off sadness, at least temporarily, like an animal coming in from the rain. Rolls back to her desk and opens her calendar to check the day's schedule. She buzzes Phoebe, says, "Send in Mrs. Cravens," and the troubled woman enters, seeking Grace's solace.

Outside the city limits, a half-dozen housekeeping cabins lie along a stretch of road neither urban nor rural. Scraggly pines screen the cottages from the road, and behind the structures the thick woods of a hunting preserve offer their own dark primitive privacy. For the nine months that Grace has been coming here on irregular late afternoons (sometimes weeks go by without meetings with Kent), she's found the place alternately sordid and beautiful. When both responses collide in her head like two planes gone wildly off-course, she trembles over the wreckage for days. But this afternoon, pulling her car in beside Kent's in front of cabin 3, she perceives the setting as merely undistinguished, drab, hardly worthy of wild flights of feeling, high drama or low. Simply dull. Yes. She knocks timidly, as if a more forceful fist might disturb this crucial neutrality.

Kent greets her with his fierce hug. She stiffens. He pokes at her ribs as if she were a piece of fruit he was testing for ripeness, or rot.

"What's the matter?" he cajoles. "You forget who this is? I'm the one who makes you feel *better*, remember?"

She does remember. She stares at the bed they've shared for scores of therapeutic hours, and it's as if she's looking at a prop in a long-running play in which she, Grace Jaffee Kessler, assumes the female lead.

He strokes her head with one hand, soothes the ribs he'd jabbed with the other. In her ear he's making little noises, coos or gurgles, hard to tell, hard to know if he's playing infant or parent. Such differentiations require a distance which she cannot seem to maintain, here, in his hug, in the midst of his hand's motions, in the enveloping rhythm of his voice, in this dingy theater where, now, knowing her part as well as she does, she finds herself playing it out again, with rising conviction, on top of the faded chenille spread.

Afterward, still pinned beneath his weight, she reads him her new lines: "Kent, this is the last time. It's become destructive, very destructive."

He rolls over. "I figured that. I knew it was coming."

"I didn't mean to hurt you," she says. "I'm just not able to handle—"

He props himself up on his elbow, looks at her face with an intense curiosity he's never evidenced before. "Tell me one thing, Grace."

"If I can."

"Is it because you're tired of me, or because you're afraid of Mitzi? I mean, is it me or the situation?"

"The situation, Kent, but—"

He grins. "Just so long as it isn't me. I've always been —*admired*, y'know? That way, I mean. Y'know?"

She does. She watches the shy pride color his face, and it reminds her of Scott, years ago. She dresses quickly, finishes before he's even got his trousers on, stands mutely at the door. He knows this scene much better than she, allows her a fast, friendly exit, sends her out on one of his harmless puns. Not until she's halfway home does she need to pull off the road. Grief, that old dormant ache, stirs again in her bones. The situation *was* terrible, but Grace, without script, mourns the man.

At the end of his two-o'clock class, Kessler forces himself to the library, tries to immerse himself in the monastic silence of the microfilm reading room. After twenty minutes, he gives up. He needs darkness, the covers pulled up over his head. In his rearview mirror, the campus recedes, then vanishes. As he approaches the house, he's struck by its sheer size, its intricate architecture: Could he possibly live here? Is there any way to imagine that he belongs behind this ornate façade? He opens the door gingerly, with a cat burglar's finesse. Familiarity falls over him like a net. With resignation, he takes off his coat, picks up the mail at his feet, shuffles through it in the hall. Several bills, the *Journal of Medieval Studies* (a special issue devoted to the Norman Conquest), an invitation to a dinner dance sponsored by the Suicide Prevention League, and a letter from Scott, who's been living for a year in a Berkeley collective. "Dear Mater and Step-Pater," the note reads, "I've decided to bless you with my presence during, as they say, the Holiday Season. Expect me by Thanksgiving, depending on my thumb's luck and the kindness of strangers." He signs it, "Your son, Oedipus." Kessler tries to smile, but it's too much work. He sighs, puts the note and the rest of the mail on the kitchen table, climbs the stairs, undoes the bed and succumbs, with shameless desire, to sleep.

Grace inches the nose of her Chevrolet up to the rear of Louis's. Their bumpers touch. Like dumb elephants linked together for the umpteenth parade, they wait in the raw dusk. Grace goes inside.

The sound of his snoring rattles down the steps onto the slate floor. She tiptoes upstairs, watches his shrouded bulk rise and fall, rise and fall. He holds the pillow the way he once held her. For a moment she wants to intrude herself into his arms, but she would first have to displace the pillow from the ferocity of his grip, and it no longer seems possible. She can't compete with his dreams, with the formless perfection of down, with the perfect soft smoothness of the pillowslip. *I am going to take a shower*, her mind tells his, as if he could hear anything she said to him, deep as he is in the ecstasy of oblivious repose.

In the shower, she scrubs and scrubs. Kent's fingers mark her flesh with invisible prints. Louis's weary pain sticks to her like a fungus. She lets the water beat on her long after the last trace of soap is sucked down the drain. Finally, the water turns cold. Grace refuses that extra dose of punishment. She climbs out, dries, robes herself, and pads down to the kitchen. In spite of everything, she still believes in nourishment.

On the table, Scott's scrawl: a hieroglyph, a Rorschach, a code buried in her cells. "Dear Mater and Step-Pater . . ." Grace holds the paper to her heart. What she feels defies analysis. She sculpts four perfect hamburgers, fries potatoes golden, and flutes the radishes before she puts them in the salad. Nothing compared to the feast she'll make for Thanksgiving. Blessings will rise like biscuits, warm•and filling.

When Kessler descends, she's humming.

He says, "Grace."

She nods affirmatively, sure, at least temporarily, of who she is.

During dinner, civility holds the air. As if one of them had sprayed purification out of an aerosol can. The morning's bad smell fades, gives way to a subtle fragrance of humility.

"I think it will be good for us to have him here," Grace says, dunking a french fry in catsup. "I think we were so . . . taken aback . . . when he left. We couldn't, I don't know, *incorporate* it." Traces of catsup ring her mouth. "What do you think, Louis?"

He lifts his eyes from his plate. "You've got catsup on your mouth," he says, as if to a child. "You look like somebody hit you."

She dabs at the stain with her napkin. "There," she says. "Now nobody will know."

He gives her a grimace that borders on a smile. It's the best he can do. She accepts the offering graciously, puts another hamburger on his plate.

"I think I'll make ambrosia," Grace says. "It's not traditional but he always loved ambrosia."

Kessler pushes back from the table. She's building up into an excitement, he can see it already, a high pitch, an evangelic fervor which will rise in intensity until Scott arrives. She'll get angry at Kessler for not sharing in the fun, not helping her plan. She'll probably even accuse him of not wanting her son to come home at all.

"I think I'll catch the news," he says.

Grace seems not to hear him, takes down her *New York Times Cook Book* from the top of the refrigerator. "Sweet potato soufflé," she reads, begins to chant aloud the ingredients. Kessler, the heretic, retreats from the sanctuary, flicks on the television in the den and makes himself, once again, dour witness to the unending disasters of the species.

ORDINARY
MYSTERIES

L ast night I had a seizure of some sort. Perhaps a stroke.
They won't put a name on it. I called it a power failure
and the doctor smiled appreciatively at my metaphor, but still
refused to give me the reality behind the image. I can't move:
a weakness as heavy as a boulder is sitting on me, it is the
most powerful weakness I have ever confronted in my
sixty-two years. This morning an orderly lifted me off of my
bed, put me on a stretcher, and strapped me down.

"Why . . . the . . . straps?" I asked him, each word a
painful excavation.

"So you don't fall off."

"I can't move."

He seemed not to hear and I remain unnecessarily pin-
ioned by these belts. Will people think I'm down from the
psychiatric ward, these straps protecting me from myself?
Will they surmise a mad destructive energy around which
these restraints are wrapped? I will have to live with the
misconception. I could dredge up speech and tell them I'm
sane, but that is the most common contention of the
disturbed and no one would believe me. I can see it is just the

beginning of a long series of capitulations which I will be forced to make in this place.

I'm waiting to be X-rayed. I have been here for what seems to be an hour, but I can't be sure. The clock is just out of my line of vision, I have pushed my eyes to the limit and they can't reach, they fall just short of the mark. Well. What would I do with the time if I had it? Still: a day makes more sense when it's organized into hours and minutes. It's the difference between living in a cave and in a house properly divided into rooms. You have to feel some control over the space you occupy, you have to be able to put up walls and close doors. Time's the same: it needs the partitions of schedules, calendars, seasons, clocks. If only the orderly had placed me just a bit to the left, I'd know how long I've been waiting. As it is, I can't be sure. Another relinquishment.

They have me hooked up to an intravenous contraption. I can see the glucose—I assume it's glucose, though they haven't told me. As if I have no need to know what's nourishing me. At home I have a large vegetable garden and nearly a dozen fruit trees. I can watch my sustenance move from seed to flower to table, so food's my friend, I *know* it. I'm the only vegetarian in the family. When Matt was alive he scorned my eating habits and made me cook him meat. Ellen moved away from my diet as she grew older. Like a great threshing machine, the world separated her from the habits of her childhood and she finally leveled the inevitable crushing insult: "Mother, you're old-fashioned." "Ellen," I told her, "I have never attended to the fashions of any particular age." Now my meatlessness is chic and she is reconsidering. I miss my girl. For years I've been hungry for the hours we used to spend turning the soil, raking it smooth, planting the seeds, waiting for the first frail sprouts. I've kept on with it myself. But since Ellen left, the spring has holes in it, gaps into which I stumble and from which I find it difficult at times to extricate myself. I do, of course, and later I send her a carton filled with cans of stewed tomatoes, jars of cherry preserves and garlic pickles—things she likes and shares with her New York friends. What will she think when she sees me lying here in this void of time and motion, my garden consumed by weeds, fruit falling to the ground? "It's that place," she'll say. "Mother, I've been telling you for years it's too much for you, you're too old." Too old to eat, Ellen? Perhaps. The glucose feeds me now, drop by drop into my stricken arm.

Beside me a wall of pale-green tiles rises like an algaed sea. When I was a child we lived near the ocean: I know water as well as earth. My memory dives now into the tiles and I can nearly taste their salt. If I could get my hand to the wall, I think it would give way to waves. . . . Oh lord, the lady's about to drown in hallucination! That I will not abide: one thing I've always been is a realist and I won't give in now to the rolling away of truth. It's a wall beside me, nothing else, hard and unyielding to my stymied touch. Ellen takes drugs—she told me this, flung the words at me like arrows: "I've heard colors, seen music, I've held the air in my hands and learned its shape." Why aren't the ordinary mysteries enough for her anymore? I've built my life on their strength, but they can't hold her for an instant. If I could get my hand to this wall, that would be miracle enough for me.

I must look nearly dead, an inert bundle of flesh and bones, a tethered corpse if not for these restless eyes. Two other people, a young man and a young woman, are waiting to be X-rayed and I can tell from the way they try not to see me that I frighten them. When I was a girl and had my appendix out, I was put in a room with a dying child. Day by day I watched her fade and shrivel, and when I left she dangled by shallow breaths the way I hang now by threads of sight. If a nurse came and covered my eyes, would I still be alive? Or just a collection of thoughts whirling around in the darkness? If only I could touch the tiles. . . .

The young man is a patient here; he's dressed in a hospital gown and his leg is in a cast. The girl's in street clothes and she holds a limp injured hand on her lap. To keep from seeing me, the two of them focus on each other with embarrassing frequency, and I can feel the sweet tension pass between them, signals traveling back and forth on delicate wires. Their soundless exchange takes me straight back to Matt, finding him on a streetcar thirty-two years ago. My mother insisted from the start that he was coarse, but I ignored the indictment. From the beginning, he made my bones bend, my muscles turn to feather; if he was a hard man, his hardness softened me, lightened me. Right now I think his touch

188

would lift this weight from my body and I'd rise healed and nimble from this stretcher. Not long ago, Ellen told me, "Daddy was a male chauvinist if I ever saw one." I told her that love had little to do with ideology. What do these two waiting to be X-rayed know of each other's ideas? Not a thing. Aren't they filling up each other's lonely spaces just the same?

"Keep politics out of the bedroom, Ellen," I told her, but she smirked at my warning.

"For God's sake, Mother, he made you cook him steak when the smell of it nearly nauseated you. Is that love?"

"It was love that made me cook it."

"Sounds like oppression to me."

Later I wrote her in a letter: "Regarding that discussion we had about your father and me. We were very different, sometimes he lost patience with what he felt were my strange notions, sometimes I flinched at his ways. But he understood that I wouldn't change, and I never tried to alter him. In that way we were the same. Maybe we should have negotiated one of those contracts so popular today; maybe there would have been more fairness in how things were done, fewer arguments and less confusion. I don't suppose it was easy on you, his flare-ups and my tears. But how to convince you of the *feeling* between us? What if *that* had been leveled out, along with the conflicts? I wouldn't have risked it." She never responded, which tells me I got through to her. Nothing, after all, is more modern than passion.

What would they think, those two across the room, how would it strike them to realize that this sick immobile old woman is at this moment racked with the yearnings of youth? I think it would disgust them: they like to think that lust is their private province, that wrinkled skin doesn't burn, that withered loins don't ache. I know: I felt the same way when I was young. Matt grew bald and weathered, I turned gray and my skin sagged: still we crawled like newborns into the curves of each other's arms. This arm struggling now for the wall cradled his head on his last living night, stroked his cheek until it turned cold. To the end, he had my touch. I could use his now. . . .

A nurse comes to check my intravenous solution, her eyes fall to my face and she flashes me pity. Wiping my tears, she consoles me: "Now, now, dear, no need for crying. You're going to be just fine."

I ask her, "What . . . time . . . is it?" All my energy poured into a whisper.

"Oh, it's early," she says and rustles away before I can pin her down.

The young man has heard my question: I see his eyes dart to the clock and I watch him struggling with his fear of me. "Ten-thirty," he blurts out, eyes barely grazing mine.

I drag a "Thank you" out from under this rock on my chest, but I'm not sure my words reach his ears. Nevertheless, we're bound for a moment in friendly conspiracy: oh, it feels wonderful to move in tandem with another heart—since last night I've been feeling so . . . *separate*. Not that I'm unused to being alone. With Matt dead and Ellen away, it's been seven years of solitary waking, eating, gardening, cleaning, reading, sitting, sleeping. Still I could throw out lines when I felt myself floundering—letters to Ellen, a warm pie for a neighbor, a trip to town to stock up on goods and conversation. And naturally—with no shame!—I've talked to myself, it's got nothing to do with senility, it's the natural inclination toward community that permits—encourages—my selves to converse. So I have managed to cope with the lone place setting, the one toothbrush, the single stick of butter, the empty side of the bed. But since last night's attack, I've been so enclosed, walled off—as if the last seven years had returned in a sweep of vengeance at my having held my ground for so much lonely time. . . .

The link between me and that boy lasts a mere sliver of time: already his aversion to me has pulled him away, he won't speak to me again, he won't look unless forced. I don't hold it against him. I'm just grateful for that tiny revolution, his joining with me in our small assault on the treachery of the stupid. *It is ten-thirty!* I would like to hoist a flag on my recaptured territory.

The nurse is coming at me again, she sees me smiling and thinks it's for her. "Now that's better, dear," she says, as if I were a child emerging from a sulk. "You'll be going in for your pictures very soon." Then the young man is wheeled away, through the doors marked X-Ray. Pictures, indeed. What an exhibit they'll have from the three of us: my eroded brain, his splintered leg, the girl's smashed hand. Studies in pain strung across the luminous gallery wall, white-clad interns debating the aesthetics of our anguished bodies. Ellen lives with a painter whose canvases are of nothing but corpses: dead bodies arranged in all the positions of life, dead babies suckling dead mothers, dead lovers locked in permanent cold embrace, dead dancers frozen in stiff arabesques. Why, I asked her, did he spend his gift on such despair, when there was so much life to celebrate? I know a little about art. I can look for hours at Cézanne and Gauguin, their colors pulsate, sing, explode. Even Rembrandt's dark solemnity exists within the warmest light.

"He doesn't believe in romanticizing things, Mother," she tells me, as if the sun did not rise, as if renewal were not proven each year in my garden, as if Matt and I had never gloried in the way the moon lit up our bodies if we left the shades undrawn and the curtains open to the night sky. . . .

"Are you . . . all right?"

The young woman has risen from her chair and crossed half the space between us. She leans toward me with the tentative, nervous concern of a reluctant witness. My eyes must have closed for a moment, she must have thought me dead. Now I give her tears and the best testimony I can summon: my hand, for an instant, makes it to the hard, unalterable green-tiled wall, its reality stamped forever across my living crippled fingers.

Ellen is in my room when I return from X-Ray. She trembles when she sees me, the cigarette falls from her hand and her eyes, wide and unblinking, are two brown marbles lodged in her drained face. She plucks the cigarette from the floor and grinds it out in the ashtray that rests on a small table beneath the room's only window. As the orderly unbinds and redeposits me on my bed, Ellen gropes her way out of her shock.

"Mother," she says softly, as if just recognizing me. "Oh Mother." She sinks to a chair beside me.

I manage a quick grin and a very weak "Don't . . . worry." Then, like an infant, I fall away from her into the sleep beneath dreaming. When I open my eyes—how much later I have no idea—she is still sitting beside me, wrapped up in her own arms. As if she has been kidnapped, this illness of mine has ripped her out of her world and tied her to my sudden helplessness. And what is the ransom, what is the ransom? When my own mother was struck down with cancer, I prayed for her death and encased my prayers in the rhetoric of mercy; but I knew it was my own deliverance as much as hers that I sought, and when she slipped away, I was as dizzied by release as by grief.

Days pass. I get no better and no worse. I am still unable to move, except for an occasional spurt of strength in a limb, or an overall twitching sensation that rushes through me and out of me like an electrical current. Each time it happens, Ellen—who sits with me from morning until night, reading magazines, writing letters to her abandoned painter, smoking a forest of cigarettes—rises in hopeful alarm to summon a nurse. By the time the nurse arrives, I am once again pinned down completely and she records my fleeting movements with noticeable routine disinterest. The doctor comes each morning and Ellen recites like a litany the signs of life from the previous day. "She was able to lift her leg . . . she reached toward the phone when it rang . . . for a second, she looked like she was going to sit up." He nods (it is all written down on the chart he has read) and lets her speak, but I can read his face and it is no poem.

Today I tell her, in this shadowy rasp I have come to recognize as my own voice, "Go . . . back to . . . New York."

"I can't leave you like this."

Years I spent planting in her seeds of love and obligation, now come to this sad harvest . . .

Neighbors appear for brief, awkward visits. They feed me small doses of gossip, placebos of encouragement. Good honest people reduced to these hollow prescriptions. Oh, the quackery of well-intentioned pity. I hate to see them shamed by their truthless cheer. Mr. Benjamin, from whom I've bought gardening supplies for nearly twenty years, has come twice, and his refusal to humor me is a great relief.

"I can't believe it's you lying there so helpless." He sits quietly awhile, then says, "You look terrible."

When he leaves, Ellen tries to apologize for him. "He didn't mean it, Mother, he's just so upset, he . . ."

Ellen, I want to tell her, he's in the gardening business: he knows blight when he sees it. I remember how he and I lamented the Dutch elm disease that took three of my trees and more of his. We loved those trees, but which of us would have thought to suggest that they weren't drastically ill? Matt cut them down to stumps, and we shared the firewood with the Crawford sisters down the road and Matt's Aunt Rose in town. If this sickness ends in my death, I wish my body could be put to some similar good use. But these occasional quivers, these flashes of energy, this still-speeding mind. I'm not yet a ravaged elm. . . .

For two weeks, they've poked and prodded this body of mine. Pushed down tubes and pulled up fluid, siphoned off blood, eavesdropped on the most private murmurings of my heart and brain. One improvement: I am off the intravenous, taking soup and pureed fruits from a spoon, fed by Ellen as if I were her baby, she who's taken a vow to remain childless. Between these feedings, a therapist comes to massage the powerless arms and legs, to keep them supple in case my brain manages to reach them again, is able to dig them out from under this enormous weight. The rest of the time I sleep, or lie silent in thought. It is as if I have left the world of society and cloistered myself in a convent, my life pared down to the simplest regimen, contemplation my most important activity. I am trying to see it that way—this illness a long-delayed retreat into my soul—but I must admit to a deep restlessness, a growing sense of imprisonment. What I want is to work in my garden again, to attend to my kitchen, to get dressed up and drive into town, drink up camaraderie like a man on a binge, lie in my own bed with an imagined Matt, cradle the deserted pillow, fall away into love's remembered urgent rhythm. . . .

"Mother," Ellen tells me, "the doctor says it's time to think about a nursing home. Or hiring a companion to live with you." She keeps her watery brown eyes fixed on the floor. "I'll sell the house. I can find you a nice apartment in town. . . ."

Reason tells me I ought to agree, but reason, after all, is just a shadow of life's form: I've always been after the *substance* of things. Did I just hear my feeble voice lift up to an irrefutable, roaring, glass-shattering "NO!"? Or did I only imagine it? Ellen's face is an unanswering stone, pale as smoke.

RELICS

I ra used to say I had no sense for what was of real value in life, and I would acknowledge that he was no treasure. For thirteen years we bartered with the primitive currency of insult. Finally the economy collapsed. Realtors and prospective buyers, huddling together in remote corners of our house, whispered, "Divorce. Desperate. Bid low." We hung price tags on most of the goods we'd accumulated, and strangers carted them off. A small civilization, dismantled in a day. There I stood, in the middle of my bankrupt life, making change for the pillagers.

In the rubble of pain, I discovered a new archaeology. I conduct my expeditions on weekends. Estate sales, apartment sales, house sales, garage sales, porch sales, yard sales: the nomenclature depends on season and terrain. I carry very little cash with me; it's not bargains I'm after. Think of me as a student of artifacts. This morning, Saturday, I'm driving deep into the heart of suburban Chicago, less than a mile from our old address. This has always been good territory for digs.

"Hey, Mom," Petey says from the backseat, "didn't we used to live around here?"

It's been more than a year since the boys and I moved to the city, to a low-rent rowhouse in a neighborhood not yet slummy enough to attract the wealthy renovators. Petey and Josh have learned to curse in Spanish. They have found their fists. They've shed their former habits with the ease of birds dropping their feathers at molting time.

Ira moved to Carmel. "My new life-style is so humanistic," he writes. "God, how I've grown."

I, myself, have put on a few pounds.

There: 27 Valley View Drive. A contemporary house, redwood and glass at severe odd angles. A metal sculpture looms in the yard. My boys, those Philistines, race from the car and begin to climb the twisted, weathered form. I walk alone up the bricked path to the front door. It's ajar. "Hello," I say into the house. No answer. I go inside.

I pass through a slate-floored foyer into the living room. All teak and leather. The odors of saddle soap and linseed oil hold the air. The ad in the paper reads "Everything Must Go," but I see no signs of an imminent move. The walls are a gallery for abstract oils and small matted lithographs. Hanging in the windows, a floating forest of plants. Books and pottery fill the shelves that rise to the ceiling on one whole side of the room. No cartons anywhere. Beside a free-standing red metal fireplace, sitting on an Eames chair with his feet up on the hassock, a man. Polished, yet scruffy. Rumpled chic. He's reading *Ragtime* in hardback. I record all of this with my photographic eye. He looks up and smiles engagingly. Before I can speak, he begins to read aloud from the syncopated prose. He keeps time with his foot. When he finishes a page, he says, "Brilliant, isn't that brilliant?"

I say, "I think I'm in the wrong house."

"No, you're not."

I edge my way backward toward the front hall.

He leaps up. "Believe me, this is the right place! You're here for the sale, aren't you?"

I nod yes.

"You're my first customer. It's early. Everything's for sale, everything."

I look around skeptically. "There aren't any tags on anything. Nothing's set up. For a sale, I mean."

"I don't want it to look like a *store*," he says. "I want it all seen and examined in its natural state. The prices are . . . negotiable. I wanted the economic aspect . . . muted. Played down."

He's nervous, perspiring under the arms. I can see that he lacks confidence in his business acumen. In a rush of empathy, I tell him, "That's a very good approach. Very —humanistic."

He grins like a boy. "You think so?"

"Yes, I do."

"Well, just look around," he says, and I begin with the books, but he rubs his chin, grows serious, contemplative. "I think it would be better if I showed you things. I won't high-pressure you, but there's a lot that needs explanation. Background."

"I hadn't intended on staying that long," I say. "My children are waiting out front."

He gestures magnanimously. "Bring them in! Bring them in! Fantastic playroom in the basement, they'll love it down there. Jungle motif. My boys were always in that playroom."

"Are they grown?"

"No." He looks at his shoes. 'They just don't live with me anymore."

A chilling silence encloses us both. Is this how Ira feels when his California friends ask him questions about his sons? Does he shiver there on his radiant beach? I bring my children inside. I tell them about the playroom and they dash downstairs. Their voices rise like music through the quiet rooms.

"Let's start in the kitchen," the man says, and I follow him, this eager guide, across the buffed oak floors.

He opens up the pecan cupboards and exposes dishes, groceries, gourmet cookware. Everything glistens with high-toned taste.

"My wife," he says, "was an expert cook. A superb hostess."

He points to a Plexiglas shelf of cookbooks mounted on the wall beside the double-door bronze refrigerator.

"She was particularly good with French and Chinese. Mandarin was her specialty."

"I prefer Szechuan," I say.

His mouth gapes. "I do too! That was the one kind she never tried. Too hot, she said. But I like it, I order it out whenever I have a chance."

"How much do you want for the wok?"

"One Szechuan dinner."

We both smile, but sign no contract. The doorbell rings. He sighs wistfully, and goes to answer it. I, too, am somewhat disappointed. I was beginning to enjoy the banter. Archaic perhaps, but I have a certain nostalgia, a sentimental fondness, for the antiquated hieroglyphs of flirtation. Oh, I know: Ira and I began with just this sort of joking, but the edges grew hard, the tenderness calcified, we honed our one-liners down to arrowheads. Nights, they pierce me again and again, those verbal knives we flung at one another, those fossils lodged in my dreams. Still: when the man comes back to the kitchen and announces he's sent the customers away and put a sign on the front door canceling the sale so that he may give me his undivided attention, I am only mildly alarmed. What should I fear from a man who's essentially extinct? There's no risk in a relic.

"Where *are* your boys?" I ask him.

He fills the tea kettle with water. "They live with their mother on a commune in New Mexico. They eat a great deal of raw vegetables and drink goat's milk."

I nod gravely.

He opens the refrigerator and takes out a pitcher of red juice, holds it up like a trophy. "Hawaiian Punch. I still keep it around. For the neighbors' kids." He fills two paper cups and bellows for Petey and Josh. He sets out a package of cookies, and makes two cups of tea. The four of us sit at the butcher-block table, on chairs that look like oyster shells. The kids go on and on about the great toys and the trapeze and the thatch-roofed playhouse and the wallpaper that looks like real jungle animals. The man and I smile benevolently at their dear chatter. Please take a picture of this tableau. I'll send it to Ira; it will help him remember his ancient history.

When the children go back downstairs, the man leans across the table and puts his face so close to mine, his breath warms my cheek. I feel dizzy. "Everything's yours for the asking," he says, "including the food in the fridge, and if you take the whole kitchen, I'll give you a special price."

"Just the wok," I tell him evenly, pulling back, regaining my equilibrium.

For a moment, he looks like the old man he has not yet become. "Let's try the dining room," he says, and leads me through the swinging louvered doors. I move into an environment of absolute neutrality. The bare teak table stands with its eight matching chairs on a flokati rug, its strands curling like bleached grass around the legs of the furniture. Against one of the chalky walls, a long buffet of the same natural wood rests like the petrified trunk of a tree sliced open to its grain and laid on its side. A macrame construction of knotted jute hangs above it. A frosted moon on a chain drops from the center of the ceiling. Ira and I had a room like this, and we would bring our dinner guests into its stark interior, willing them to transform it for us into a festive, celebratory site. We, ourselves, had forgotten the rituals. As the years passed, we could not remember, for the life of us, the old incantations, the venerable customs, the simplest tribal songs.

"Aside from the pieces you see here," the man says, stooping to open the doors on the end of the buffet, "there's all this as well."

The cabinet is filled with photo albums, and he begins to spread them out on the table.

"I really don't—"

"Oh, but I want you to see them. There's a wealth of information here. If you were a writer—"

This is the way it operates now: the vanquished provide the commentary on their own defeat. Unlike the Maya, who disappeared centuries before their ruins were unearthed, we preside over the cataloguing of our own bones.

I tell him, "I work in a mental-health center."

He brightens. "Then you *know* about life. I thought you did. I could tell immediately that you were *sensitive*."

Actually, I'm the receptionist. I started there as a client myself. After two sessions, my counselor declared, "What you need is a job that will take your mind off of your own problems and make you feel like a productive individual." I've been at the front desk ever since. They come in a constant stream, the refugees from love, the stunned survivors from New Pompeii. "Listen," I want to tell them, "I just do this for a living. I'm as much an exile as any of you."

I spend the next half hour looking through the man's collected intimacies, candid and posed. He watches me so closely, I think his eyes might pinion me to one of the pages. But I continue to turn them over, one after another, the finished books piled on the floor. I find nothing remarkable: my own albums are nearly interchangeable with his. When I'm done, it's as if I've seen a silent movie of my life in which I did not appear.

The children call me. "In the dining room!" I answer, affirming my existence.

"You can have each one separate," he says, "or the set at a savings of—"

"I don't understand why you would choose to sell them."

He looks grim. "What good do they do me? They're the dead past, as far as I'm concerned."

"So why should *I* buy them?"

"Well," he says, using his hands to shape each word, "you would reinvent them, so to speak. Make the old new, the past present. Through you, I would reinvent my life."

The children are pounding up the steps. "I'm not able—"

"I'd have to explain *everything* to you, every picture, all of it. I would have to find a way to tell it that made *sense,* that made it seem—believable." There are tears in his eyes. "It might feel like a life if I told it right."

"I don't have time," I say. "The boys are getting—"

They materialize. "Can we walk to the Mall?" they demand in unison, a prepubescent Greek chorus.

"It's so far," I say.

"It's less than a mile," the man says.

"It's less than a mile, Mom," says Josh.

"You might get lost," I tell them. "It's been so long since—"

Petey says, "We remember everything, Mom. It's like we never left."

"You be back in one hour." Feigning calm, I give them each a dollar. "In one hour we're going home." And they disappear into the streets of their memory, their rich ancestral land, those cul-de-sacs I thought they'd forgotten forever.

The man says, "We have just enough time to look upstairs."

For purposes of scholarship, I assent.

"Let me show you where I do my work," he says. He opens the door on a cork-walled room. In the center of the wood floor stands a drafting table, stately as an altar. Above it, a Calder replica drifts on invisible currents. Tacked to the cork, I see blueprints, coded messages on notecards, ink drawings on parchment-like paper of houses and stores and one that looks like an entire subdevelopment of split-levels and ranches.

"Architect?" I ask.

He perches on the drafting table's stool. "That's it. Fifteen years in the shelter business."

"A funny way to put it," I say, pretending to study the scale-model plans for a five-bedroom Colonial with attached garage.

"My wife used to call me the Frank Lloyd Wright of American Obsolescence. She said I had sheer genius for coming up with designs that were outmoded and reactionary."

I turn to face him. "And what did you say to her?"

"That she was a pseudorevolutionary. That she was a—"

"Stop!" I cover my ears with my hands. "Don't tell me any more! I can't stand abstractions!"

He smiles. "I can't either. Believe me. Absolutely wore me out. I'm much more comfortable with the concrete." He offers me his T-square. "You want to buy in? Partnership? Fifty-fifty?"

"I have no training in your field."

"You have good instincts," he says. "That's worth—"

"I'm sorry. I'm not interested."

"Well," he says, "that's a damn shame. I just can't handle it all myself anymore." He stares at the mobile. "It gets lonely, you know what I mean?"

"Yes," I whisper, my throat tight. I imagine him hunched over his table, a solitary scribe inside the catacombs, a monk at work on his medieval calligraphy. In the late afternoon, does he lay his head down in his arms for a rest from the day's hard work? Once, when Ira was still a lawyer, I found him in his office at four o'clock, asleep at his desk in that schoolboy's position, the rules and assignments of his grown-up days too much for him to bear any longer.

I tell the man again: "I really am sorry."

"Let's move on," he says. "I haven't given up yet."

His bedroom is across the hall. Attuned to danger, I ford that space as if it were a turbulent river. He raises the blinds. I enter the province of magic and taboo.

"Extra firm," he says, patting the mattress of the king-size bed. "Best you can buy."

I ignore the pitch. "This is a nice chair," I tell him, examining the scrolls of the bentwood rocker.

He bounds over, puts his hands on my shoulders and lowers me to the cushioned seat. "Go on," he says, beaming. "Rock a little."

I do. I have to admit it's comforting.

"Nothing like it," he says. "It's the motion of the womb, but I guess you know that. After all, you're a mother."

Oh, I can feel the weight of my babies in my arms, those tiny infant mouths taking my milk. Aboriginal lullabies rose up out of me then, the most enduring melodies of the species.

He says, "You ever think about having another?"

"I'm too old." I stop rocking. "I'm thirty-five." My voice is hushed, small, I can hardly hear my own words.

"That's not too old!" he says. He drops to his knees and takes my hands in his. "Lots of women—"

"Recent studies prove—"

"The hell with recent studies."

And then he kisses me, lifting me gently out of that chair, our arms encircling each other's bodies, heat coursing through flesh with enough intensity to meld us into a single living icon of sacred and ceremonial significance. Of all the remnants I've unearthed, this embrace could be my most important discovery. But I'm in no condition now to analyze it in its cultural context. He's maneuvering us to the bed. With all the will I can muster I pull away from him. Free again. Severed.

He deflates. "I know. Sure. Wouldn't want to get carried away and go on a spree you'd regret later."

"I'm glad you understand," I mumble.

Suddenly, in a sort of frenzy, he yanks open his closet, pulls out jackets, pants, a rainbow of shirts, and throws them across the bed. From the lacquered chest of drawers, he scoops out socks, underwear, monogrammed handkerchiefs, and dumps them in a mound on top of the other clothes. "Anything here you might like? Something for a Christmas gift? Birthday? Take your pick. I won't even charge you. On the house, so to speak."

"I couldn't."

"What you mean is you won't."

Just like Ira: a semanticist. How we wrangled over meanings, connotations, precise definitions, until finally we realized that our language was dead and the old alphabet no longer spelled out anything that mattered to either of us.

I tell this man, "I think I'll wait for Petey and Josh outside."

"You haven't even seen my boys' rooms."

"I don't need to."

He shrugs. "I guess not. I guess it's pointless." He sinks down on the chair, shuts his eyes, and begins to rock. As I close the front door behind me, it seems I hear him chanting a dirge.

In the shadow of an aged elm, I watch my children move toward me in a glad processional. Petey, then Josh, skip across the low stone wall that borders two of the yards, leap over the boulder at a driveway's edge, cover the span of the next lot in four cartwheels, race each other to the sculpture, and collapse in glee at the totem's base. I intrude on their revelry, summoning them to the car, insisting on solemnity for the long ride home. They regard me dolefully.

As I drive, the man's lamentation plays itself over and over in my mind. I feel increasingly funereal. Finally, my vision blurring, I pull over to the side of the road and cry.

"What's wrong, Mom?" says Petey.

'Don't you feel good?" Josh asks, leaning over the seat to stroke my head

I turn around to look at their fearful loving faces. Blubbering into a tissue, I tell them, "I forgot the wok."

"So what?" says Petey. "We can go back for it."

"Sure," Josh says. "We can go right back, Mom."

I bawl like a mourner, or a newborn, my sons the uncomprehending witnesses to my tears. Then I blow my nose, turn on the motor again, step on the gas, and swing us out into the confusing rush of modern traffic.